A RECKONING

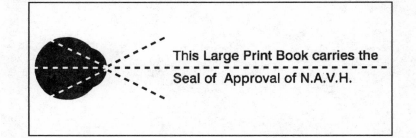

A RECKONING

LINDA SPALDING

THORNDIKE PRESS
A part of Gale, a Cengage Company

Farmington Hills, Mich • San Francisco • New York • Waterville, Maine
Meriden, Conn • Mason, Ohio • Chicago

LIBRARY OF CONGRESS CIP DATA ON FILE.
CATALOGUING IN PUBLICATION FOR THIS BOOK
IS AVAILABLE FROM THE LIBRARY OF CONGRESS

ISBN-13: 978-1-4328-5431-7 (hardcover)

Published in 2018 by arrangement with Pantheon Books, an imprint of The Knopf Doubleday Publishing Group, a division of Penguin Random House LLC.

Printed in the United States of America
1 2 3 4 5 6 7 22 21 20 19 18

For Michael

Just look what the water's carrying up this four-armed river!

— PABLO NERUDA

It was Sabbath and my father was preaching on an angel coming to our town. Said we would beg it hard to bless us, hold on hard to do that. Hold on and beg! Pa kept on shouting, and I was watching him jab the air with his hand when a stranger leaned upright against my tree and took off a hat full of colored feathers and wiped his brow as if he'd been walking for days. I said: Good timing, mister, and gave over the shade as I was just then wondering if angels could sweat. He'd walked twenty miles on the lookout for loggerhead shrike, which meant nothing to me but I told him we had some and later I made my way home through the woods. I'd be in trouble for that detour but I'd take my beating in order to earn some time to think about an angel come among us. What I should do.

1

The stranger carried a leather bag with his drawing pencils, a book of rag paper, a pair of trousers folded small, spare collar, neck scarf, stockings. Other ingredients were weightier — bowie knives, hand-drawn maps, a packet of compasses, the dials of which rotated as he traveled first by coach and then on foot. A pair of field glasses, unusual in 1855, hung on a strap that crossed his chest. Boots laced up to the knees with treads enough for slippery banks. He was going to tour Virginia but he had lamed himself after removing the boots to cross a creek and he needed to rest. When he paused at the edge of a campground, what he heard behind the noise of shuffling, coughing adults and crying, whimpering children was the hectoring diatribe of a shouting preacher. Coming from a pavilion open on all sides, the voice was first trumpet then flute, describing an angel that Jacob had refused to release from his desperate grip. I will not let thee go! Unless thee bless me! howled the preacher. And now the angel is come amongst us! Do you hear? Do you see? Hallelujah! Amen and Glory! Each and every one of you will be tested in the coming days! You will beg for the angel's blessing. Beg! But deserve it!

Limping slightly, the stranger made his way to a sycamore tree, large and cool, that sheltered a boy who was whittling at a stick.

An angel! shouted the preacher again, and the boy rolled his eyes. Good timing, mister.

Who's the preacher?

My pa. The tone betrayed nothing.

It was early spring and the boots of the stranger, whose name was Ross, left moist dents under the sycamore tree. The boy studied them. I never saw him labor with more zeal, he said, as if thinking it over. Then he grinned, showing crooked teeth.

Ross edged in closer to the pavilion, peering past a column to see the preacher clothed in black with arms raised like branches over his head. I do so desire your company as we wrestle this angel together, the preacher cried, and the mortals in the pavilion began to fall on their knees or dance on their feet. Ross had given his life to a naturalist's logic. He was a believer in the evidence offered by rocks and bones but the moaning and praying unhinged him and he clung to his post as if some alien being might really descend and take hold of him. Good timing, the boy had said. Zeal, he had said. And that grin. Meanwhile, a girl began to turn in circles until her hair came unpinned and people grabbed one another shouting, Glory, glory! Heal me, Jesus! and the preacher moved among them, stepping around outflung arms and legs. Hold fast to the angel!

The pavilion was swaying as if a storm had hit. Cries of Save me and Bless me. Ross went back to the tree, unpacked his scarf, and mopped his face. He had given little thought to salvation. His desire to free slaves was about justice rather than virtue; he hated the slaver more than he loved the slave. The boy said: You never been at a revival?

Ross said: Not to this day.

I knew you was a Northern.

I'd like to meet your father.

Easy as pie. Just cross that field is our place. But pass on by the big house 'cause it's the day off and my uncle's none too friendly when his people play.

His people. So, Ross had found his battleground after walking for three days. He had

13

been hoping for this and waiting since the first abolitionist meeting he'd attended the previous winter in New York, where his professor, a hydrotherapist, had made a fervent speech. Ross took a breath of clean spring air. He looked around, gauging his adversaries, and decided to leave the Christians to find their angel among the wagons and tents. *Rectify.* It was a word inscribed in his mind, his professor's word. He walked away from the campground with his leather bag and the field glasses favoring his sore left foot. There were huts scattered around and these would soon have fires lit for the warming of basket-brought food. Having trudged twenty miles that day, Ross was ready for his own small fire and the comfort of his bedroll, but first he would learn what he could about the lay of the land. Scripture say knowledge increaseth sorra, an old Negro man had told him a day or two before, but Ross had picked his way very slowly down the western side of the Commonwealth of Virginia and he had seen few signs of knowledge anywhere, although he'd been keenly observant of sorrow. He took note of the trees and the lack of them. Dirth, he called it, seeing man as the ruination of the natural world. Once, the whole continent had been as balanced as a pendulum. Swinging here to there to here again. Even the ancient fires brought growth. Clouds of birds had filled the sky, whole races of birds that knew the vagaries of weather and migration and yet there were fewer trees and fewer birds and where would it end?

As he walked, he thought of the slaves he planned to free. For those who could read, a map. For the rest, quilts askew on laundry lines or nails pounded into crossroad trees. He stumbled, as the road was rutted, and he kept to the edge, where sprouted grass pushed up through pounded earth. He remembered walking along the dunes in childhood by the never-ending lake at the edge of Ontario, scuffling feet and ruffling plants without a thought until Eva Nell pointed out the error of this, saying all things were bound together, even including the tiny biters that plagued them and must not be swatted. Bugs and ruts, trees, birds . . . I can't say how it all connects, she'd said, but each of us is bound to all the rest. It was the start of his education. As a newborn, she had been carried to Canada from Virginia by her mother and a runaway slave. Mary Jones, Eva Nell's mother, explained it as a rescue mission. But Eva Nell thought there was more to it than the saving of old Mama Bett. Why would her mother risk such a trip with a baby? Why did the family in Virginia never contact any of them? Who is my father? she had asked a thousand times. And always she had been told not to question the past, which was left behind for good and all, her mother had said. Once, Mary Jones had said: Your father was lost in the war up here. I mean, he never came back. Another time she had said: Bett was enslaved. What choice did I have? Usually she had said nothing and Bett, who was Eva Nell's nanny or Mary's servant, was equally silent about the past. They had come out of Virginia together. That was all Eva Nell needed to know. Bett lived in the city called York now, helping other runaways and immigrants. Ross had gone to her for advice. Where should he start? What words should he use to convince a slave that the risk was worthwhile? Bett knew about the Underground Railroad, which had helped her avoid capture years before. Warn them of the catchers, she told Ross. Catchers everywhere these days now. But Ross thought such warning might imperil a man's enthusiasm for escape. He would focus on pride when he talked to slaves.

He began with the same stretch of wilderness Eva Nell had traveled as a newborn child moving in the opposite direction. She, who had attended his mother's school in Belleville, where girls learned to spin and weave, but also to read and use well-formed cursive script. It was more trade school than academy, but it rose in the estimation of Belleville residents as the children grew up and became usefully employed. He could almost see Eva Nell now, with her hands on her hips and her dark eyes squinted, defying him to make sense of her unexplained life. So he went on walking while his foot went on swelling from the twist it had taken, and the sun was uncertain, casting shadows that he moved through time and again. Time and again he looked for some mark of house or plowed field or even a fence until he noticed a wood grouse fluttering in the sticky underbrush. Getting down on his hands and knees, he called, chick-chick and crawled along in order to capture the grouse, his clothes picking up seeds and burrs so that when he rose up with the bird in his hands he was a mess of scratches and torn trousers and shirt. The bird's wing was apparently injured. She had set her eyes into slits of no mind to find her reserves, if there were any to be found. Then, upright again and tucking the grouse into a soft canvas bag he kept inside the leather one, Ross saw a gleam of window glass through a stand of elms, a fine brick house with four white columns reaching all the way up to the roofline. He studied the sweep of grass where a child was squatted, clipping at it with a long curved blade. In Canada, Ross had studied to be a naturalist. Then he went down to New York to take a medical degree and now he stood on a back road in Virginia watching a child wield a lethal blade. It was a sight that went to his heart and he turned onto the clipped lawn and went up the walkway to the door of the red-brick house with its sunbitten windows even though he'd been warned by the boy to walk past. Day off, the boy had informed him, and that meant there were slaves on the property who were not required to work on the Sabbath other than to wash their own clothing and cut the sweet grass.

I want the master, were his words at the door when it was opened by a girl of ten or eleven years. She was wearing only a shirt that barely covered her knees and when she didn't speak, he said: Child, tell me, what is your name?

There was a muttered answer, Lou, and then the door was closed firmly. He heard a bolt slide into place.

Ross knocked again and stroked the bird

through the canvas bag. I shall wait! he called in warning, and he sat down on the wide porch steps and took the bird out and looked closely at the wing, absorbed in the set of the hollow bones and the blank staring eyes in the fading light that was making it hard to see. He was a medical student and any focus on healing calmed him so he stroked feathers and bones and sat on the steps as the sun sank behind the elms. The fields around him were soon drained of color, and he thought about the two children again. Usually slaves live in quarters, he thought, and he wondered where their mother was and where the quarters were on this gray property. When he heard hooves on the road and the snort of a horse, he covered the grouse with his hands and watched the long path leading up to the house, where a dark shape was approaching on a horse apparently homeward bound. At the base of the steps, the horse swerved, the man pulling too hard on the reins, and Ross looked directly up at the glowing, ruddy face of a man in his middle years. I waited a long while out here, he said, while far below on the road he saw another rider streak by on a dappled mare. It was the long-armed preacher fully bent over the neck of his horse. Ross introduced himself and said: I am here in your county studying birds.

The landowner rolled the whip handle in his hands and jumped down from his mount. From whence do you hail? He regarded his guest's torn clothes and muddy knees with a look of slight scorn.

New York, said Ross, thinking it was safer than the truer fact of Canada.

You trap our birds? He looked at the grouse.

This one is injured.

And my fields must not be; they are newly planted, the land-owner said as he turned back to his horse and loosened the cinch of the saddle. Stay off my land.

Ross held the grouse, running a finger across her beak, as the young grass cutter came around the corner of the house keeping his head down and his face averted from the master's gaze.

The homeowner handed the reins to the boy and mounted the steps of his house, roughly grazing the shoulder of his unwanted guest. Stay away from my fields.

Ross took his leave, heading for the road and being careful not to limp.

In a grove of trees he spread out his bedroll, took off his boots, and moved his toes in an arc, the way he'd been taught by his New

York professor, who insisted that his students and patients rotate ankles and wrists three times a day, take no liquid but water, use no sweetener, take no meat. Ross had bread, he had cheese, he had a raw turnip to slice. Then, having eaten those delicacies, he checked the wing of the grouse and laughed at himself. This bird had fooled him with the oldest ruse in the book of bird. She must have had eggs or chicks in the underbrush and was trying to lead him away from them. He would find the right spot and put her back where he had found her. Limping again he walked barefoot down the road a few paces and set the bird under a sheltering tree. Then he returned to his bedroll and lay in the scent of shield ferns remembering a long-ago night stretched out beside Eva Nell with a hundred thousand shooting stars overhead, great pieces of falling sky. What year had it been? He remembered the thrill of those heavenly deaths and the girl beside him, older by some years and always his secret ideal, his youthful fantasy. When her mother became ill, Eva Nell had begun to help with his mother's school, bringing in feathers and rocks and shells for the students, hoping for paid employment. Soon she was teaching the girls to sew and weave. Wonderful days those were as he sat

21

at the back of her little classroom, the only boy allowed there, and now Ross rolled over and pillowed his face on an arm. Look at me, she had said that night of the stars. And he had looked and blushed as she removed her outer clothes and lay down with him in the dark. In those days, Eva Nell was so lively and curious that when Ross began to examine the wings of damselflies, she tried to learn about insects although little information was available to her. They went to the library and looked at books. She took him on long walks and introduced him to the thrashing lake, which caused a temporary fright, for the restless, splashing water seemed unrhythmical, its smell brackish. But one day there was a discovery that made him forget his fear and discomfort. Stomping through the shoreline vegetation, they came upon a nest propped against rocks, a nest holding two baby gulls, barely feathered, two lumps. These were Bonaparte's gulls, but Eva Nell did not know that. She knew only that they were common birds, pretty enough, and loud when they moved in flocks. She had seen them forever from her mother's lakeshore house and now she lowered herself to a squat and promised the birds that they would not be touched lest their bird parents decide to abandon them.

Lest you be orphans like me, she said, and Ross was caught by her voice, by her tender intelligence, by something in her outlook that rattled him. By then, her mother was dead and she'd never known a father and Ross crept back a few feet and held his breath and took home with him not so much as a feather from that stone-bound nest.

Eva Nell was eighteen that summer and he was eleven. She lived in a house on the cusp of Lake Ontario, a house with its boards beaten by wind and ice while ships rode by on waves that crashed like cannon fire, and now Ross had come to Virginia to satisfy his need for action against slavery. And perhaps to solve a mystery for Eva Nell.

2

Martin's way home from the revival was through dense woods that abutted corn- and cotton fields. He knew the path by feel and he could whistle and sing and spit without much fear. He could cuss if he had to. His father said that the woods were unclean. They harbored dangerous, unreasoning beasts. In any part of nature, it was important to exercise reason. But Martin felt tempted by the privacy of wilderness, where he could unbutton his trousers and feel the air on his tenderest skin. Such were his pleasures and now he got down in a crouch and made a turd on the narrow path. What would the angel think of that? A message to the other beasts. Maybe that Northern man was behind him, finding his way along in his feathered hat. He rubbed himself with a dry leaf and made a whoop to try its effect. He moved across a piece of land that knew the footsteps of its earlier inhabitants and he thought of them. When he came to the field behind his uncle's big house, he skirted it widely in order to miss the cabin where his father might be talking to God after the long hours of preaching. Man to man was the way his father talked to God. Martin thought about the angel again. Why did Jacob hang on to it? Why was he wanting to be blessed? Had he done something bad? I will not let thee go except thee bless me, is what Jacob said. Martin thought of old Reuben muttering, Bless my soul, well, bless my soul, and he knew it wasn't the same.

He could ask his father about it, but that would entail another lecture to be followed by a beating since he had run off without permission after the camp meeting. He could ask his brother about the angel but Patton would tease him. He could hear Patton's voice without even trying. Is Patton the same as me, Martin wondered, when it comes to being crumply? He didn't think so. He thought Patton was superior and not afraid of their father, who was himself not afraid of anything save the Lord's earned wrath. But the Lord couldn't make a bruise on your arm or a lash mark on your leg, or box your ears, which meant their father was harder than God and thinking about it made Martin feel crumply again. I'll get a beating for leaving Mam and the girls, he thought, but I don't care one heck about it. He said the word out loud to himself.

Sunday supper included cold meat and suck-eyes with collard greens and sometimes rice pudding, and because he was hungry Martin decided to go home and face the beating and he even hurried a little until he reached the cornfield behind his own house. It was the acre he plowed up every spring — riding on the plow to level it — and he could already see the corn coming in as he jumped across the rows he'd made. They were straight as string this year and maybe his father would not be in a bitter mood if the collection bowl was full from the meeting and there would be rice pudding.

3

The preacher was sitting in the cabin his own father, Daniel, had built long ago. Since the old man's death a year ago, this place had become John's harbor. He came here to sit on a chair his father had made. He came to write on the table his father had constructed so that his family could gather to eat when they first came out of Pennsylvania to escape the scorn of his community. Daniel, a widowed Quaker, had married a young Methodist named Ruth Boyd. Now Daniel's son by Ruth sat at the old table when writing sermons or bills, and this time it was a bill of sale and a letter to his half-brother, Benjamin. He should not work on the Sabbath but he managed Benjamin's business, selling cotton as well as flax and cider and the brandy he distilled. John had no day of rest. Had he not given his heart to his gathered congregation that very day? Wasn't exhortation a form of labor? And wasn't his pastoral income too scant to keep a family housed and fed? He recorded accounts for Benjamin's farm and was paid a percentage of the profits. *In my father's house there are many mansions.* It was John's bitterest joke. His father had created wealth and John's older half-brother had transferred it all to himself while John and his wife and children lived with a Christian minimum of worldly goods. You see, he said to the ghost of his father, I am my brother's keeper. He stared at the fireplace as if a waft of paternal affection might be smoldering there in spite of Benjamin's lifelong wastefulness. The problem had been there for years — an inclination to buy and trade and sell and, what is worse, an attitude of Devil-may-care regarding the outcome. There was, first, the Mill and Comfort House, given to Benjamin by their father in order to keep him home from the war in 1812. There, Benjamin made his profits and drank his own brandy and challenged travelers to games of chance. There, the gristmill built by their father — the small but steady business that had first given them hold on Virginia soil — became a venture too small for Benjamin's greater talents. This because, while Daniel had been content to copy the simple waterwheels he'd seen in Pennsylvania, Benjamin wanted a gravity wheel fed by a sluice. He wanted a saw frame and sliding carriage to hold logs rather than grain and with them he turned out floorboards for the brick house his slaves would build. Benjamin's first wife, Elizabeth, had come to the marriage with two black men as her dowry and Benjamin had soon purchased more. Wives were found for them. Babies were born. John tried to remember the various histories, but most of them didn't have stories that he could know. Rakel had suffered a mysterious illness that rendered her useless, but Elizabeth had allowed her to stay because her sale would not bring any profit. Josiah had come a few years back from an auction near Rosehill. Abe. Jule. Young Jim was the newest. Nick was born on the property to a woman who was later sold.

It should all have been sufficient but Benjamin took on loans from the Jonesville Bank. And when Elizabeth died, he married a girl who would not be satisfied with life on his farm and he took more loans. There were payments due every season and now, after a long, dry winter, they were low on cash.

As a circuit-riding preacher, John was accepted whenever he threw up a tent, but sales and bookkeeping suited him just as well. He was, in spite of his mystical leanings, fastidious with accounts. Of course this served his interests, but there was also the pleasure of numerical balance. Today, along with the bill of sale for cider, he composed his monthly statement for Benjamin. He wrote these letters in order to impress on his half-brother the facts of their finances, which might otherwise be deposited in a column called Denial. *Dear Brother,* he wrote, *It is my duty to inform you that you are required to make a court appearance on May 5 unless payement is made on the bank loan. Money must be found before the day in court, so I ask you to have care where expenses are concerned. We must improve the output of the workers and repay our debts.* Here John laid his quill aside and sat looking at the wall for several minutes. It was so familiar to him, this log wall, that he could use it as a mirror of sorts, a means of introspection. How had he and Benjamin come to such mutual dissatisfaction? Their father had no brook with slavery after his purchase of a young boy ended in tragedy. But a lack of workers meant that his land earned no profit and he finally gave or sold it at a loss to Benjamin, who was born of Rebecca, Daniel's first and beloved Quaker wife. Benjamin was the favorite and now John picked up the quill and finished his letter. *Apparently with our father's passing, the bank has lost trust in timely repayment. We must remedy this. Your brother, John*

Counting himself the original sinner by purchasing so much land that required more and more slaves, Daniel had retired to his cabin and closed the door behind him. It was possible that Benjamin had housed his workers in his cellar so as not to irritate his father by building quarters that were visible, and now there was no end to the discussions in Jonesville of that unwholesome practice, which was an embarrassment to John.

The one exception was a small cabin placed a good distance from the barn, where it was not much noticed. This habitation had its own tiny plot of land with a few stalks of corn and a chicken nesting on a pile of hemp bags and now John got out of the chair and knelt on the floor in order to feel the spirit of the Lord and to pray for the patience he needed to stay away from that little house, and from the barn, although it was nearly milking time, when Emly would be alone with the cows. Sabbath is Sabbath but thirst and hunger do not disappear on the Lord's holy day. Milk does not dry up and cows must still be tended. Life in a barn is separate from life in a house. The same rules do not apply. In the sweet reek of hay, a man can be ardent as he is nowhere else and love the webs that hang in the stalls and the light that eases through the cracks and the woman who lies down with him amid the cows and horses and mules and the flight of the swallows tearing in and out and, beyond the roof, a hawk screaming dutiful warning. John stared at the log wall again, mirror to his shame. It had begun when he'd gone to the barn one morning to saddle his horse and had come upon his brother's milkmaid with her brimming pail and her face with its features defined by the early light that came pouring so generously through the wide-open door. Her mouth that was broad and quiet, her eyes that so calmly searched his. He'd put out a hand with its fingers groping. No right had he to touch his brother's slave, but she dropped the pail and what was the use of arguing as he pulled her to the floor of the barn . . . as he came to believe that she cared for him?

Dear Father, what is the suffering of man to that of the Son of man? Can we point to a grief that He has not experienced? Except! He never loved a woman, did He, Father?

You spared Him that consuming pain.

John's month had begun at the home of Brother Moses Hume in Rosehill. After prayers there, he'd been given thin soup and cold bread and his next stop was at the cabin of a family without winter stores where he took no nourishment but offered a quiet sermon on gratitude. We must be thankful for adversity. John included himself in that category since much of his preaching was of a controversial nature and he often felt called upon to defend himself. Once or twice he had met the local Shakers in private combat, but John was not eloquent in debate and some of the settlers had been swept into the muddy pools of an ungodly faith that did not recognize marriage as a Christian sacrament. On this latest trip he had been compelled to travel many miles out of his way over high and steep hills where there were few roads to guide him. Riding into a valley he had erected a tent and preached to a settlement of Baptists while tears dripped from his face. Christ preached among the infidels. He next found himself near Brother McCarthy's farm, a ride of more than forty miles, and coming home he had preached on both sides of the river. Forth and back, the horse wading or swimming. This was his route and it had taken twelve days to accomplish, but he was no mere circuit-riding preacher, he was *paterfamilias* wherever he went. Praise God. John got up off his knees, which were stiff, dusted them with both hands, and limped to the table to peer down at the lined account book. He was short-sighted. A little dizzy after his prayers. A twelve dissolved when he looked at it, lost in the margins, and he shook his head. If only his eldest son would assume some responsibility for the farm. Patton wore a chip on his shoulder but it was framed in a golden light. How many times had John convinced a neighbor that Patton meant well, never mind the theft of apples and chickens and one thing and another? Oh Emly. I need your arms around my shoulders, your legs around my back.

So John sat through the milking hour in a cabin that was softened by time and abrasion. He sat at the table his father had made, puncheon, much abused, and he went over the books again and found the errant twelve and folded the letter he'd written to Benjamin into thirds. He tapped the dry wood with his quill. Total value of property twenty thousand, including eighteen workers worth twelve thousand dollars, which could never be redeemed. They needed those workers in order to live. In Britain, the mills were hungry for cotton. Who can eat cotton? Not human beings. He picked up his father's Bible and thumbed its soft pages. Daniel had once said in anger that the Good Book could so easily be turned and twisted to any man's intention that it offered no guide . . . *All things go to the bad, lose their power and slip backwards* . . . those were the words of Virgil, who had comforted the exiled Quaker more than all the Testaments . . . *If he happens to relax his arms for a moment, the current sweeps him away headlong downstream* . . . Daniel had brought five children out of Pennsylvania and now there was only Benjamin, born of wealthy Rebecca, and John, born of a small, sure-footed orphan whose wit was learned in a poorhouse. There was no record of Ruth Boyd's life, not even a birth certificate. He glanced over at his father's trunk and nudged it with an outstretched foot. There were three keys in a clay jar on the mantel, two large, one small. John got up and went to the mantel, which was layered with a variety of things, including a recent portrait of his eldest daughter painted by an artist passing through town. John would never have permitted Electa to sit in an unknown room with an unknown man and yet she had made the decision and gone off on her own during the Easter school break, proclaiming that it was a gift to him, so that he could not complain.

Next to the portrait, a saucer held straightened nails. There was a book of cookery made by his half-sister Mary in her youth. She must have been about twelve at the time and such a trial to her stepmother, Ruth, because the two were actually close in age and Mary had profited nicely from her mother's polished ways. Then she had fallen in love with the son of Frederick Jones, the town's founder, and he had run off to the war in Canada without saying goodbye. Ran off with Isaac, the third brother. Never came back. Without slaves, Daniel had needed the help of a willing son, old enough to work and think and take direction, and John was too young. So it was all given over to Benjamin. John reached up now and took the cookery book down from the dusty mantel. It had girlish drawings of kettles and spoons and baking pans and described the manufacture of corn pudding and the pecan biscuits they had loved as hungry children. There was a dried snakeskin on the mantel too, another remnant of their childhood, and John thought of his father saving it. Was the old man sentimental? Or was it Ruth? She might have saved anything found or invented by her stepson. There was that jar Benjamin had fashioned one day by the creek and then baked on a fire he'd made by himself. Now John took the small key out of that jar, reaching in without looking because he knew its feel, and he went slowly to the foot of his father's bed. Daniel had been buried twelve months before and surely a son must emerge from the bones of his father. A son must emerge and gather the dirt in his hands and build his hut and may it become a village, a town, a country. May it become a future if he has the courage to survey the past. My hut, thought John, such as it is, and nothing else left to me by the man whose second and unloved wife was Ruth Boyd. He turned the key in the lock and felt the contents with his right hand while he held up the lid with his left and he picked out a folded piece of paper he had read several times over the past few weeks. *Dear Papa:* it was dated 1816. *We are safly on the east side of the most wondrus of any cascade on this earth. East in this case means North, Papa, and that means we are Safe. (there is a mill on this river that excedes anything you might emagine.) The river takes its rise at Lake Erie which you once showd to me on a colord map. I would tell you of our crossing but I was stuck under canvas so I onlie heard the cataract although was wet throoh and I canot think our Creator would punish us after such trials on the road as we had with the motherless babe. We were dashed by the spray but there are two Falls the water almost Emeralde on the far side and there is a gap I would not enter on any dare. (rememeber Benjamin dared me to cross our creek when it was high?) Then we were met by Friends, Papa. Quakers. They are the last station of the railroad as it is known here. All-ways Yours*

John knew that Mary had run away with her sister's baby on the night Jemima had died in childbed, shunned by her family because she had lived unmarried with Rafe Fox. Mary had stolen the baby to hide her from the eyes of the local residents. But shouldn't Daniel have told the family that Mary and the baby were safe? Neither of them was ever mentioned again. Not once over the many years since Mary had disappeared had her whereabouts been discussed. It was a local scandal. Rafe Fox went mad with rage and made every effort to find the two slaves who'd run off with Mary. Bett had run off and so had her young son, Bry, who was later brought back.

John stared at the letter. In small towns, disappearances are not forgotten. Speculation was endless. Mama Bett had provided medicines to people in Jonesville for many years. She and Mary had worked as a healing team. John was rummaging in the trunk again. *I wonder if you, dear Papa, should not take up the employment of sugering? Here the season is one long festival, especially among the indins who mack suger when the hunt is compleat. (most of the work done by the women I should say.) What I lick best are the flowers growing in the Ontario woods. Day lilies the Turk's Cap We are favorud by clear sky even in coldest winter.* John rubbed at his eyes and began to indulge in the anger that was habitual to him when he did not take pleasure in facts. His father had betrayed all of them by keeping these matters secret. And at what cost? How hard it had been to work against a growing sense of family oddity. Perhaps I chose my ministry, he thought, in order to placate our wary community. It was my job to keep them busy with Christian thought and prayer. He slammed down the lid of the trunk, which was full of more letters from a half-sister he could clearly remember. He had been fourteen years old when she ran away.

4

Sore from his beating, promising himself that he would never eat breakfast again as long as his father presided at table, Martin went off the next morning with his brother and their father's gun.

Patton had chided him: You're never any use, boy. Let's get Mama a buck.

Off season, said Martin. We can't.

But Patton carried the forbidden gun across his shoulder, caring nothing for rules. Patton had a great spirit, an enviable spirit, and Martin looked up to him even as he led his little brother through the fields and into the woods until they came right up close to Rafe Fox's dreary farm that sat in the middle of the Dickinson property with only a narrow right-of-way to the outside world. It was the family victory. Benjamin had surrounded Rafe Fox by purchasing all the land that abutted his. Which made it all the more interesting to Patton, who lectured Martin as they walked along Rafe's fence line. One shot has to do it. That's all the time we have. Aim for the head.

I thought we wanted a buck. You can't shoot a cow.

Just you watch me.

Patton, I already got a beatin.

That was for yesterday's sin. You are what now? Thirteen? Almost? Years and years older than yesterday. And you have a father with no love for sport, which leaves me the job of tutoring scared-of-his-shadow you, little Marty boy.

I'm not scared. Martin so wanted to *be* his brother, to somehow fit into his skin. He said: But let's stay on our own side, okay?

You are such a jackass.

Keeping to the trees, the boys walked until they found a place rough enough to give them foothold. Then it was up and over the fence. Nineteen-year-old Patton was known for his stride; he was known for his laugh and for his Virginia courtesy. He was never awkward, never fell down unless he had too much brandy. He was one to lift his hat, bow from the waist, and speak to ladies most politely, and now Martin was at the mercy of this older brother on the unholy land of Rafe Fox. *Old Rafe, old Rafe, beyond compare, gelded a boy and made him a mare.*

It was a rhyme never said except at school by boys who smoked and cussed. Still, the phrase was there in Martin's mind as he followed Patton on the wrong side of the fence. Gelded a boy. Gelded a boy. Over and over it went in his mind. His thoughts were jumping, his throat closed tight. Rafe Fox was the devil incarnate, according to their pa and Uncle Benjamin, but Patton was forever hunting, trapping, meeting the local daughters with a flask of brandy and forgetting to respect any boundary. Devil or not, Patton had a bottle in his pocket and Martin could hear it rattle and clank against loose coins. He kept a worried eye on the pocket because if Patton drank and then fell asleep in this field, he would have to know what to say back home come suppertime. She's all yours, little brother, Patton coaxed, pointing to a brown milch cow nibbling on a tuft of grass.

We are off our land, Martin noted with his small voice, but he was diverted by a strange-looking toad that he stopped to touch with his thumb and the cow moved along amiably. He tried not to think about Rafe Fox, who might come after them with his gelding knife. Patton had found a screen of prickly laurel and was hissing at Martin to come over to it fast. Get on over here!

Hell, boy! Duck down and shut your mouth. And when Martin pointed at the bottle sticking out of Patton's pocket, he heard a growl that seemed to come out of his brother, a deep, angry throat sound, and he ducked his head as he had been told to do but raised it again in time to see his brother lift the gun. No! Please! Martin whispered. No. Because they were in a trench behind the laurel screen on Rafe's private land and it was a wild, angry noise above them that made Martin's skin prickle and the hairs on his neck lift up. It was a growl that he had heard only once before in his whole life, and now it came from a large black bear high up in a tree some few yards off and the bear was climbing, paw over paw, stroke by stroke through branches shedding their needles and growing new ones on that bright spring day. She was climbing to get to her cub and Martin's protest went entirely unheard under the sharp, resounding crack of the gun, that clarifying sound that shattered the bright green world as Martin watched the big bear fall backward, rolling slowly in the empty air, her mouth tearing open, her legs paddling, and her eyes focused on the tree where her cub was clinging to the trunk, not much bigger than a puppy, all arms and legs, and Martin grabbed the gun by the burning barrel and shoved it hard at his brother's chest. Then he ran at the tree and leapt up to reach the cub's furry legs, the claws so sharp they tore at his hands, which were already torn by the laurel bush. Was there another shot? Was Patton shooting at him? Martin zigged through snapping trees with the small burden tight in his arms as out of the bush from nowhere, a man stepped solid and hard in front of him and grabbed his arm. Just hold on, the man said. Let's see if it's hurt. Hold still. It was the stranger with the feathered hat, the wanderer in search of birds. He seemed larger now than he was the day before and he gripped Martin's shoulders. She has claws, he said. Be careful. She'll need milk. I'll come back to the house with you. Speak to your father.

Martin's breathing was shallow, old and new tears streamed down his face, and he rubbed at the tears with his bleeding hands. He looked up at the man and was obedient, holding tight to the bear cub, feeling the fear in her panting. Got to climb the fence, he said.

No, there's a gate. And it opens. You might have tried knocking. It's considered polite. The birdman tousled Martin's hair. Wipe your face. You'll scare your poor mother to death.

Martin wondered about Patton. Was he hiding? Maybe he didn't even care.

Their walking was tangled by things underfoot, but Martin could almost keep up with the stranger, who opened the gate and closed it behind them, and whose stride was direct while the weight of the bear in Martin's sore arms seemed to increase with every step.

At the house they went first to the kitchen, where Clotilde reached out to feel the bear's furry head. That's a comfort, she said. I'll warm up some milk. Clotilde had been in the kitchen forever. She had a bottle used for orphan lambs and she might have settled the cub on her lap but Martin said: She's afeared just now, and he sat on the kitchen stool and put the rubber nipple into the groping toothy mouth while Ross stood watching and Clotilde went about her work.

When they left the kitchen, which was separate from the house in the Virginia way, Martin led Ross through a garden planted with stakes and lattices for peas and beans. My father's garden, said Martin. There were already squash vines, onion sprouts, and peas. But all around this feeding garden was an acre or more of flowers planted for color and shape. My mother's garden, Martin explained, and Ross saw peonies and early roses, a trellis of wisteria, and he recognized the symptoms of a woman's wish for beauty over necessity. He was taken by the Japanese magnolias, which were white and pink and a dull color in between. He thought such a garden would make anyone kind.

Through the door and into the dining room, the preacher sat alone at an oblong table drinking black coffee from a saucer that had belonged to Ruth Boyd. When John looked up it was to see a stranger in the doorway with an arm around young Martin, who had not come to breakfast and who seemed to be holding something tucked inside his shirt. Martin's face was blotted with streaks of blood. He was breathing hard.

Father, this is Mister —

Doctor Ross. I'm Doctor Ross. The bird-watching abolitionist put out his hand.

John half rose, still focused on his boy, but he glanced at the lump of bear.

Your son rescued it when the mother was shot by some rascal in the woods. Ross smiled to show his goodwill and took off his feathered hat and held it in the crook of his arm and smiled again, shifting uneasily.

John stood then, son of small orphan Ruth

Boyd, stretching for height. He had been taking his second coffee of the morning and considering economies. His hair, which was fair enough, was clipped from the forehead halfway back to the crown but the rest fell lank to his shoulders in the way of the Methodist ministers. The hairstyle was a kind of uniform and he saw that Ross was noticing, which meant he was unreligious and John found that he felt unwelcoming. Who was this man fastened to his son? He stared at the field glasses Ross wore as if they might contain portents, and Ross lifted the strap over his shoulder and held the big glasses out. Made by an Italian, he said respectfully. It's a new way of carrying distant images to the eye. He took off his bag then and kicked it to the wall, still clutching his hat with an elbow. I am here in your county to study birds. Well. And it's a pleasant task, pleasant enough, although, he added, while Herr Goethe said the senses do not deceive, I sometimes think we see what we want to see.

John nodded vaguely. The glasses were heavy and as he put them up to his face, Ross said: A bird is a league away and each feather is detailed. It could be inches. But there is more to it than that. Adjust the focus and it is possible to feel close to a

47

subject who has no suspicion of your interest. Spin this here, this brass ring, Ross said. Try closing one eye and work it that way. We want the bird to be one thing or the other. We want to classify. I'm in pursuit of the loggerhead shrike, which should be migrating north about now.

Minister of the Lord and wary of science, John looked through the field glasses and wondered that time could be so wasted. He reminded himself that he had once brought home a cotton gin from Baltimore and that object was the result of someone's pursuit of knowledge and it had made the Dickinsons wealthy. But was this not the demand of the land? Did it not demand to be useful, John wondered, as he held the glasses to his face, seeing nothing. Of what possible use was the study of migrating birds? John did not like jokes, especially when they were at his expense. His own economic research had been interrupted and now he had a stranger to contend with in his dining room. He handed the glasses back and told Martin to take the cub back to the woods where it belonged. He told Ross he might look for loggerhead shrike on the Dickinson land if he did so with all due care. All but one field belongs to my brother, he explained, but I manage all of it. John enjoyed that claim of authority over the soil he and his brother and father and sons and nephews had tended. He turned then to see his wife coming swiftly toward them with a bowl of cut flowers for the table. They were daisies and roses, an unlikely mixture, but Lavina put them down and went quickly across the room to examine the bear.

John looked up at his wife. This is another black mark on Patton, Mother. I did not give permission to use my gun. He made a curl of his mouth to show his displeasure and to show that he would take things in hand. He would threaten to send his eldest son away, to prove his point. Lavina relied on his authority. One more mistake and you are on your own, he would say in her hearing. Out west, where you can work off your sins, is where you'll go. It usually worked to calm Patton down for a week or so. John spoke calmly now, introducing the bird-watcher as the one who had come upon the murderous scene, and said: I've told Martin to take it back to the woods.

But it isn't weaned!

John opened both hands in a gesture of forbearance: Listen to the sentiment of women, Doctor.

Ross tilted his head, male to male, showing that he understood. Although perhaps your boy has a rare opportunity here, he said gently, angling his gaze at the preacher while he took the cub out of Martin's arms and laughed when she pushed up to suck at his ear. Wouldn't that be something for the history books, raising a bear? To train? And a good way to keep a boy occupied in the summer months.

John stood by his chair. He wondered what the birdwatcher would find in the fields that he himself might not notice. If the senses do not deceive, were his less competent? He thought of the land that stretched out around them. He stood wavering. He considered and made a decision that would change everything in their lives. The bear could recover in the barn.

Build a closed stall, coached Lavina. Warm and dark. Lots of milk.

John grimaced, but he invited the birdwatcher back. For supper, if you don't mind, Mother. He then regarded their guest, who would see birds, yes, but who would also see oats and flax already seeded, and cotton, which is delicate and tiresome and unknown in the north. He would see timothy grass and clover cut by scythe and gathered by rake. Such sights had no need of an Italian device. Such sights were God-given to the eye and gratitude must be enjoined. Blessings abounding, now that he thought of it, blessings upon us endlessly. In the orchard there were blooming pear trees, plums and apples. Birds, too, taking off for someplace else. He would ask Lavina to put her good plates on the table since she had so little chance to enjoy them. There would be the light of more than sufficient tallow candles and he would lean back in his chair and speak of the natural world that surrounded them since he was born of this piece of earth and its sap ran in his veins.

5

Jonesville, three miles away, was a small collection of merchants and a few others who served the needs of the families scattered across the county. It boasted one general store, one bank, a blacksmith and wheelwright, a courthouse soon to be built, and a school where John could preach on Sunday when he wasn't at the campground or out riding his circuit. There was a rival chapel for Presbyterians at the other end of a street wide enough for two wagons to pass without touching. Because this street was part of the Wilderness Road or turnpike, there was a regular throb of big wheels and groaning beasts with people of want wanting more, restless, going west. Three miles out of town in that direction, Benjamin Dickinson held three thousand acres, some of it inherited, some traded, some won. Martin said: You want to see birds, they'll be over in the field there pecking cottonseeds.

Ross said: They don't like cottonseed.

Yessir, they do.

Ross touched the ground. Warm. Moist. They don't like cottonseed, he said again. How many slaves do you have?

We don't say that.

Ross had the glasses up to his face. How many?

They're not ours anyway.

They belong to your uncle . . .

I thought it was birds you like.

That's right. And what do you think might be the effect on birds of planting all these acres in cottonseed?

Martin was holding the little bear and she was clinging to him, belly to belly, sniffing and sucking at his ears.

Ross said: Can I trust you, Martin?

Yessir. I always tell the truth.

Truth is a temptation, Martin. It can be dangerous. But listen. I'm curious about the slaves around here. On the various farms. How many would there be, do you think?

Martin had no idea. Thirty? Fifty?

Where would they be at this hour?

In a field. Different fields.

What about tomorrow? Morning? Can you bring me to them?

We'd have to . . . You mean . . . I don't

53

think Uncle Benj—

Would like it. Let's go make your bear a nice safe place to sleep. Have you named her yet?

Leaving the sown field, they were careful to stay between the rows, hopping from one foot to another over the long narrow mounds, Martin pointing to some striated rock when they got to the edge and Ross saying: That was once at the bottom of the sea, son. I'll wager there are fish skeletons in it. Take a look.

There's an owl comes to that tree over there, Martin replied, to show that he knew his whereabouts and could not be fooled about fish in rocks.

And what does your owl like to eat? Cottonseed?

Martin hugged the bear cub. I could name her Cuff.

Why?

She cuffs me. Then bites my ear.

Omnivore. Do you know that word? A jay will eat the babies in another bird's nest.

That's a cannibal. And rocks got made by the Lord, Mister Ross.

Ross pointed down: Just look here. This old ground was formed by operations that repeat themselves over and over. The law of nature is constant change. Flux. Nothing is ready-made.

Martin suddenly shouted a perfect imitation of his father's preacherly voice: And the disappearance of languages! And the return of the Jews to the holy land!

What's that? Ross was taken aback.

Confused by the talk of constant change, Martin asked: Don't you know about Jesus coming back?

They took their time in the woods, doing a count of birds, Ross making marks in a notebook. They did not find a shrike on the wing or on a branch and Ross wondered out loud if he might be too late, if they were even now nesting in the marshy lake country of Upper Canada. He used his field glasses. He crouched and peered. Jesus is coming back. Here?

We have to *earn* the sight though.

Isn't it all predetermined? Who gets saved?

No sir, that's Calvinist! Martin looked up at the birdman slyly. And not very scientific.

6

Martin was late to the supper table. Having spent the afternoon in the barn nailing down pieces of wood to cover a mule stall so his bear would be safely confined in a warm, dark cave and then going back to the house and upstairs, where he went straight to the cot for overnight guests that sat in a corner of the hall and looked through the birdman's leather bag. He could hear Patton whispering threats from their shared room on the other side of the wall: I'll get you back for telling on me. My baby brother! What a pal.

Martin whispered: I didn't tell! But he thought of Cuff's mother, who would be chopped up for meat, her fur to be spread on the floor of the parlor as if it had never known life, never had a little baby to protect. Patton was not allowed supper and Martin didn't care. Serves him right. Maybe he would bring something up to their room at bedtime, but it wouldn't be anything nice. Patton had to learn his lesson. That's what their father said and now their mother was upset by the threat of sending Patton out west. It was easy to look through the birdman's leather bag. But why so many compasses? Why so many knives? Maps of Virginia, Kentucky, and Ohio. There was also the notebook containing pitiful sketches. *Thrush — largest of the sparrow kind, with bill somewhat bending at the point. Also the stare or starling, though with flat bill. Also the blackbird in same genus*

note: more snares laid for thrushes than for other birds — esp song thrush and redwing

note: the starling damages Indian corn in its milky state.

a farmer would require guns to protect his crop

Martin skipped through the pages. No mention of loggerhead shrike. He thought: The birdman doesn't even know starlings feed on grub worms, which makes up for the early corn damage.

note: In the woods: wild grapes, blackberries, raspberries, gooseberries

He was thinking about the mistakes in the notebook when he got to the table, last to arrive. No wild grapes in these woods, he was thinking, pleased by his local knowledge. The birdman doesn't know so much. He scraped his chair legs on the floor and got a frown from his mother while John introduced his daughters. Gina, the little one, and Electa, just home from school in Carolina. His tone underlined the feat of sending a daughter off to any form of education. There was no mention of Patton, no point in identifying him as the "rascal" who had killed a mother bear. Instead, the preacher took up his favorite subject. We cured this ham our own family way, he began, gesturing at the heavy platter Clotilde was balancing on her forearm. Our best pig slaughtered in the fall. He tucked a napkin into his collar and next explained that the smokehouse had been built by his late father, that the customs of the family had been set long ago, that they were traditions by now, and he rubbed his hands when the smothered cabbage and spiced beets were served up by Clotilde spoonful by spoonful to each plate. Ross seemed surprised by this show of earthly appetite, but Martin knew his father well in this regard. His father consumed everything. He hated waste is how he put it, and now the hungry preacher was watching Clotilde cut the ham on his plate into bite-sized pieces with an expression that made Martin look away. It's the acorns, John said reverently. And the peach pits, plus smoke, which we learned from the Natives. Who were plentiful around here until Mister Jefferson cleared them off . . . Martin's father had slipped into his preacher voice and now the diners relaxed. Six-year-old Gina's eyes were closed, ready for prayer, and Electa was clasping her hands while Lavina was impatiently moving her lips. Let us give thanks to our Heavenly Father, said John, bringing his voice back to full volume. You will note we do not imbibe, Doctor Ross.

Nor do I, said Ross nicely. Although there is the problem of Communion, isn't there?

At which water will suffice as it did at Cana.

Martin's mother was staring at the loaded plates.

For what we are about to receive, may the Lord make us truly thankful, John said, keeping his eyes on her.

Was that the Cherokee who got run off? Ross asked after everyone said Amen. By Jefferson? He stared at the frayed cuffs on John's jacket. I guess they refused to work the fields?

John frowned. Have a pickle, he urged, passing a cut-glass bowl. Good for the digestion, as you would know. And as to the meat, it is first coated in salt, that's the ticket. Three days, no more, it sits in our smokehouse on slats so as not to turn soggy.

Ross was burying his ham under cabbage leaves.

Then in spring, we take the meat off the rack, wash it, dip the joints in boiling water, and coat it with borax. Borax! John thumped his chest. Then we hang it up in sacks to the rafters of the smokehouse and keep a fire smoldering . . . and . . . we . . .

Ross was nodding. Hmm. I meant to say that I attended your ministry. Ah, yesterday. Although it seems a long time ago now, thinking back on it, when you mentioned an angel . . .

And you think the concept of angelic interference is lacking in evidence, I suppose. John leaned back in his chair, preparing himself, obviously pleased.

Oh, it isn't evidence I want, sir. That would be pointless. I am trying to remember the biblical story is all. I remember an engraving. Doré, I think it was, in a library book. It's Jacob who begs the angel for forgiveness, is that right?

Makes supplication. Promises to repent. As I said. Yes-ter-day. John made each syllable of the word a little joke on the frailty

60

of the human mind. Jacob, he downright bullies the angel, don't you see, although you'll remember that his brother has been cast adrift. He has cast his brother out entirely. Utterly! John stretched his legs out under the table and looked at the tips of his fingers as if they had earned the right to hold his fork. Yes. You see. And he knew it well enough, didn't he? A brother made homeless for twenty years. What right had Jacob to beg for a blessing? And yet, what choice after such fraternal indecency?

But a man who treats another so abominably has a right to expect forgiveness?

Expectation should play no part in it. John shook his head solemnly. Besides. I thought you men of science had no interest in such questions. Angels. Forgiveness. He was still enjoying himself.

Ross looked down at his water glass. I'm wearing a cotton shirt, sir. I'm not guiltless. He lifted his eyebrows.

Which we . . . Oh! I daresay you are pulling my leg! Cotton shirt! John cleared his throat. But back to the Natives. He took a deep breath and then another bite. He was embarking on a favorite subject. Man is made of many types, Doctor Ross, as I am sure you will acknowledge as a scientific thinker. Some of us are born to lead, some

61

to sow, and some to reap. The Native's historical time is spent, I'm afraid, although social position has no importance in the eyes of our Lord. John took a piece of ham on his fork, looked at it, and shoved it in his mouth. He laid the fork on the tablecloth, smearing juice and fat. We are part of nature, he said, which claims exactly the same differences in all species.

Exactly, sir. We are not even the only species to kidnap or capture our own kind, making them work for us without gain. Many insects do the same.

Martin heard this as a kind of thunderclap and he watched his father lean forward, bracing his weight on his hands, lifting himself a few inches from the seat of his chair. He was turning a little red in the face, which was not unusual, but this was the supper table and his mother was tapping her foot and once again moving her lips, even squinting some at the visitor, as if she could not believe what she had heard. His father's question was almost a hiss. Do you not call food and shelter fair reward for labor?

Gentlemen, Lavina interceded.

Not without choice, sir. Which always depends on advantage.

John looked at his guest and frowned.

As in *Woe unto him that useth his neighbor's service without wages.*

The children had now lost all interest in food. They were sitting in their separate chairs, Martin having pushed himself to the edge of his. He was frightened and pleased. He would not have moved for anything in the world.

John said tightly: The people who work this land were born in America, Doctor Ross. Not a one of them was captured. Virginia does not allow importation! And we shall gradually improve the race, I assure you, John finished mildly, picking up his fork and running a finger over the stain on the tablecloth. Pass the beets.

Shall we do that through crossbreeding or education, I wonder?

Martin said: But, Papa, Bry was captured!

John snapped: Electa! Take your sister upstairs right this minute! He pointed a finger at Martin. You go now with the girls! He clapped his hands. He said to Ross: According to your theory, the drone ant resembles the queen?

Martin was frozen in his hard chair. He watched the pulse beating in his father's neck. Probably his father had hoped to engage the doctor in some subject of scientific interest, but it was not going as he wished.

Before dessert, Papa? They were the first words Gina had uttered and the voice was a whine and Electa said: Don't worry, Papa, I've heard worse at school, as the door was flung open by Clotilde and the scent of peach cobbler covered them with its hint of relief. Lavina stood up, reached for a small silver pitcher, and moved quickly to John. At his side, she began to pour nutmeg sauce on his portion of cobbler while everyone else waited to be served. There was no tenderness in the act of pouring, only Lavina's usual custom while John jabbed a spoon at the latticed crust. Electa, you children are excused. I won't say it again. He dabbed at his mouth with the napkin still attached to his collar.

Electa was pushing her chair away from the table. She said: Doctor Ross, if social position is of no importance to God, then slavery is as good a system as any, isn't it? The look she gave him was not easy to read.

They were born right here, John repeated.

Lavina made a clatter of dishes, gathering some of them from the table before holding them out to Clotilde, fluttering her arms as a signal to take them away.

In the kitchen a few minutes later, Clotilde was humming to herself, grinding newly roasted coffee beans when Lavina came in. She kept pots of herbs on the windowsill and she reached for a sprig of the lavender because the scene at her table had made her head ache, the guest using knife and fork at the same time, and further offending by engaging in sordid politics. Lavina's day had been long and sad. As the preacher's wife, she'd attended the birth of Sister Eliza Ely's first child. It went on the whole of the day and she could not clear her mind of it now for so much as a minute, even considering what had occurred at her table. She had watched poor, young Eliza die in a pool of blood. She had watched the bereaved husband while she thought of John putting his own little newborn Martin outside on a rock the night he was born. She had made every effort to forget her own past as she took Sister Eliza's baby in her arms and washed him with tears and then Eliza's wealthy mother had arrived in a rush and made a show of taking the baby away in her carriage. This is my baby now, she'd said, while Lavina had looked at the father and pitied him. After that awful scene she'd fled home in her buggy to find a strange man in her house and another unpleasant scene. Stop that! she said of the coffee grinding, her voice sharp. John was particular of his coffee and it must not be too fine, which Clotilde should certainly know by now, if she knew anything at all.

On the other side of the door, John was gazing at his table, seeing the tallow candles, more than were necessary, and the porcelain plates muddied by peaches and nutmeg syrup. He lifted his face to glance across the table at his guest, having forgotten Martin, who was sitting as quietly as he could manage to sit so as not to be sent away. Ross was saying: By way of thanks for this fine meal, I might mention that some churches in New York have a concoction of boiled raisins and water to serve for Communion. Because. It doesn't ferment. For some reason they add the white of an egg, though I can't say what the purpose of that is.

John said simply: I suggest that while in Virginia you should keep your opinions as to insects and Communion to yourself. We have the law with us, is what I mean.

Ross interrupted: Although surely you believe Christ's law is superior to civil law. Give the Jewish law of bond service to

Virginia, and there will not be a slave left to wet the soil with the sweat of unpaid labor. Then, rising from his chair, Ross apologized for abandoning the table. It is the hour of the owl, as I like to call it, he said, though others have more useful names, I've no doubt.

I suspect you have many a doubt, John said coldly, putting his hand on the pocket where he kept a cigar. Then he added: Doubt being no shame to a scientist.

7

When Martin left the house the next morning, John watched from an upstairs window. No boot clunk or door squeak. The doctor had already left his cot and gone off with his Italian device and a notebook tucked under his arm. Now Martin followed him, slipping out silently in the dark, a boy in bare feet, a boy not easily awakened, a boy born twelve and a half years ago on a cold October night, blue of skin and not expected to survive. The midwife had advised John to put him outside, as the cold air would decide things. Four pounds at birth, and Lavina left the birthing bed to go out in the dark to lift her newborn off the ground. Now John wondered: Why would the boy wake up to run after a man who was looking for birds? Why would the boy want to follow at an hour when he was usually soundly asleep? Martin had rescued a bear cub with the help of this intruder. And why did I allow the cub to be kept in the barn when the last thing I need is a nosy boy playing in a mule stall? Was it Lavina's entreaty for the cub or something darker — a tinge of guilt for a baby left out in the cold?

8

In the woods full of pitfalls and whipping branches, Martin was as quiet as he'd learned to be when he ran off with Franklin, Emly's oldest boy, who had reached an age when play was forbidden during the hours of work, and even afterward he had to curry and feed the master's horse and bring him around when the master called, so he could never go off out of earshot. Now, if they met, it was usually on the sly, and they'd want to go back to building their dam that washed away every spring, but that was too far from the house. Anyway. What was the rush? Shouldn't the birdman be strolling, studying branches, looking up through dew-heavy leaves for the starling with its flat bill, the thrush, largest of the sparrow kind? Instead he was heading at a wobbly run toward a cotton field cold in its rim of grass. He had a sore foot but he was running! The pale sun cast a vaporous light across that bare field and men and women and children moved along in single file, turned by the unrisen sun into silhouettes. Martin recognized each walk or shrug or shape. Mean old Sutter kind of stomping in that way he had and Reuben dragging along and the five children clutching hoes that wobbled on their narrow shoulders like metal flags. There was Franklin in the lead trying to march, asleep on his feet. A week ago he and Martin had played their favorite trick on Uncle Benjamin's bull, hiding behind the laurel and bellowing until his head went up and he cleared the cows away and came charging, pawing at the ground in a bullish rage. There was a good fence between the laurel and the bull, but sod was flying and the boys laughed. Now Martin stopped behind a tree and watched his friend stagger along in the line of slaves while the birdman hurried to catch up. He saw the men shade their faces with hands or hats as the stranger approached and the two women bowed their heads and then he heard the hooves of a big horse, and he wanted to warn the birdman about Uncle Benjamin. Who else would be out here at this hour? But he hid behind a bush and watched Ross explaining something to the silhouettes. The horse was coming. The iron feet nicked the stones in the field and Martin ran off fast.

He had forgotten Cuff's milk. He should go back to the house. The barn was closed up and the bear seemed alarmed at the creak of the door. She let out a few furtive squeaks. Then she was making mewing sounds and hissing through her baby teeth. Black as night in the barn and Martin climbed into the stall through a little door he unlatched. Were there creatures that might hurt his bear, as the birdman had warned? A snake? The mean father bear? I name you Cuff, he said, when she pushed at him, looking for milk. Was a bear like a horse or cow to be fed at a certain hour? Can't you just wait a minute?

Then the big door opened again and the boy and the bear listened to the sound of light human feet. It was Emly quietly speaking to the cows, bringing them grain to tempt them closer. She dumped corn at the heads of the first cows to be milked and Martin heard them move forward to eat as she readied the pails. In a moment the others began lowing, asking for shares, and Martin crawled back out through the stall door and got up on his feet. When Emly turned, she said: Oh! You came for the bear?

I forgot her milk.

Come here, Martin. Emly was like this, always nice and soft because he was Franklin's friend. Or because she was nice to everybody, even cows. She said: The girls can share their milk, I guess.

There was no bottle but Martin went back to the stall with a half-filled pail. The cows were lowing again, waiting now for hay. The three young calves were bawling and Martin heard Emly moving toward them with full pails. The sun had risen and the floor of the barn where he sat was washed with a cool striped light.

He did not hear his father's entrance. Only the softest call: Emly? He had come to feed his mare, of course, although it was early. And Emly answered: Here. Then she said: Martin, too, in the stall.

Quietly, Martin held the pail of milk and the cub grabbed for it, slopping it up with her tongue and dribbling it on the floor. When she finished she moved to Martin's neck, greedy to suck now, as if she had missed this pleasure while taking milk from a pail. It made Martin feel strange in his stomach when she sucked on his ear and he wanted to pull away but he pressed his back against the stall and let Cuff have her way. If Emly or his father saw this, he would be embarrassed. Hey, stop that, he would have to say gruffly, but the bear was a motor and Martin felt expanded, his heart beating hard. He might have identified this as a symptom of love but he had no experience of such an idea, no memory of his own infancy or the nurture his mother had provided. His present life was a test of propriety, one test after another. His father spoke of Heaven and Hell as if he had a formula. His father believed an angel was coming. His father believed in each person's need to work toward getting blessed. He had a balance sheet. Some days Martin gave the balance sheet a check mark, but then he would think back and erase it. Oh, bear, he said: What is Mister Ross doing out there in the cotton field? It's the workers who always get punished, no matter who does something bad, Martin thought. They don't know about birds, so he should leave them alone. And from now on, Martin would ask Emly to save some milk every morning for Cuff.

That afternoon he stayed out of sight and the day leaked away. But that night he picked his way along the edge of things, following Ross again. The birdman had taken leave of the family just after supper. I'm heading on up the road, Ross had said. With many thanks for your kindness.

At this hour?

I have an appointment with that owl. He said goodnight to Martin, even shook his hand, then shouldered his leather bag and set off as Martin quietly followed, keeping well out of sight. Uncle Benjamin's brick house rose up like a fortress while Ross went the long way around it, front to side to back, leaving the road far behind. Beyond sat the smokehouse with its steaming bricks, and beyond that the barn and past the barn and into the bush, the soft shape of Emly's cabin against the softer night.

Martin was following furtively, keeping to the shadows, wondering if Franklin might be outside. Hopefully he would not make any noise about Martin sneaking around. Martin had never been inside the little house but Emly had once made him a shirt because Uncle Benjamin allowed her to gather the wool his sheep deposited on thorns and fences. This wool she washed and carded and spun and when time allowed she wove it into cloudy cloth, making warm shirts for her children that fell to their knees. Martin's shirt had a collar so it was better than Franklin's. He was thinking about that when he saw Ross tap on Emly's door and he knew then that he should not be watching. Such a man should not be knocking at such a door. Not at night. Not ever. Martin crept up close and hid behind an azalea bush. No star shone yet; it was dark all around.

When the door opened for Ross, Martin heard the low hum of voices inside the house and he could see a group of men crowded in there, all standing up for lack of any place to sit. He saw Bry and Reuben leaning together. They were the oldest. They had been on the farm forever except for when Bry ran away and got captured. Martin recognized the voice of Nick asking something and then there was quiet. A smell of roasted corn filled the air. A few whispers lingering. Nervous laughter. Martin's teeth chattering. He pinched his arm to calm himself down and, when the door closed, he went closer, putting his ear up against the logs. He could hear breath hissing out of throats. How many in there? He turned his head to listen with the other ear. The bird-man was going to tell a story. That's what he announced in a loud whisper so that everyone got very quiet. But what a thing to do, after he'd said he was going off to find an owl! The birdman was a liar and Martin felt tricked even though the lie had been told to his father. A long time ago a baby got carried up north from down here near this farm, he heard the liar say. I know that because her mother's certificate of marriage lists Jonesville as the wedding place and I came here to tell you about a slave woman who carried that baby to Canada and then found her own freedom there. Because Canada is another country, where slavery is against the law! She was helping the baby's mother but she got herself free! And so can you.

Mister? Somebody was interrupting.

There's catchers the whole way up to there.

Bring you back. Make it worse on you.

Renau from the Morgans got took back.

We down the bottom of this Commonwealth, Mister.

Renau got branded.

Burned his face.

Bry got worst!

A bevy of voices and Martin pressed against the logs trying to make them out, but the birdman was quiet for a long minute on the other side of the wall. Then he said: I myself will travel around the Commonwealth this summer, which is a risk to me, but I heard the story of the slave getting herself up to Canada, just a woman, and how she made herself free being brave and I wanted you to get up there to where she can help you find a good life. The birdman's voice took on a cadence now and Martin knew in his bones that no one should trust a cadence. He had heard that same tone too often from the pulpit and he also had proof that the birdman was a liar because of the owl. Ross was shaping his words, telling about the glories of a country owned by England where no fugitive slave law grabs you and sends you back down to bondage. And if anyone here is willing to risk that long journey, he said, I shall provide a compass and a knife and a map and you will be safe on the other side.

What of?

Martin could have answered that. He knew geography. How could a person cross such water, even finding the narrowest place? The Ohio was nothing but a river, but the lake up there was more than a man could cross without a ticket on a steamboat and it was unfair to tempt anyone who couldn't buy such a thing! Angry now, Martin started to cuss under his breath. Hell! Piss! He began to hear panting too because the men had to breathe as one creature in a house without windows and a door closed tight and he thought he heard the leather bag get opened and then get shut with a snap. Here rises the sun in the morning and here is the way you walk at night. Hiding. Always hiding. For if you are picked up, you will be beaten, sold, brought back to this place in chains. Just as you said.

No sir. I ain't tryin.

Martin had fallen against the wall in such a trembling state he could hardly move. Those men listening would be found out and punished. Emly would be punished and even Franklin, all of them. Martin had seen Sutter and Billy whipped, which was way worse than a beating, clothes off and skin torn and Uncle Benjamin used to make his sons watch every time he did it. You know the North Star? The birdman was challenging. That is your guide. You take dry bread for the journey, which will be many long days of hiding and long nights of walking where you can barely see your own feet in the dark. And you rush. You hurry on. Carry no light. You are listening, looking at the sky. There will be signs that are secret. You know about them?

Sure we know.

So! Read every sign. Quilts with a blue border mean that house is safe, from what I heard. Be careful though. You are risking your life because in Canada you will have no master. You will have Freedom. And Mama Bett can find you work in a big city and you will earn money and . . .

What city is that?

Now Martin made himself stand up straight, not to run away but in order to concentrate. In the morning he'd better talk to Bry, who could read and write and help the others understand that this was a terrible idea. Yes. They would talk man to man. There was more and more talking in low, anxious voices and the chimney was growing cold by then but heat of another kind had boiled up inside the house, so many men in there with women in the neighboring houses or quarters. There were children. There were issues of one kind and obstacles of another. When the door finally opened, there was no light from the house, not so much as a candle, and at the side Martin stood stock-still watching Emly hold the hand of a man with a doubled-up fist. He was saying: I got a mama up there and how could I ever know it? Maybe I got a child.

Martin closed his eyes and said a prayer because it was the old one called Bry and tears were running down his face as if every lie he'd heard in Emly's house could be true.

And the next morning, he was gone.

9

Bry's first escape had taken place on the night of Eva Nell's birth, when Mama Bett carried her away from the house before Rafe Fox could lay his eyes on her dusky skin. This happened while Jemima's dead body was taken off in a wagon: it happened when Bett grabbed the baby out of Bry's arms and he ran away, hiding in caves and eating dead things and maybe Mister Rafe never knew the part Bry played in begetting the baby who carried his name but he hunted the slave boy down anyhow with the hounds he had raised. He hunted him also with legal notices and bribes: *runaway boy in my yellow shoes I never gave to him;* and a few days later, Rafe had him brought back tied over a mule and he did the punishment himself, using a gelding hook on a boy who was just fifteen.

The extent of the damage would take years to acknowledge. No growth, no knitting of bones, no advance into manhood for body or voice; *gelded a boy and made him a mare.* Bry's legs often ached and his knees never quite unbent. What use is there for a capon man? After the punishment, Rafe gave the boy to Benjamin in payment of a gambling debt and all these years later Alexander Ross had given Bry the one incentive that could make him want to run again. Then, within hours, Bry became an inspiration. Rafe lost four men, and some of the neighbors lost two or more. Benjamin lost three more — Billy, Josiah, and Sutter — and everyone turned on Preacher John because he'd sheltered the man who tempted their workers to flight. It was said like this: A man might go out to relieve his bowels or his bladder in some stand of bush or tree, but what is inconceivable is that he does not return to his pallet, which is a place among his own kind, unlike the road or the woods, where beasts and unwelcome others lurk. What is inconceivable is that a man so well fed and housed would risk his life to run away into nothing but starvation and eventual capture because, by the time the defections were counted up, Benjamin and his neighbors had created a posse of men and dogs. Notices were posted. Rewards were offered. In the North, the fugitive slave law would bring them back.

Some ten or twelve miles from Benjamin's farm, Bry had built a feeble shelter in which he slept exhausted for two long days and two chilly nights, not being strong enough in body or young enough in years to move fast. He had eaten a mere hatful of berries and he was too tired to forage so he lay in his shelter curled around himself and chewing at a sapling stick and trying to remember the details the birdman had spoken about where his Mama Bett was living. He rubbed at his knees and worried about the others and wondered if they would follow his lead and maybe get caught and that would put him to blame. He thought about the girl named Rakel, who had been confounded by a tragedy some years before when Benjamin purchased Josiah, who loved her and married her. It was a blessed event, or so it had seemed, and for some days after, they waited, foreseeing the time when they would find an hour to spend alone. It would not happen in the dismal cellar but out somewhere in the forest beyond the field on a Sunday when there was time to give to each other. Bry could so easily remember the rush brought about by that hammering kind of love and he had jealously watched Josiah go off alone in order to meet his bride in the privacy of leaves. He had remembered the portion given to Adam and the portion taken by Eve and he had let himself fret but he could not even imagine that what happened to Josiah was poor Rakel's fault. He imagined them as they must have fastened themselves to each other giving no thought to the rags they were wearing on tired bodies. Time being short, they had never unclothed or stepped out of their boots and a week would pass before such an hour would come again and they determined to stay separate until they could disentangle their swollen hearts and relieve their great hunger to be known to each other. And so it was that Rakel on that second Sabbath had fashioned a bower out of branches and they lay against the receiving ground and examined arms and legs and bellies and then Rakel pushed her lover with a firm hand and rolled him over in order to breathe her breath on his back and she saw a long scar that matched the gash she remembered on her little son some years before when he had been whipped by an overseer on a different farm where she had lived and given birth at the age of thirteen. Josiah was her husband. Josiah was her son.

They were punished for coming back late but their pain was something else entire.

Josiah explained it while beating his head with his fists and Rakel went to the corner of the cellar so that she would not look on Josiah's anguish. A parent and child should never be separated to the point of unknowing, Bry thought now. Sold apart and something bad could happen. What if he met his daughter and loved her as a man to a woman except that he couldn't. He had no heart between his legs, and he huddled alone in the shelter he'd made, thinking these thoughts and was therefore surprised by the sound of grief coming out of his mouth. Maybe Josiah would take Rakel with him if he left and they would all meet again. But Josiah couldn't swim and he wasn't careful of himself. Can't swim any more than me, Bry thought. He could hear the trickle of water as he lay there trying to bring back his earlier boyhood escape. Saleem, Mama Bett had called those yellow shoes Jemima gave to him, and it was nothing but a word made up because she liked to make up a word for the two of them so that Mother Mary would not be in on it. Mother Mary was the owner of Mama Bett, and those two women, white and black, had raised him until he was taken away by Mister Rafe. And now. Will this bird fly into another net? The land was some cover and there were caves known from the past. Huts and houses, barns and fences all to avoid, grown out of the forest as all things are. First the forest with its perfect order and then the rest of us come and chop it down and build up towns with the wood of the murdered trees. Out here, sweet birch to suck, the markel good in spring. What will heal and what will feed and what will cause a dream. Onions in the open. Ramps in the dark. And water. Stay close to it. Moon a hook like the castrating knife and he walks all night and his stomach growls and the wind blows through him so a hound couldn't smell him passing by. Gutted by terror. Great swell of heart. Someone had thrown out bones. I'll snatch them up. I'll walk under the gourd and away from the knife and be smarter than the boy I was when I got caught. Bry reached down to his separate thing, its duty nothing more than watering, and had himself a freedom piss.

10

In the reading room of a Cleveland hotel, Alexander Ross picked up a Richmond paper that contained a lengthy account of a slave escape near the small town of Jonesville. "THIRTEEN NEGROES FLED," the headline read. The article noted that an organized band of abolitionists had invaded the town, supplying slaves with directions and illegal means of escape such as knives to be used on their masters' throats. Authorities were urged to offer a reward for the apprehension of the cursed Northern thieves and Ross put his feet up on a cushion, drank a glass of water, and laughed. He would clip the article and share his success with Eva Nell to soften the things he had learned about her past in his short morning meeting with Mister Rafe Fox on the day bear was shot.

11

Crouched in the stall with Cuff, Martin did not hear his father enter the barn. He heard a soft call, nothing like the voice of a father. It said: Are you here? and Martin thought it was meant for him and that he would stay as quiet as possible so he would not have to help his father with the mare, who was mean as gravel and sometimes kicked. Martin shushed his bear. He took her paw. He stroked her head.

Then he heard Emly's whisper: I'm here.

There was nothing to do but listen. He gathered Cuff in his arms and let her suck his ear. The mare was stamping her hooves, as if to answer the footsteps she knew so well but when Preacher John coughed and cleared his throat, Martin covered his ears. He felt a sharp curiosity and a strange sense of shame. When he at last took his hands away from his head, he heard Emly saying:

With a child to come. I am . . .
And Martin's father said: Is it mine?

12

Four men unaccounted for! Benjamin was shouting. It was June and he had found his brother in the confines of their father's sun-struck cabin. The river's running high and no one holds out the slightest hope of them! How do you plan to make it up to me, Brother John?

John looked down at his account book.

If I catch that sly nigger who started them off, I'll beat him to death.

You'll feed him and mend him as you did when he was a boy. Come harvest, we can hire . . .

Harvest? A hired boy costs forty dollars because prices went up to the roof when the men ran off. Harvest? Benjamin ran a hand through his hair, gray at the edges, his face also gray. God damn you, he said. If He placed you on my land by divine decree, I do not thank him for fouling my nest.

Not until that hour had John considered

his complete dependence on this half brother, half human being. If Benjamin's fortunes failed to revive . . . The thought made him cold and he said meekly: We'll have brandy to sell when the pears come ripe. He tried to meet his half-brother's eyes.

Pears!

Wind was bringing down branches. There was rain like wrath.

John made an entry in his account book: *hands replanting potatoes, which under the Season rotted in the ground and we have only slips.* These days, his entries were more like bad dreams than balance sheets.

And Emly's body swelled with life. He wanted to say: Does he use you? But he could not make the words leave his mouth. What was use and what was need? What was lust and what was love? John loved Lavina and yet it was as if the clocks of the world stopped when he lay between Emly's legs. Circe, he called her, and he resigned himself to the logic of minutes piling up somewhere to be spent at another time. Better to need than to use, he decided, and Emly put his hand on her belly while inside lived a tucked and restless child. She rolled toward him so they lay face to face. She put her hand on his brow. Stormy, she said.

13

Bear learns the varied smells of leaves and nuts, learns everything by sniffing. Bear must practice — to forage, to taste, to climb, to fight. Bear is a million years innate. As the wet summer advanced, she sniffed at trees and logs and the sniffing was loud, like a horn in reverse. She favored poplar leaves and liked to hold them in her mouth. Then she would spit them out, bluntly, in some distress, making a rude *pff-pht* sound. When she charged at Martin, it was all bluff. She never trailed far behind him or ventured far ahead and sometimes she wrapped a forepaw around his thin boy leg to hobble him and make him fall down. Then she would suck on his neck or ear. One day she went up a tree. Instead of resting at the first branch, she went higher, then even higher. The old pine bark crumbled under her claws and Martin, frightened almost to pain, opened his arms and Cuff fell into them. For a few moments, she was all grace, but the memory of another bear was there in the boy and he thought he must teach Cuff to climb. Her safety depended on him.

As she grew past twenty pounds, she stopped more often at one place or another, smelled and tasted more plants, mouthing them as if some part of her palate could decide what was right for her. Martin loved to think over her every move. Why did she eat soil? Why did she eat deer droppings? When offered a little frog, Cuff politely spat it out, but she had begun to dig for ant eggs and wood beetles and ate them like treats. The boy spent more and more time with the growing bear.

Meanwhile, Martin's father was pre-occupied every minute of the day. He was taken up with his circuit — riding through wind and rain or plain summer heat — or with worries about Benjamin, who was spending his nights at the Comfort House. It was not lost on anyone, this state of affairs. Benjamin was beleaguered. Everyone watched as he quietly fell apart. Patton bought a horse and charged around the neighborhood in search of distraction. Lavina's attention was carefully kept on Gina, who had a cough that kept her in bed.

Electa was weaving, sewing, helping Lavina in the house, and Martin, with all his chores, found more and more time to spend with Cuff. He memorized her different huffs, different growls, and her small but dramatic moans. There were her various ways of walking, sometimes bowling along in a rush and sometimes walking stiff-legged to hide in the trees when she felt threatened. School was closed for the season and Martin could take up the challenge the birdman had given him. To train a bear. He would do it gently, not like Preacher John. He wanted a happy pupil. He would teach Cuff to dance. He would create a livelihood for the two of them.

Once, Martin saw a woodpecker on a large dead log. When it flew away, he went to the place it had been and knelt down, which usually brought Cuff to his side, then lifted the bark to expose a colony of ants. Cuff ambled over and took no interest in the larvae but went straight for the big ants that came to the surface. The taste of those ants seemed to surprise her, or perhaps they were biting her tongue, but she shook her head after a single mouthful.

By the end of July, Martin had taught Cuff to wait while he ran off to hide. She learned to sit on her haunches while he counted to ten. Then she would pant and sniff and come after him. A rare opportunity, the birdwatcher had declared. To train a bear. And sometimes Franklin came along. Who you like best, the bear or me? Franklin asked.

Well, she's faster than you, Martin teased. And they ran off to the woods with the bear loping behind to visit the old bear tree. This was said to be a place male bears left marks and scent. It stood above the trail on a narrow cliff and Cuff regarded it from below and then worked her way up the steep slope, but in minutes her screams brought Martin and Franklin to the rescue and they took her back down and led her around to the side of the rise where she could climb up easily, finding a trail of bear tracks straight to the old red pine. Why do bears come here? Franklin asked.

And Martin wondered how Cuff even knew about the tree without a mother to teach her things that matter to a bear. He also wondered: Were the tracks made earlier in the spring, when the ground was soft? Or were they recent? If so, was there a male bear close by? Could it be Cuff's father? Franklin hopped up and down at the thought of a male bear, but Martin would not go home until Cuff was ready to leave.

He did not want to see his own father just then. His own father was in a disruptive mood. A Baptist had come through the town and several Methodists had agreed to be immersed.

14

Alexander Ross was very glad to be back in Canada. The United States had tired him with its various oppositions. No one in that country seemed to agree on anything. One thought the foundation of democracy was capital, another thought it was sacrifice, one bled the land, and another fostered it. Arguing was the primary occupation. It was not a communal country but rather devoted to the individual and to personal gain. Ross found his mother on her front porch having tea. She had given over the classroom to Eva Nell so that she could have a break. Lately, Eva Nell had taken on more teaching, walking from her house on the shore to the schoolroom at the back of the Ross residence, where she taught the girls to dye linen and spin wool, then to weave and sew, offering them useful industry while Missus Ross taught them to add and subtract, to read and to write cursive script.

When she heard his voice at the front of the house, Eva Nell excused herself from the schoolroom and ran to the hall to stand at the door to the porch. She and Ross were closer than siblings and he had been gone all summer long, and Eva Nell wanted to see his face; she longed to hear his wonderful laugh and the high points of his trip because fighting slavery was a fine thing to do. It fit his character better than studying birds and trees. He would make a good doctor but there was more to him than that and later, when they had a few moments alone, she would learn the results of his secret assignment. Surely he would have discovered the truth of her mysterious past. She was older than Ross by seven years. She had no inheritance and no real father she could claim. Jones? It was a name on a marriage document found with her mother's few papers. I have learned your history, Ross would say, crossing his legs and settling into his chair while a cup of warm water wobbled on his thigh. For the moment though he was leaning forward, telling his mother about the slaves he had met. He was saying: Remember when I first asked Nell's mother about her background?

Missus Ross said: Which she would not divulge at any price.

But she told us about slavery and Mother, it's so much worse than she said.

Unseen in the hallway, Eva Nell was waiting for her turn with Ross. She did not want to share him with her employer. She wanted to feel his arms around her in that protective way he had with her, but Missus Ross was pouring tea and rambling on and finally Eva Nell stepped out to the porch because she could not wait any longer.

Missus Ross looked up and said: So, she was listening behind the door. All right then, Nell, I'm sure the students will keep well occupied, if you must join in. I am hearing about my son's efforts for the slaves. She allowed herself a sigh.

Ross went to Eva Nell gladly, putting his arms around her while he kissed her lightly on the cheek. He then turned back to his mother, mimicking a Southerner's voice: Oh but we don call em slaves, ma'am. We never saaay that awful word.

Missus Ross pursed her lips and shook her head, the long ties on her cap swinging fitfully, and Ross admitted that he did not know which slaves had escaped due to his efforts or even how many, but he had visited several towns where he had seen notices advertising for missing Negroes and one article in a Cleveland paper had proved his

99

own personal success, he said, bowing formally and tipping an imaginary hat. Mother, before you send Nell back to the classroom, may I have a moment with her?

Missus Ross rose from her porch rocker and called to a former student who was serving as her maid. Jilly, please take in the tray. My son drinks only water, which makes life so much poorer for the lack of flavor, but leave him his glass. And she swept up her full, stiff skirt and went inside as Ross said quietly: How have you been, Nell? Is the school holding itself together for you? I've worried. Was the summer pleasant? Did you find entertainment? Any sales?

Well, I've been making new dyes. Finding new plants. A strong black, wonderful for patterns and outlines. And indigo. I boil it down. Yes, thank you. But please, Alex, tell me what you learned. I am . . . I cannot wait another minute longer. There is a gentleman . . .

A suitor? But that's wonderful, Nell. Although you may find some of what I have to say unsettling. Will you sit down and let me do the same?

Eva Nell sat down without bothering to smooth her skirt.

I found your father on a farm near Jonesville, Ross said, taking his seat. It wasn't difficult. I think you always knew he would be there, didn't you? He may have fought up here in 1812, but he must have gone back home. As Ross spoke, he watched the wariness of Eva Nell's expression while, from the interior of the house, the sounds of the schoolroom were pleasant and familiar. He leaned back and took a deep breath. Eva Nell was waiting for his report as she had never waited for anything before and he must be careful.

Her hands gripped the arms of her chair. She frowned and her warm skin began to pale.

Your father's name is Rafe Fox, not Jones. He's a neighbor to your maternal family and it's not a pretty tale.

I'm listening, Alex.

The point is . . . the fact is . . . well, the worst of it is that Mary Jones was not your mother. It is, I mean, the truth is that Mary Jones was your aunt. She was . . .

Mama? My aunt? Why would she say what's not true?

To protect you. Ross looked across the porch at the woman sitting in the shade of a climbing vine and he said gently: Your mother was Mary's younger sister, Jemima, who died giving birth to you. He paused, as if he had just comprehended the sorrow of this, and then he said: She fell in love, do you see? She was too young to know the harm of it. She must have been carried away by her feelings if her parents' approval was of so little consequence and . . .

And?

She ran away with Rafe Fox, an older man, a neighbor who . . .

Didn't marry her?

You don't sound surprised.

I am surprised that my mother . . . that *she* never told me.

Nell. She was a Southern lady. Your safety and reputation were paramount.

A Southern lady who did not tell the truth! And my father? Did you tell him about me?

I did not. He is no friend to your family.

Eva Nell bowed her head: He is my *only* family. I will write . . .

Ross said: No. And I will not mention this to my mother, Nell, and you must do your best to forgive your aunt and keep the facts of your birth to yourself. You see the importance of that, I'm sure.

15

Emly's new baby bore a striking likeness to Granny Ruth Boyd, or so John believed. White people do not look closely at black babies but this one smiled and cooed and her nose was a little hooked and her chin had that Ruth Boyd shape and the brow too; well, it was plain as day but then it was late July and five of Emly's dewberry pies were getting pulled from the outside oven while the workers — those remaining — held out tin plates. John stood to the side, taking note of mood and relations among them. The cotton harvest had made everyone giddy with fatigue and there were jokes that John didn't understand but his heart beat hard at the sight of the baby girl tied to Emly's breast. He was wondering what the workers would make of her sixth child. Unable to read their faces, he shifted on his feet, watching Emly as she cut steaming chunks of pie and served them up. Her clothes were clean and pressed. How did she manage? How could she look so regal when she could also wrap her legs around his shoulders like warm, thick vines and roll onto her stomach when he asked or put his most private self into her body so that even to think of it meant . . . he moved away from any eyes that might notice the bulge in his trousers. But he could feel Emly through any distance and he turned and left the oven yard with a sign to her, then went to the barn.

To be undone. Like this: Say my name. Say it to me. Say, *John.*

The breasted baby blinked at him.

Why won't you use my Christian name? Is it my brother? Some rule he made that . . .

Your brother . . . she dropped to her knees. Will sell me. Me and my little children, may the dear Lord Jesus save us. On her knees with her breast wet and the barn light so unexpected, changing from shadowy to bright, and the child pressed between parents, Emly wept for some time without stopping, pulling at John while he fell into a timelessness where they were as no other man and women had ever been. One flesh as he poured himself into her bones. My name, he begged. Just say it and I will never see you sold, I swear this to you. How could I let that happen? Say my name, he said, meekly pleading . . . Please, opening her blouse and pressing his mouth to the milky flesh. And he muttered the promise again and wept his own salt on her milk. He is driven, he protested, speaking of his brother as well as himself, and there was the ache right through him as he unclasped the leather at his waist and he wondered for just a moment if Benjamin had sent her on this errand in order to enlist his financial aid. But what a contemptible thought that was, and anyway what could John offer his wealthier brother, he who was prone on the hard, strewn floor, he who could bear anything but the loss of this? A mother and child suckling.

John, she said.

16

When more rains passed over the fields, drenching the corn, Benjamin visited his brother in the cabin again. Six hundred acres gone to waste . . . He kicked the old table their father had made.

We'll hold, I tell you.

One good hill of corn in ten and me with fifty hogs to fatten. Benjamin put the blame on John again. I should take you to court for giving that nigger thief shelter.

I couldn't count the study of birds against him, could I?

Birds flying north, Benjamin snapped. I'm going to sell the females.

No! We won't do that. They are . . . we need them to keep things going. John studied his options. What would Rakel bring, anyway? But Emly had been frightened and for good reason. He thought of Lou, Emly's ten-year-old daughter, who was too young to weave but who would be useful in time. He thought of what they had built, he and his brother with the help of their workers. He thought of any way he might save them, his mind floundering. Emly. A silent cry.

With them sold I can get me a man.

No! I forbid it.

They are mine, Brother John. My farm, my workers. My decision to make. Benjamin's use of the word *brother* was meant to remind John that his work as a preacher was less important than Benjamin's work, that John's vocation had saved him from the gamble that farming involved.

John was thinking out loud. We can rent out the men.

As breeders? Maybe. But . . .

John interrupted with a groan and walked to the window their father had long ago cut in the front of his cabin. It helped him in many ways, having a room in which to think and a window from which to look out. He stumbled through the next two words, Our father . . . and he squeaked: A worker is not to whore! He rapped angrily on the glass with bent knuckles.

Benjamin laughed: Of course no man of the cloth will profess to an interest in profit. He looked down at the account book, seeing John's scrawls and jottings. I trade three females for one man. No one has to know Rakel's condition. Lou is near ripe. He smiled at John, showing teeth, almost a grimace. Do you mind so very much?

John's chest a knot. Another loan will tide us over.

With what collateral, Brother John?

John waved at the window. All that out there.

Mortgaged. Every inch, and you know it. There's the loan in addition and nothing paid up for three months.

Now John saw in Benjamin what he had not seen before: the heartlessness of a man who had control of their lives. Had his brother noticed the nose of Ruth Boyd on the face of Emly's newborn? Or was it the influence of Matilda, his second wife, who would have a new buggy, who would have breakfast brought to her bed. John said, looking out the window again: Our father built this farm acre by acre and you'll lose it *all* if you start . . . Voice cold. We need . . . Voice wheedling . . . I will sever our partnership, Benjamin.

You're not my partner. You work for me.

Then. John closed his eyes and spoke at the nothingness in front of him. I will apply for a loan. Co-sign whatever is required. If you promise not to . . .

Benjamin had been pacing but now he stopped and pointed at the preacher's threadbare jacket. You are worth nothing.

I have fifty acres. Two pigs. Four sheep. Two milch cows. A house. And a bear, John added, to ease the terrible strain he felt. If you promise that . . . they . . . are safe . . . I will sign. We'll go to a New York bank this time. Nothing local.

Benjamin lowered his head as if in a game. As if he might reach out and jab at John's arm and John would jab back and they would then run outside to play as they once had played when Benjamin, so much older, always won everything. He found a square piece of paper where John put his name, first and last.

17

Bry had studied the hand-drawn map and learned its rivers, although the ink had smeared during a fall in a puddle so that two of the rivers bled into each other as if a geologic drift zone had been opened between Virginia and Kentucky. His plan was to get to Point Pleasant. Avoid Kentucky and cross the river just above the state line. Ohio, river and state. If he kept north. River. State. And free. Meant going through the mountains that rise up on the left all brown turning green. Meant knowing how far to go north and where to stop and how to see a river buried in a forest too far down to keep an eye on where it sits. There was a place named Holderby's not to be trusted as a crossing place. So had said the birdman in his quiet, secret voice. Better to pass on to Point Pleasant, the Northman had said, but he was talking fast and he was hard to hear in all the whispering and hum of fear. Lord, Lord. He had that map that showed the river in ink and around Point Pleasant there was a swamp where French people put their money on bad land. The birdman had a story to tell about that but it was nothing the men needed to hear. Buying land? What's that about?

The map with smeared ink. How to keep paper dry? Keep paper in your mouth? Tucked under your hat? There were places he could mention as a joke but he flattened the wet paper on a stone and made the lines stay fast in his head. He knew the course of the Ohio by now in his sleep and the fact was that in order to get to Point Pleasant he had to cross the big Sandy and next the Kanawha and they were the ones run together in a smear on his map but maybe he would smell the difference in the waters or see a change in color where they met. This he said out loud because, having no one to talk to, he talked to himself. He made up things that did not exist or he made himself remember true things from the past. A day when Mama Bett saved a neighbor's brown foal. He had seen it born and seen it fail to take in air. And that was a good day for a boy of nine, running as fast as his legs could go to fetch his mothers, who had ways to heal anything, even a foal. And it was Bett who got there first. Bry remembered how the neighbor didn't trust her to touch his animal but she put her hands on it and brought it back to life and that was a memory to think about when he was too tired to sleep on the wet ground under the cypress trees where he was doing his best to hide. Was Bett alive? How could that be? He remembered the strong parts of his life and put aside the weak parts and the suffering parts and the gelding knife that was so sharp he didn't feel the first poke cutting into him but the next jab made him scream and he didn't now remember anything except the rope tight on his neck and that first little painless nick under his limp man sack before the sharper slash and even now he cupped his hand over that missing part where he could feel blood making everyone jump away and the thought made him sick but he could also think of the newborn foal who got up on her legs even before Mary came down the road and collected a dime from the farmer along with his thanks.

18

Maybe Cuff was lonely. This is what Martin reported to Clotilde, who made pecan biscuits for the bear. He also said it to Franklin, that Cuff seemed to be missing someone and it had to be his mama because who else could it be? Martin said to Cuff: Your mama is a rug now. He spoke the truth in order to earn her trust, believing all parents should do the same. When he led her into her stall, he stayed with her, telling her stories or singing hymns and these were Martin's happiest hours.

His brother and sister were getting ready to leave for school. He had to watch Patton pack up his clothes in the old satchel he always took with him when he went away. Patton was pretending to be sad. He was playing more with Martin and even with Cuff sometimes, but Martin knew Patton was glad to be going because their father was lately so hard on him. It's the way of the world, Patton would say, slapping Martin on the back. Fathers want sons out of the house! You'll see.

Even Gina was going to a class for six-year-olds. It was an experiment, since children learned to read and write at home, but Lavina was forward-thinking and she had enlisted a few women of the parish to collaborate with her. The Jonesville school shared space with John's church in a two-story wooden building. That is, on Sundays, desks were moved aside. On the second floor, the lodge met once a month. Therefore most residents of Jonesville knew the wooden building in one guise or another.

That fall, John preached hope wherever he went, but he said to himself: Another harvest is upon us and we are not saved. He took his mare into the woods and put his face against her neck. We are not saved. He thought of Emly, her hair in a knot, bent over a vat of cornmeal. Emly had moved her pots outside because food must be cooked even if it is too hot in a small log house. We are not saved. Another worker had slipped away and how were pears to be picked or apples? First there was rain and now there was none. When will you finish? he had asked in passing the vat of cornmeal.

She had not lifted her eyes.

The first drift of leaves, the first wind from the north, made John wonder. Would the loggerhead shrikes come back? Did Doctor Alexander Ross have any idea what he had caused to happen in Jonesville? The loan from City Bank of New York had come through and payments were due and John was off riding circuit, gone for ten days, his parish hungry after the waterlogged summer. There was talk of a human exodus, this one west in a wagon train. Some of John's people looked to him as their leader. There were opportunities. The Kansas–Nebraska Act was forthcoming. Land for pennies. Land for corn and wheat. Land best settled by Southerners who would know what to do with it. Bring their slaves. Make it into something pastoral that would work in the grasslands. What do Northerners know except commerce? Manufacturing has no place on the prairie. Would John gather pilgrims for such a trip? It would be long and none of them knew the way. None of them had traveled so far, forfeiting land and history, forfeiting this extreme point of Virginia once so unspoiled, so clean, so generous in its sun and rain, each of which used to come at the proper time. Once, there had been men to plant corn and cotton, men to pick fruit, and no more Indians to bother with so it was a paradise. Now, with so many workers gone and the land left untended, it was not the same. Would John lead the way? The tawny races of the west were in need of conversion, some said, and they praised John's oratory and his limitless faith and offered him soup when he slept in their homes and daily John prayed that all, all together by the cross, should be lifted. Through their efforts. Through their efforts. He sank into any chair that was offered. He was privately exhausted. He had, at last count, given sixty sermons in the past four months. His church in Jonesville was in disarray, although the arguable sins were pathetic. Should jewelry be allowed? Can we shave on the Sabbath? Can we sing? One parishioner had donated a silver chalice that John returned as too worldly. What does Jesus want with silver? He chastised a woman for attending the Presbyterian Church for its melodeon. Cavils and skirmishes. A Sister was with child and a Baptist had made a mark on her door. Was the baby defiled? John listened and hushed his people and told them time and again: Let us devoutly pray that simplicity and hard work will suffice. Did he believe his own words? What in the foundering world would bring his people, his own family, back from the brink? Without enough workers they were unable to make their harvests, which were anyway rain-mired. Who had a dollar to spare? Benjamin, for example, could not make the first or second payment on the New York loan, which had been taken to pay off the former loan from the Jonesville Bank. He could not make the third payment in September and the notices were coming like bullets in the mail. On the mare's back, John drooped and all his bones ached. He remembered his brother's youthful promise: Lend me your faith and I will make us wealthy. Now his throat was raw and his thoughts were all on the future — not on wealth but on the barn in the far distance, on the new child with his own mother's face. How strange that he should think of that dark child, who'd been given the name Pleasance, when he surely missed his Gina in the usual, aching way. Little girls. He had a soft spot for them.

Coming home, there was the road ever winding, there was the great brick house in the distance and his smaller place behind a grove of elms. There was all of that and eventually the small chimney he always looked to, Emly's small chimney, without a hint of smoke. Around and about, the clean sky told of nothing on the hearth, nothing at the ready for the children who would need a meal of corn cakes and buttermilk. The clean sky frightened John more than any part of his long month, any piece of his blemished week.

I sold her, Benjamin said on John's return, without being asked. And there was his smile, tolerant, as he said: Her children are scattered to the winds. No offer for Rakel, but Franklin brought a good price.

John had by then, by the finish of his brother's words, entered a grief secret and unyielding. He might have said: You made me a vow. I signed that blank piece of paper. He might have added: I signed my life away. Instead, he said: Only with cotton will the bank get paid. His voice was a mere suggestion of voice when he added: You made a terrible mistake. It was the sum total of his spoken rage. He did not display his pain nor did he mention the note of debt he'd co-signed, which lay in a drawer in a distant bank. He might have reached to the shelf behind him and brought forth a copy of that blank piece of paper he had signed so that no slave would be sold. He was sleepless. Emly, where are you? How can I help those

I hurt by sheltering the abolitionist? True it was that some of them still clung to him, begging for aid, but he hid in the cabin his father had built and stayed on his knees until they had swelled up enough to take the sharp pain from his head. *Scattered to the winds.* Those words beat at him as if they were actual things that could be picked up and weighed. Scattered. He could not speak to his insolent brother or admit how much he cared. John and Benjamin lived in separate, hazardous states.

And they were hit by an early blizzard. It was out of season. It was a rebuke from the Lord. In the cold cabin, John paced. With stores too small to hold through the winter, Lavina begged John to butcher a pig although it was too early in the season and it was a task always supervised by Emly. No one else had her skill with the cauldrons. It was Emly who managed the rending of fat, the making of sausages for both Dickinson households. But the weather! We must get it done, said Lavina. We need to eat; all of us can agree to that.

John called on Reuben, the most ancient of Benjamin's servants, and the two men along with Patton and Martin went the whole task of slaughtering, dismembering, and salting the animal, while Lavina and

119

Clotilde awkwardly handled the trying of the fat and the pickling of feet for Lavina's jelly. Throughout the afternoon there was yelling from the mistress and there were tears from Clotilde, who had come with Lavina from her parents' inn when she married John. They were close in age. They had grown up together, one always in charge of the other. But in an unfamiliar circumstance, they were not at their best.

Hog killing had been a favorite time for Emly's children. Now, in the chill of an October afternoon, John missed their greedy hands and eyes. How they had danced around the cauldrons, waiting for the fat to harden and the rising of the cracklings. Little Lou, who had sat on his shoulders while shouting at the others to stay back from the hot oil. A bossy little cuss you are, John would laugh, and Gina would emerge from the safety of Clotilde's kitchen to enjoy the sizzling treats along with the others. To John it seemed now that no more joyful time had belonged to him in all his life. Franklin's sly humor, the way he counted every bite given to the others, even as to size. One, two, three, my turn. Those children made the place ring with their antics and John had wantonly taken it all in stride. He had watched the children grow and he had watched their mother and then there had come that morning of the beautiful head against the flank of a beast who gave and gave and when would that giving be finished so that John could put out his hands, his arms, move closer, press himself against his brother's favorite?

19

One night in October, Bry was leaning against a fence, having eaten a turnip, an apple, and a stolen oatcake. The cake had been left on a windowsill that morning while the baker's family had taken a wagon off someplace, maybe to church, where they could pray for the life they wanted. Bry didn't feel shame in the stealing of food that was left in such rare company as a tied-up dog and a yard full of heckling chickens. He thought of taking a hen, but the carrying would be awkward and the killing of such a fighting thing was not to his liking and the cake would slake his hunger because it was big. So he was leaning against that log fence enjoying his meal when he heard the low hornlike bellowing of a red deer bull. Bry had heard the males call their own into the hills and down again but he had never seen what afterward befell, which was a herd of two hundred or more . . . first the soft thunder of hooves and Bry dropped his food and turned and saw them running like water over sand, like a river over a precipice, and he savored that running and envied the deer their good legs and clear minds. With night in their legs and hearts, with feathery darkness descending, they were innocent of guns, of pursuing wolves. They all lifted their heads and moved like one body, males first, calling, taking a stand at a distance in order to watch over the does and the fawns, calling them into a valley where they would be safe, the does taking up the thrum of hooves against soil, some of them eager, each of them having a body of muscle and blood, a mind of intention, protection offered by the few to the many, by males to females, by fathers and mothers to their young. He picked up his cake from the ground and watched the formality of families. He had wondered sometimes how it was that his people were driven so far to the slave ships in Africa. He had wondered what means were enacted to drive them across deserts and rivers and forests.

20

Martin went to school with his collar turned up and his boots leaking into the heated schoolroom. He could not seem to listen to anything there. His ears were stinging with words shouted out at home — his father to his brother, his brother to his father, his mother rocking in a chair without rockers, just herself going back and forth with her hands over her face. I give you my last fifty dollars and you waste it on song. Martin knew his father would never say: wine, women, and song. This was a shortcut to protect Lavina's feelings. Your days under this roof are done. Now go get a piece of land with your warrants. No, Mother, I will not be silenced. We have put up with enough from your big spoiled boy! He is now on his own.

Sitting on his school bench with his elbows on his desk, Martin thought about his father's sermons delivered in this room three Sundays of every month and wondered if his father knew God's purpose as he claimed to do. He wondered if his father knew that he, Martin, was the cause of all the trouble that had come down on them after he'd listened to the birdman tell the workers to run away. It wasn't Patton's fault! It was all because I never told anybody about what happened that night. It was my fault the workers left. I could have stopped the whole thing if I'd knocked on the door and told the men to go back to the cellar or else I'd tell Uncle Benjamin. Then he thought: And if I'd never gone off with my brother that day with the gun, Cuff would still have a mother and everything would be the same way it was. He put his face for a minute on the cold surface of his desk. How would he live without Patton?

21

It snowed one night in November and the snow kept falling the next day and all night again. It was usual to take ice from the creek and store it on straw in the icehouse but the snow fell so hard no one could get to the creek. Eight of Lavina's chickens froze in their coop. Within hours, the Dickinsons — both households — were running out of firewood, which seemed an issue of more importance than cutting and storing ice for the summer months so far ahead. The house was cold and Gina developed her usual cough. Weak chest, her father said.

She needs to get out of bed and play. Electa had said it a thousand times. You treat her like a baby. It's only a cough. Let her play outside in the fresh air. Electa had been away to school, and she had strong opinions.

But the parents were joined in this particular mission. Gina must be cosseted. She was timid and sensitive and sickly.

Then Benjamin caught the fever and began to cough in the way of a man whose lungs are worn thin. Lavina provided Matilda with the syrup Gina used, but it made Benjamin's head swim and he refused a second dose. His young wife slept in another room and left her husband alone in the cold marriage bed. Marriage bed twice over, and now the floor around it was strewn with Matilda's stockings and boots and shirts and silk handkerchiefs and Rakel would not tidy Matilda's things. Rakel said she heard Emly walking in the house, looking for her children. She said sooner or later the big house would come apart without Emly to supervise the kitchen and milk the cows and weave the linen and wash the windows and clothes and iron the sheets and polish the silver and wax the floors and make the cheese. Rakel had always helped Emly some and worked in the fields, but she swore she could not take that good woman's place. As the snow fell and cold blew through the house, the slaves in the cellar snarled at the second wife, who now had full authority since the master lay abed. They stayed below stairs when Matilda called down to them and it was not for a lady to say what she said when the slaves refused to mind

127

her commands. She called them names; she showed her spite, she slapped. Too old or too young or too tired to run, they had no warm clothes and what does a cotton picker know of snow? This is what they said: What do I know of snow, Miz Matild?

But the cows must be milked! she yelled. Never mind your bare feet. Get on out there to the barn!

Lavina had her own household to run and she was no friend to Matilda, nor were Benjamin's sons, who had fled to other towns and other work. John was as good as useless now where his brother was concerned. He seemed to have lost interest in the three thousand acres that fed all of them. But one afternoon Lavina pushed herself through the snow to help Matilda bring hay to the cows and grain to the horses and mules. She had once been a girl of some beauty with parents who owned an inn. Now she was a preacher's wife; she kept her hair up in a cap, kept her dress simple, and hardly remembered her lively childhood. She had only Clotilde to remind her of pleasant meals with foreign guests and Clotilde thought of farm life as beneath contempt. Dirt, she called the workers who tilled the ground, and now it was Clotilde to whom Lavina turned for help. John's mood was too dark to decipher. He had thinned in the face; his eyes were larger and his back slightly bent. He did not offer solace to a worried wife. He sat in his father's chair in the old cabin, which was warmer than the house but not warm enough. He counted things, moving his fingers in the air. Lavina had seen him do this when she went out to the cabin with his coffee jar wrapped in a heated towel. John seemed despondent, he seemed to grieve. He could not ride circuit due to the weather and surely, thought Lavina, he needed activity. But when he started to deliver a sermon on the first Sunday of Advent he sat down on a chair near to hand after muttering a few words and stared at his concerned congregation without a grain of tolerance for any of them. He did not sympathize with the plight of his dying half-brother or his half-brother's wife. He did not sympathize with Patton, who'd been sent into the wilderness. He had lost the ability to care.

One night, lying beside Lavina in bed, he spoke of a toy he had stolen when he was eight or nine. I can't sleep for thinking of it, he said.

What was it, Father?

Oh. Well, I believe it was a ball that belonged to the boy who was raised by my sister. Mary.

Bry? You mean Benjamin's Bry? Why on earth are you thinking of him?

Well, he was the first to leave last spring.

It wasn't for the loss of a toy, Father. Take your rest.

On the following Sunday, the second of Advent, John went into his church and found he had nothing to say, not so much as a prayer. Lavina watched him fumble through the Psalms. He looked out at the shivering Methodists whose feet were cold, whose arms were clenched, whose eyes were averted. The church had no heat and neither did he.

During the Christmas break, Lavina took Electa with her to Benjamin's house because Benjamin could not leave his bed and his frantic young wife spent her days running from barn to kitchen and back to the barn again. When Electa was sent out to the chicken yard and the storeroom to check on the state of things, Matilda said she felt judged. She stood in the iced-over garden made by Benjamin's first wife with its unfallen leaves hard frozen and said Benjamin had seven children and she hadn't created a one of them and all of them were in league against her. Everyone was, or so

130

Matilda claimed, and there were envelopes to her husband from City Bank of New York that she was afraid to open.

Lavina left her alone and went off to make tea. The big, separate kitchen was a masterpiece of planning on Benjamin's part, made to please Elizabeth, but it was too far from the house during a winter like this. Now Lavina and Matilda and Electa sat by a frosted window in the small indoor kitchen and Electa offered to take some tea up to her uncle Benjamin, but Matilda said: No, thank you, leave him be. The snow was a wrap around them and Matilda had taken refuge under a shawl while Lavina sat on a hard-backed chair and looked through the window at Martin gamboling in the snow with Cuff. The thought came to her that there was nothing so pretty as a bear in snow, and she smiled as she watched Cuff roll over and over and then stand and shake and start the whole thing again, rolling and standing and shaking. Cuff usually slept during the daylight hours since winter had started but she would come out to play at the slightest temptation and Lavina watched Martin throwing snowballs at his bear and Cuff trying to bat them back with her paws and she told Electa to excuse herself and go join them. It will do you good, she said kindly, and I will enjoy the sight.

22

Late that month, John went over the accounts again, rubbing out a numeral here and adding one there. Benjamin's debts exceeded by two thousand dollars the total value of his assets.

19th, more snow, no one to do spinning, Tom and Jule to cut wood, Edward sick.

Winter was the time for women to spin and weave and sew while men cut and split timber to rebuild fences, grubbed out new ground, and hauled topsoil to the fields from the wetlands. Now with a foot of snow and five men run off and with Emly and her children sold, John divided the seven remaining workers into groups — a plow gang made up of Tom and Abe and Young Jim, and a hoe gang composed of old Reuben and Jule and Edward, who was sickly and thin. He made lists. Rakel must tend to the animals. She must cook for Matilda and see that the workers had something to eat.

He added and subtracted. It gave him a measure of calm but it was a small enough measure because most of his mind was caught up in imagining an endless morning in the barn when Emly and her children had been sold and scattered. Had it been bright or cloudy? Weather was always company on John's circuit but now he could not remember his rides through the woods and valleys during that terrible week. He had no recollection of rain or sun or wind. He had preached with his usual fury out in the hinterlands while Emly and the children were pushed into a corner of the barn in spite of the promise — the vow — he had made. Were there tears or screams? Were they bound by ropes? One woman, five children, and a suckling babe and what was the profit in it? How could a person's worth be counted in dollars? It was a question he had never asked himself. Benjamin's begotten. And his. Why had they been sold apart from the mother who fed and protected them? Where was the record of those dismal sales? At what fraction of a dollar had his little Pleasance been valued? Pleasance of the turned-down nose and doubled-up fist . . . He remembered her tiny grip on his finger and touched his own hand wonderingly. She, too, had needed him. He had seen it happen dozens of times over the years. A family disrupted, sold apart. Human histories severed. He had seen it and accepted it as necessary to the lives that must be lived in their world. He had made Emly a promise but, in truth, it was not for her. He was looking after himself. Yes. He must speak to his brother, like it or not. He would do it. Shame or no shame: he would force the question or his mind would crack.

And one cold afternoon, when the north wind came straight down from Canada, John left his hat on a hook by Benjamin's front door, having come in without knocking. The house was silent, as if no one lived above or below, no one slept or ate or loved, no one wept or bled or felt the cold. Silence, and John went quickly up the stairs, gripping a banister covered in dust, taking the steps two at a time. From a bedside chair, he stared down at the man who had betrayed a contract between brothers, a man who had thereby caused him to break his own solemn promise. Wake up, John said, poking at Benjamin's arm. Then, without preamble, he spoke of a day when he'd built a fort with Bry. Do you remember how you knocked it down? How small we were then, Bry and I, born the same year.

In the mess of blankets, Benjamin stirred.

His voice, unused for days, was unpleasantly hoarse; it was raspy and thin, and when he opened his eyes they were red-rimmed and bleary as he pushed himself up on an elbow. What?

I was thinking of Bry because he was the first to run away last spring, John said. When the abolitionist came down here from New York, Bry was the first to run and he's far too old to survive such a trek and no doubt he's down some hole in the ice or drowned or been shot. Consumed by a hound. Why would he take such a risk at his age? I wouldn't do it. John lifted his head and studied the unswept bedroom. A cobweb dangled at the front window and the curtain was torn. There were clothes and shoes strewn on the floor and the fireplace was cold. He had not been in this room since he'd come to view the body of Elizabeth laid out with the flowers she'd nourished. He could remember the day Benjamin had brought her home from the east with two slaves chained to her pretty cart, but he said to his brother now: Do you remember how you didn't allow Bry to play with me after you tore down our fort? We were two little lads and yet you used your boots and fists because he was born to a slave who lived in our sister Mary's house.

A swirl of ashes drifted across the floor-boards and mingled with the clothes left in piles.

Benjamin pushed himself up on his pillow and the effort made him wheeze and a rack-ing cough went on for several minutes, dur-ing which John sat stoically, and when all the coughing and choking subsided, he said: In fact, Bry was raised by our sister. And yet we never looked after him when he ran away that first time and got caught. We took him in trade and enslaved him again. Yes? Broken, castrated. Ruined, is the fact of it, but we put him to work in the field before he could stand up straight or walk without soiling the cotton with his blood. I suspect his pain was as real as yours or mine.

Benjamin licked his cracked lips and swal-lowed. He said: What difference now? I can't get my breath.

I used to run off to play with Bry, John said, where you wouldn't find us. Eight years old and I was afraid of you, afraid you would put out my eye or break my arm or put sand in my mouth. Things you some-times did when you were roused. And do you remember? Bry made me a sword, but our father didn't let me play with it although you were allowed a musket. John was talk-ing to himself in a darkening room. A clock was ticking. A hand clung to his sleeve. He was sitting by a brother who was sick to death. He was thinking of their lives lived so close to each other, thinking of what they had used; what they'd abused. He put his hand on Benjamin's wrist to feel its pulse. On a shelf over the door the clock ticked away. Where is Emly? he said, pressing hard on the flesh.

Benjamin said: Out to whore.

23

In Kentucky, Bry was working on a horse farm. Three days of that fine life although his manner of getting there had been fraught with hiding by day, walking by night, and crossing two rivers, first Big Sandy and then Kanawha, which had coal-lined creeks running into it so the water was distinct. He felt fortunate in the miracle of that dark water and in the fact that, raised by Mama Bett and Mother Mary, who owned her, he could read any posted sign. *South to river,* one said. *East to Bap. Chr.,* said another.

He found a place he could float across the Ohio on a flatboat if he stole it, although a boat is a danger to a man who can't swim. He'd been following trees in Virginia — nails in them at every crossroad — and he made a mistake because he'd never known, in those hungry weeks of nighttime wandering, in those weeks of sleeping in forests and haystacks by day, that at Point Pleasant the river was not flowing up to Ohio. No. At Point Pleasant, the river flowed south and west.

Bry wondered if Josiah had run off by now. Josiah had reached in the leather bag and pulled out a compass. Said he needed no map. Said he sure as the devil would know the way from the look of the sky; said any fool knew that, but Josiah could not read. What good was a map? What about Nick? What about Billy, who used to help Bry fill his cotton sack? What about Jule, who was the most frequently lashed? Josiah always said he had nothing to lose so why not try. Josiah took chances, leaving a field to hunt or fish, but he looked after Rakel, finding an extra bite for her when food was thin and checking on was she warm and quiet enough in her sleep. Josiah was the watchdog of the cellar and Nick was the clown and Jim was the youngest and Bry wished he could find one of them by some chance, but he wouldn't wish that river on Josiah, who couldn't swim, or on anyone who had better sense than to jump on a flatboat that was soaked through and when the river slowed down some, Bry had climbed out where he thought it was Ohio and walked in his careful way for some nights and kept to a valley, surviving on mushrooms and onions and berries and the yams he dug out of farm fields. He was walking north but he never saw a living soul until he came upon a white man in the canebrakes, dead and stiff. The man had a dense and vicious smell about him and the face was crooked from lying sidewise and Bry felt exploded by the thought of this person's lost life. Did somebody wait for him? The man was dressed pretty well and his hair was cut straight. He was white but turning dark and he'd be hard to recognize in another day but Bry had found him and so they would say he killed him and he would get hanged on the spot if he went for help. Knowing that, he ran himself out of breath to get far enough away, the sight staying with him for miles and later in his life it would come back, a man lying dead in a field with nobody around him to grieve. There was some fighting going on in those days about German and Irish immigrants. Bry had read a paper to that effect tacked on a fence. So maybe this man was a German or an Irish not desired in these United States. Like me, Bry thought, only he knew himself to be desired as a slave. At night he walked in the dark and by day he found a place to sleep. Once, he killed a squirrel and skinned it with the bowie knife given by

Mister Ross, closing his eyes when he had to take off the ears and face. Once, he cut his hand and the blood made him weak, but he bound the wound, never looking, using leaves wrapped around his wrist. He sat with his hand in the air for some hours and sang because it took away his fear. Bry had never prayed for help from the Redeemer because to do so wasn't right. What help he had — knife and compass — had been unasked for and given freely and now he was currying a horse, brushing the mane. Why do such a thing to a beast?

He curried too gently in respect of this horse that could kick and bash. The long legs might break and he knew that was the end of a horse and would also be the end of him. He had to laugh at his luck or lack of it. Walking to find Mama Bett and maybe that child born when Jemima died and got rolled away in a cart. How old would the child be? What color eyes did she have? All that walking to get to Ohio and on the other side of the river he'd stumbled into a farmhouse pursued by starvation, beyond caring if he got caught.

His arrival was an opportunity for Mister Lappeton, breeder of horses, to assess a wandering man of another race and to offer comfort and food. Indeed, sore and bitten,

Bry was looked over and taken in. It was the first time he'd come into a house for five months and to top that he got offered a chair and a glass of beer and a cloth to clean his face. Missus Lappeton herself came in to serve up ham hocks and rice, black-eyed peas, cornbread, a hot cup of coffee, although he took this fine meal out on the porch. Had two mothers once, he muttered, and yet I forgot how to eat from a plate.

The horse breeder had noticed Bry's poor, cracked boots. I have a pair to fit ye good enough for work. If you'll take it. You'll be out to the barn.

So it began, the idyll of three days in a barn with geldings as fine as anyone had seen in this horse-raising state. You be firm now, the farm wife said. Have a care or they'll kill ye.

Bry did not say that he had never touched a horse. He knew mules with a deal of hatred and horses were worse. In the barn he was issued a blanket, a pair of old boots, and instructions. Go to sleep. Work tomorrow. Tell us your story another time.

Racehorses have brains that are not as great as their hearts and the look in their eyes was outrage. They lifted their hooves in their stalls, pawing in agitation as if the hay was not suited to their needs. But the barn

143

was immaculate and there was a trainer who was white. The trainer did not talk to him and the horses also got quiet when he came into a stall, but Bry crept carefully past the noses and ears and teeth and never close to the rear as he'd been taught when Mama Bett took him out to a fence at the age of two and showed him Mister Daniel's horse that he'd saved from an auctioneer. That horse was broken down but even so he was loved although a worker who can't do work is known as an impediment. Know that big word? Mister Benjamin used to shout on a Sunday when the slaves were concocting suppers for themselves or hanging up some clothes to dry. Know that word impediment? What you are to me when you don't earn your keep.

Tell us your story. Another time.

Indeed, the idyll of the horse barn gave Bry a chance to consider the shape of his life and he remembered back to his first days at Mister Rafe's when he was a child in the cotton field pulling bolls, jamming them into a bag that was bigger than he was in length. Two hundred pounds or a whipping. Little boy that I was, taken from my two mothers and made to sleep on a log in the quarters and drag the bag through the field and then the day Jemima came we all

144

heard about it, how she lived with our master in the way of a wife. When Bry learned about Jemima he could not eat or sleep or move his bowels or think. He ached at the thought of Jemima with Mister Rafe. He could ache even yet because he had loved her as a boy and then for the rest of his life. Later they met in the shade hut out in the middle of a cornfield and she did her explaining. She swore that she'd come as a woman to Mister Rafe in order to be close to Bry and for nothing else. He was thirteen by then and raged out and thin after three years dragging the cotton bag. Such an angry one you grew to be, she said, and it wasn't blame on her part to say it. They were no longer children and they found relief in a field hut all around bristled with maize. Then later she was growing a baby and it was Bry's baby and not Mister Rafe's is what she said. What would Rafe do if the baby had no red hair on its head like his? If the baby had coal-black eyes like a baby slave? Which is just what her baby would be if it lived. Put out in the quarters to work in the fields.

Bry wondered about that child as he watched three white men approach the barn where he was currying a beast so much larger, so much stronger than he was. It had been three days of calm thinking, remembering, currying. One of the men approaching now was the horse breeder who'd offered him work in the big, clean horse barn. The others were larger of girth and walked with their legs set apart and yet moving fast. One of them was opening and shutting his bare hands. The other had gloves on and a tall hat. Bry reached up to the spine of the horse and felt the weight of hard muscle over bone. He wanted to climb up and ride away but there was no chance of that although he might still run on his own two feet. But maybe they meant him no harm. He must get used to the world again. The horse breeder had taken him in, offered him a fair wage, given him boots. Maybe the other two had come to look at the big horse, so he began with the curry brush again, stroke after downward stroke, even talking to the beast in his high soft voice. You an me, he said, both the same but you run faster only you tied up right now and I'm free.

Step over here, boy, the breeder said.

Bry dropped the brush and turned to the three white men.

Say your name to these gentlemen and where you came here from. Time to tell your story.

146

Bry said his name, that one word.

From around here?

Yessir.

This county.

Uh-huh. Yessir.

What's the name of it? The two unknown men were closing in.

Bry said: I never got told it but I . . .

The breeder put out a hand much dented with lines and took hold of Bry's arm. His face was frozen, eyes never blinking.

You come on with us now and we'll get you a name. The breeder reached behind him to a peg and brought down a rope and pulled Bry's arms behind his back. Bry thought of falling to his knees but instead he stepped along quickly from the barn to the house where he got tied into a covered cart with tall wheels.

24

Spring was late and Benjamin wasn't buried until the thaw. Then people arrived at John's little church in the Jonesville school riding in wagons and buggies and a few came on foot and when they bent their heads to pray, it seemed to Lavina that dead, we are all alike. Dead we are God's contract with the universe and she said this to herself although it was a heathen thing to say and she sat like a stone in her long brown dress and remembered the funeral of Eliza Ely because she had last worn the brown dress on that terrible day. She thought of Sister Eliza even as she watched Matilda sway on her bench and blow her nose on a handkerchief she pulled out of her sleeve. What did Matilda know of grief? This is my baby now, Eliza's mother had boldly announced, looking at the grieving father, whose head hung down on his heaving chest. A mother dies and her child loses every right to safekeeping. What if I die? John can't take care of Gina. It will be left to Electa, who cares only for herself at this age. She then thought of the two little hand-dug graves under the apple tree, the graves of her children unmet. She tried to concentrate. John was lately quiet at home but in public he was more and more erratic. She shifted her weight and stretched her legs. John and Benjamin worked as a team, John taking orders from the older brother, and what will happen to us now without Benjamin's expertise? John will inherit land from his brother, of course. She was sure of this because it was common sense. John had slaved for his brother, although Lavina did not like the word to be used as a verb. She imagined the windfall that might occur as recompense for John's years of service. She imagined herself in a fine Persian shawl even as John at the pulpit went rambling on about the spoils of . . . lust! She began to listen now. Was he going to expose his brother's half-breeds? They had never confronted that shameful subject and Lavina prayed that they never would. Gina had fallen asleep on Lavina's lap and Martin was knotting a long piece of string but Electa was obviously hearing every word of her father's strange rant! At school she had learned to embroider and do long division and write an essay on Rome in the Middle Ages, but she was not of an age to understand lust, and even the adults around her were scratching and shifting. They were muttering one to another behind their hands when John suddenly pointed at the coffin: Someone in this room will be tramping in hell before winter comes again, he exclaimed. And when he mentioned the tired old metaphor of the eye of a needle, Lavina discerned that it was lust for wealth that John was berating, using his brother as an example of death by greed. Trying to imagine Benjamin, even as a ghost, fitting through the eye of anything smaller than a doorway, Lavina bent her head to hide her smile.

25

An hour later, Benjamin's big house was crammed with Dickinsons — sons and daughters, husbands and wives. Matilda provided the last log of Emly's sweet cheese. There were doors slammed and voices raised while she dabbed at her eyes with the damp handkerchief. What else was she to do? She had inherited the house, which was not entailed in any mortgage or loan, and this news was a surprise to everyone. All of them should have been weeping. John took Matilda into the back hall, closing the door. He told her that the brick house was his because he had lost his own house to Benjamin's unpaid loan. He said: We are exiled by the whim of a man who cared only for himself and this will now be our home.

He cared for me, said Matilda. She added: And it's mine.

Throughout the afternoon, Martin sat on the long covered porch and Electa sat with

Gina in the parlor, remembering the house as it had been under kinder management. All she had needed to feel valued back then was an afternoon spent with her aunt Elizabeth. A cup of sugared tea with a pecan biscuit. That warm hand stroking her arm and asking about her thoughts. Electa began to cry a little as she sat looking at the room and remembering the past, and still Martin stayed on the sidelines, trading remarks with cousins or tickling a younger child, oblivious to the outcome of his uncle's death. He sat on the porch rail swinging his legs as if everything would go on as it always had although he was old enough to know how thin the membrane was between life and death. Everything is fatal, Electa thought, feeling sad and adult. The house held a string of sun that crossed the floor and climbed the papered wall of the room where the Dickinsons were collecting. Matilda was smiling, offering brandy distilled from Benjamin's pears. In a few moments everyone was clustered, gripping tiny glasses of the dark liquor and avoiding John's scowl, as she set the decanter down on the little side table and sat back primly. All eyes were pinned on her and none more hostile than John's. She pulled herself up, tucking her handkerchief into her bodice so that the lace stuck out between two pearl buttons. Do go on and help yourselves to a second drop, for heaven's sake! Her accent was from elsewhere — Georgia or Alabama. Oh, my goodness, she said. What a long day!

They all felt the loss of Elizabeth, who would have drawn them together with appropriate charm and sensible wit. She would have resigned herself to taking on the burden of her children and her nephews and nieces since Benjamin had failed them so utterly. She would have managed it somehow, or so the bereaved were prone to believe. But this newly married child bride was no match for such a family. Benjamin's sons had begun to plunder the closets and drawers. While the elders stood somberly in the parlor, nursing their grudges, grown children went on a rampage, collecting silver and china and flinging their findings into cloth bags. Then Matilda, dressed in black, her curly hair pushed under a cap, and, duly noted by Lavina, wearing Elizabeth's sapphire earrings, and Lavina noticed that sacrilege. She said: I must inform you all of my dear husband's last will and testament.

They were astounded by Matilda's calm demeanor as she calmly explained that the fields required to support the porch, the red bricks, and the four stone chimneys of the house were forfeit to a New York bank. To prove her point she read out the list of properties Benjamin had lost.

374 acres on Powell River
300 acres on the east side of Glade Creek
647 acres on the west side of Glade Creek
17 1/4 acres adjoining Jonesville
640 acres on Milton Creek
610 acres on Glade Spring
500 acres on Glade Creek, location to be determined along with eighteen Negroes, among them two females and five tots. (It had not been reported that five of this number had disappeared and six had been sold along with an unlisted newborn.)

Can you just imagine it? Matilda asked. All that land gone up in smoke and I am barely a bride and now a widow with nothing left! She looked around and blinked her eyes at the affront of it. Except for this house, she said.

John growled: I have explained. The house reverts to Benjamin's partner, who has lost everything by co-signing his loan.

Not at all, said Matilda.

26

John stormed through the rooms of Matilda's house in the following days as if the noise of boots and shouting could get the cotton planted and harvested before it was claimed by the bank. We'll pay it off! Perhaps he thought noise would erase the memory of Emly's children in their knee-length shirts, and Emly, too, and Bry and Josiah and Nick and Billy and that last run-off fool, Sutter. But Benjamin had peopled his acres with creatures never made part of the success of the fields they planted and now word of impending foreclosure spread and how could anyone be induced to work? All those acres would be dust in the vault of a New York bank. But listen! John insisted: Each one of you, including Rakel and Reuben, must work ten acres of cotton and fifteen of corn. You will be roused before dawn by the clanging of a bell, given enough time to fill a gourd with water and another with dinner and then hurried to the fields while swallowing a piece of cold pork. After dark, when you drag yourselves back to the damp cellar of the house, there will be the usual chores — feeding the mules, swine, and horses; cutting wood; grinding corn. There will also be yelling and crying upstairs to be heard and withstood. Missus Matilda will be snarling and promising to bring lawyers and buyers into the house you are forever dusting and sweeping but pay her no mind; she is nothing to us. I will be snarling right back at her and lying myself down on my brother's bed and refusing to move because . . .

where oh where would I go?

Matilda had found willing buyers, the Milbourns, although any nearby land to be farmed would have to be purchased back from the New York bank. Having made a down payment, the buyers wanted immediate occupancy, but John had mounted his horse for years and ridden his circuit and preached the word of God while his brother took more and more chances, risking their worldly goods, and the Jonesville neighbors, knowing John as their preacher, eagerly took his part. John had married, buried, baptized, and chastised a thousand times over. They supported his right to the property he had managed, and agreed that the Milbourns would have to see John in court. He had kept his brother's accounts and now he went over and over the books again, sleeping no more than two or three hours at a time, then getting up to pace the floor as if he could plant it and make it bear fruit. If only he could identify the hole in his brother's design, find the mistake, and make restitution. It only meant making sufficient payments a little at a time. A little, that's all. His thoughts wandered shapelessly in and out of past and present scenes, scenes remembered and imagined, sometimes even conjuring Emly in a different kitchen, but where? Emly and the children . . . images in sepia, the littlest one with Ruth's down-slanted eyes.

Without them, the house had gone hollow. Were there fewer furnishings than before? Had Matilda sold carpets? Drapes? The overstuffed chair that Benjamin had so favored? Where was the silver tray? John commanded Lavina to make a list of furnishings and to keep her eye on them. Lavina had never been invited into the outside kitchen by Benjamin's second wife but now she opened barrels and canisters with the help of Clotilde while Matilda sulked on the second floor in her chosen room. Lavina opened jars. She tasted the contents, licked her spoon, nodded or frowned. A long table sat to one side of the cavernous kitchen and it was covered with basins and bowls. Wood and stone. Beneath the table there were baskets of onions, yams, turnips, and potatoes. It wasn't Lavina's kitchen, not for a minute, but she was amazed to find such after the hard winter and she began to distribute the food to the people who lived in the cellar. They were hungry. Everyone was hungry, most especially the workers. Her own small outside kitchen had been swept, mopped, polished. It was perfectly empty and ready for imminent foreclosure. She had moved its edible contents out to the lean-to where she was storing up foodstuff while she wandered Matilda's big lavish house, opening drawers, inspecting a pair of lace gloves and muttering her disapproval while Matilda packed her trunks.

Lavina dusted the piano Elizabeth had loved, although it now sat closed and silent. She thought of the Schubert Impromptus Elizabeth had played, inviting Lavina to come over for an afternoon to drink India tea and listen to the wondrous and emotional music of a man who had died in his youth. Sometimes Elizabeth let her tears fall as she played and Lavina was moved by that, although the music she had known in her youth bore no resemblance to anything composed by Schubert. Lavina and Elizabeth had been close in that familial way of women married to brothers. They had shared recipes and worries about their children. They had conspired on patterns at Elizabeth's loom. If Elizabeth were alive, Lavina thought, none of this would have happened to us; Benjamin would never have taken such risks in order to please Matilda, who will not be pleased no matter what. Seven sons Elizabeth had and this well-kept house, which has been invaded by a second wife aged twenty-three or less. Oh, but we wives are easily replaced, Lavina said to herself, and maybe just as easily forgotten. It was a new bitterness, a slew of dark thoughts coming at her. A woman's victories were quickly squandered, like Elizabeth's sapphire earrings and Sister Eliza's stolen child. Years before, Elizabeth had influenced John, given him a measure of sophistication when he was her sweet, young brother-in-law. She had flirted with him, wagging a finger and laughing at his mistakes. Did John remember that? Elizabeth had tried to teach him a few husbandly skills. Lavina had heard her suggest to John once sotto voce that he compliment his wife, take her in his arms now and then, and kiss her sometimes on her lips. It will do you both good, Elizabeth had said, but Lavina had put any hope of such attention aside. She had made of her home a respectable place but she could not be easy in Elizabeth's house because she did not feel sufficient to its demands. She did not feel herself its proper mistress, any more than Matilda was. And then, what to do with Clotilde, who would not sleep in the cellar with the "dirt" but preferred the chilly lean-to, where she could feel superior. What to do with Rakel, who lazed about, staring at walls. What to do with Martin, who spent all his time in the barn, where the sleepy bear was most wont to curl around him while he read stories or sang hymns. Martin was growing too old for a pet, but with all the snow, school was often closed, and now Electa, too, was home and full of moods because there was no money for her spring tuition. Electa disliked Matilda and did not like living in her house. Electa wrote long letters to her school friends with inaccurate excuses about the sudden change in her life. She wrote that she would be back at school in the fall. She wrote that her father was suddenly ill. She wrote that her brother Patton was off to buy a plantation. And John. He kept to his office in the old cabin as if he meant to inhabit his last piece of solid ground. Days lengthened, with light from the sun making more time to wonder what had gone so terribly wrong, and sometimes Lavina found reason to go to the cabin door to check on him. May I come in for a minute? I have brought your coffee. Then she might peer over his shoulder and stare down at his scrawls in the ledger book. His accounts, as he called them, although they resembled the notations of dreams.

March 30 hired a boy 17 years $37 with 2 plows going and Reub repair axel. wagon next

April 10 court. Plow wetland- 3 out Brother Lucas to hire two I cannot spare Abe, Young Jim

April 19 river risen 3 put manur plows put in corn

April 25 all day at c court

April 27 decision pending need rain care for mine enemies

Hogs $25 Utinsels $100 Plows etc $100 3000 acres = $4000 letter to Patton returned

Sent another to Louisville

Lavina missed Patton so intensely there

was no way to share her yearning with John. He might be sorry for sending their son away and then become more disheartened. And there was the hope that Patton would learn independence by going off in search of land. He might even save the family. At night she prayed without stirring the blankets. She kept her fear to herself so as not to cast blame on her husband, although she could not discern the full shape of his apparent regrets. John still sat at the old table in the cabin late into the night. His candle would burn down and he would finally slump into a sitting sleep while she climbed the great winding slave-built stairs in dead Benjamin's house. Wood. Nails. Paint. She found no comfort in any of it or in the bed that had belonged to Elizabeth and Benjamin and then to Benjamin and Matilda, all three bodies lying together side by side in her tired mind. Each night, Lavina sank unwillingly into a cavity worn by those other wives. What pleasures had they found in this bed? Were their husbands as brusque as hers? I am not finished. I am finished. Words to that effect. Was all the talk of wedded bliss an illusion maintained by unmarried girls? Lavina had no one to ask. She stretched her legs and felt the footboard as a comfort pushing back.

And one night, waking to the usual long hollow on the right side of the bed, she heard a disturbance outside the house and found no rhythm in it to recognize. She shoved her feet into leather slippers and threw a shawl over her shoulders and head. When she listened closely, the wrangling sound seemed to come from the throats of angry men and she went to the window and saw on the lawn a straggle of bearded faces lit by lanterns held in large hands. The lanterns cast flickering shadows on the faces and Lavina saw that some of the men were Milbourns and she saw that her husband was going toward them in his nightshirt, holding his gun, the old rifle brought back from the War of 1812 to prove Mary's husband was dead. Those men outside on the grass had come to declare defeat or triumph and they had accomplices, other men, who had knelt down in prayer with John but who now held a different spirit in their hearts. There is never anything so dangerous as self-righteousness, Lavina thought, and she leaned out of the window and yelled: For pity's sake, Father, come upstairs to bed! Her hair was braided and it hung down her back. Her face was blemished and sleep-dented. When John did not show that he'd heard, she turned from the window and scuffed in the slippers down Benjamin's stairs. Better to climb down a ladder than descend like a belle, but she took note of the shape her shadow made on the wall, wondering whether she'd kept any of the beauty she'd had as a girl. Mister Dickinson, are you daft? She rushed the last few feet of hall and out onto the porch.

Some of 'em my congregants, John whispered angrily, if that isn't the limit! His chin and beard twitched.

And Electa was coming down too now, stepping into the hallway, peering outside with the look of displeasure she wore these days since she was kept home from school. What is all this? Holding a candle at shoulder height, dark hair tumbling, nightdress clinging, bare feet showing under the hem.

Your father is busy defending what he believes to be his, Lavina said dryly, turning away from her daughter's immodesty. Go back to bed. A shawl might have been a good idea, she added.

On the lawn, a piece of paper was held up and waved like a flag and Electa chose to float past her mother and down the porch steps, gliding over the unclipped grass, gripping it lightly with her toes, and coming upon her father and the assembled angry men. She tilted her head and then straightened it in order to look at their shadowy faces. Hello, she said, and reached for the piece of white paper, bringing the candle in close and then moving back a few steps without turning away from the men. Certainly they could see her form through the thin muslin of her gown and they could see the concern in her eyes when she turned to her father, leaving her back exposed, and squinted at the paper to read it out loud:

. . . for and in consideration of the sum of Eight hundred dollars current money of Virginia, the receipt whereof is hereby acknowledged, Matilda Dickinson doth grant, bargain sell and deliver to Andrew Milbourn all her right title in and to a certain tract and building, it being the same heretofore claimed by John Dickinson and on which the said John Dickinson unlegally resides, the interest of the said Matilda Dickinson derived as heir at law of Benjamin Dickinson, deceased, the said undivided tract being bounded as follows, to wit: Beginning at a stake on the Fox property line . . .

Electa turned very suddenly then, having scanned the rest of the page. Papa, the court has ruled against you.

The men had tied horses to the elms at the edge of the lawn and when she handed the paper back, they were satisfied and went to the horses as nicely as students would do at the ring of a bell. Lavina stared at Electa and suffered a feeling she couldn't name. John had cheated Electa of an education and yet Electa hurt for him. Perhaps her daughter was generous. So Lavina chided herself and led her broken husband upstairs, taking hold of his sleeve. She had two bushels of peas from the early spring planting and a gallon of corn oil saved. Pork she had salted. Beans. Flour.

27

A wagon train was organized and nearly ready. What were the chances? John put young Martin and old Reuben to rebuilding the family wagon, drawing his requirements on a piece of paper kept clean for his sermons. Straight lines top and bottom. New bed of seasoned oak to withstand weight and water. Sides jointed. No nails to work themselves out of the wood on a bumpy trail. The wheels to be straightened and rerimmed by the Jonesville blacksmith, a good Methodist. When John came to view the progress one late afternoon, Martin told him that the wagon would be heavier than it had been before. They'd need another mule, he said, although Cuff would do her best to pull. And then he laughed like the boy he was.

But his father hollered: You take my wife and daughters in your hands and remain a fool. How should I trust such intemperance?

Martin hung a tar bucket under the wagon so the slats could be caulked before a river crossing. Over the ribs, Lavina had stretched two layers of muslin, one dark and one light. These she had coated with hot beeswax and linseed oil and Martin touched them reverently. The wagon was a family effort, although Reuben was responsible for its balance. In what way am I intemperate? Martin queried boldly, praying that the bear would stay hushed, although at this hour she often grew impatient in her stall. Martin's boldness was unusual, but he was working as a man with Reuben now. He was thirteen years old and useful. He said: How in this family is intemperance possible? He was not sure he knew the definition of the word but he thought it meant drinking spirits like whiskey. A forged iron rod was attached along the length of the wagon tongues to strengthen them. The wheels had been soaked to tighten the wood to the rims. He touched one of them proudly.

Do not take that tone with me, boy. Not for an instant! I can show you what I mean.

Rather than dropping his eyes, the boy stared. Winter had fallen hard on his father, whose face showed new lines. Sometimes there was no explanation to his strange orders. Along the sides of the wagon he had demanded closed boxes. Empty, they looked as ominous as coffins.

He remembered the scene in the barn with Emly. He could, if he chose to, let his father know that he had heard him in the mule stall. He had practiced some sentences that could broach the subject and show what he knew but now all he said was: I'm not in charge of anything. He could see the moon rising through the open door of the barn and he wanted to take Cuff out for her evening romp. A warm breeze blew in, lifting the sweet smell that rises in the spring as the earth exhales. He could see his uncle's house in the distance, a place to be looked at by passing travelers. On the bleakest day the sight of that house was worth the three-mile trek from town but Martin took no joy in his gaze of it now that they were forced by his father to live in it. Everyone around knew that it went to Aunt Matilda and now they had nowhere to live because she'd sold it to another family. He had a feeling about all this that he had no name for, but it was a feeling that sat on his skin.

Martin, you will drive your mother and sisters to Missouri. You will do exactly as you are told and if one crack or crease renders this cart of yours even remotely vulnerable, I will seal it with your hide and I will do it personally if I have to dig you out of a river in the middle of May. John's voice was a dangerous blast fast growing to rage. You will do as you are told! he repeated, as if he had forgotten what else to say.

But where will you be? The boy quickly added *sir* to his question. Where will you be, sir?

My plans are none of your concern. His father's arm went up straight as if it held a blade or a staff.

At this, Martin crouched down on the far side of the wagon. Tongues, spokes, axles were liable to break, but not sons. A beating would be next.

See that this wagon is worthy or you will have nowhere to live; you will all be stuck in the wilderness, the whole lot of you, your mother and the girls. Rivers are up and roads will be mud. When the wagon train leaves . . .

Martin stayed in his crouch.

. . . mud will be preferable to homelessness . . .

Martin watched his father stride off through the wide door, wondering who would tell his mother that her husband planned to stay behind in the shambles of his life. He stood up. He had made a black walnut table for the road, low to the ground. He was proud of his table, which was more of a bench, a place to put pans and food out in the open while traveling. He had painted *Dickinson Partner Ship* across the back of the wagon in red script for when Patton met them. Martin began now to think of the coming trip as a nightmare to be endured. Out in the lean-to Lavina had put by more beans. Bacon. Cornmeal. Not destitute, Martin had told a friend who had enrolled with him at Emory and Henry College, but I will not attend classes this coming year.

His friend had said knowingly: If I was to go out west, I'd go the whole way up the Platte to Oregon. Or California for gold. But no, sir, I'll finish my schooling and get a certificate, then a wife for company on the trail.

A wife would be a bother, Martin had said knowingly, although he had no such actual knowledge. In Louisville they might decide to board a boat, and Electa said the riverboats were gay with music, stopping at towns along the way to invite local people aboard. There'll be dancing, she'd warned, because Electa had been to a school in Asheville and didn't think dancing was a cardinal sin.

He compared her with his little sister, who was unbearable. Un*bear*able, he said to himself, since any bear in the world is easier than Gina, who was never fun to play with and that was because she was spoiled to death. Martin could remember when Lavina had made biblical jokes about her pregnancy because, at forty-three, her condition confused her. Consider Sarah, she said once, trying to make light of her predicament. She had kept it a secret, wearing fuller aprons and staying in the house. Now it was hard to know whether Gina's slowness was the result of too much cosseting or whether she'd been born with a disadvantage. Mama should let her walk and run out of doors, Electa always said. Spoilt, Gina was, when she kept crying to her mother or climbed into her parents' bed after a dose of syrup, which they gave her almost every night. But Martin had more serious things to worry about. He let Cuff out of her stall and led her outside. How are we going to get the females to Missouri, bear? He put his face against her fur. You have to help. You know the ways of trees and rivers and creeks. The order of the forest. As usual, he forgot his fears when he ran alongside the bear.

In his half-brother's house, John was sitting with Gina on his lap, stroking her hair because this comforted him in much the same way Cuff's fur calmed Martin. Gina liked to hold on to her papa and listen to his made-up stories, so it was a mutual comfort they found, father and daughter. Tonight John was in a state very near collapse. His eyes were closed and his head was resting on the back of his chair and he was clinging to his child as she clung to him, telling her about a horse named Pete who could fly from pasture to pasture and who one day flew into town and bought a red jacket. A real boughten jacket with brass buttons.

How did my horse find some money? Gina wondered.

Her father slowly shook his head. Now where would you get such an idea? It wasn't your Judy who was flying up and down the streets but that rascally nag named Pete who lives in an onion field and never has a dime to his name. I've told you about him, haven't I?

Horses don't care for onions.

Which is precisely why Pete learned to fly.

Martin had come in from the barn in time to hear this story. His mother sat at the table with her mending and seemed not to notice his entrance or his walking or his sitting down next to Electa. The room was missing a large stuffed chair and a patterned carpet. Some things were just the same as they had always been and some things would never be the same again. It all felt tilted. A portrait of Uncle Benjamin's best horse, about the size of a baking pan, was hanging over the mantel where it had always hung. The horse was dead, but the portrait endured and nobody looked at it as it leaned to the left on its nail. Pete should come with Judy on our wagon trip, Gina mumbled, and Martin stood up and said: Father. Am I taking Judy? There was an edge to his voice, a slight warning. Gina was pulling her fingers through John's thick beard. Electa rose from her chair and took herself to the door. She lifted the latch very softly and stepped into the evening air. The sun was setting later now. Oblivion. Erasure. Good for her, thought Martin. Good for her but there will be the wagon trip and she'll have to face it like the rest of us. Again, Martin said: Father, what animals will I take?

Four cows, John said. Plus Judy.

Lavina looked up from her mending. Her

eyes searched the back of her husband's head, all she could see of him from where she sat. Mister Dickinson, please turn to face me. She had spent the morning grinding flour at the mill. Middlings. The finest grade was too expensive and they would need a hundred pounds for each of them. Her afternoon had been given to sacking the flour in cotton bags, then in leather pouches.

John turned his chair into the gaze of the room. I shall not accompany you, Mother. I am too old now for such a trip.

You are not much older than you were last month when you planned it and only six months older than you were when you sent your son to Missouri to look out for land, which must have been part of your plan. Her voice was vexed. Then she said: And what of your followers, all those believers who want to go with you? Will you just forget about everyone who depends on you? Now she muttered something under her breath. Her hands were shaking and she put down the shirt she was mending. His shirt. Fully aware of herself at that moment in time, she meant to shame him for the thought he had uttered out loud and she set down, as well, the needle, the spool of linen thread. People joined the train on your recommendation, she hissed angrily, because now she was letting it sink in, what he had said. He had not been making idle conversation. People who need your leadership. And faith. She studied her husband's face. Faith! Lavina seemed to hold the word in contempt.

He said: I am no leader. Look at me.

Lavina brushed both hands over the fabric that covered her knees and looked straight at her husband. She said fiercely: Then I shall go myself.

Who, after all, was Lavina? Daughter of an innkeeper, she had married John Dickinson shortly after her childhood or while still in the margins of it and she had never, for a moment, looked back. John swore that God was embedded in every stick and stone and footpath. He trod those paths without a shred of fear, gone for days at a time, and yet she trusted his return as surely as she trusted the Christians who gave him shelter along the way. But now his unexpected announcement shook Lavina to the heart and bones and deeper than that, all the way to her soul. John had lost his shirt, as he had once put it. Lost pockets and cuffs, lost pride and livelihood to his half-brother and to a faraway bank. As she rose to climb the stairs, Lavina considered that her future would have a whole new set of hurdles to be faced. Alone. She stood without any support and wondered how she would manage without a husband, without John, who was all and everything. But how could she stay? How could she bear the public shame of losing all they had? Where would they live? What was he thinking with nothing left? Stunned and bereft, she let each foot fall firmly on the boards that led to a bed that had once belonged to other women and would soon belong to someone else.

In bed, this couple usually slept on separate edges of a narrow mattress, facing away from each other as if seeking fresher air. Rarely did his feet brush against hers, or her arm reach out for him. Always, she put his slippers by his side of the bed and pulled the quilt up to her chin and if she moved it was only to rearrange her legs although recently she had taken to using the chamber pot once during the night. There had never been an argument between them. It was not consensus but simply an aversion to disagreement of any kind. She had considered that they were allies, and that seemed right to her. Fine. John consulted her about matters of the church or farm. She consulted him about relations with the town or with Benjamin's troublesome new wife. The children were shared between them. Lavina was a tall woman with upswept graying hair. Her face, once plump, had sharpened. Her long legs would define future generations. Clothed in the garb of a farmwife, she kept her apron clean. Was she ever ecstatic during the long camp meetings over which her husband presided? She professed to having been saved at the age of sixteen, that being enough for one lifetime, saying: What is the point of being saved all over again? And she would never allow herself to roll or grovel on the ground at anyone's feet, most especially John's, who had too much of that sort of homage for his own good.

The night of John's surprising announcement, she lay on her back looking up at nothing and wondering what had become of her marriage. The words she had spoken amazed her and certainly she would not take them back. That much of her future was settled, although God's commandment was that husband come first and wife abide. She turned onto her side with an arm firm against the quilt and felt a ringing right through her that took a minute to recognize. So then, I am furious, she thought. I am furious.

28

The next day Lavina was scrubbing at a spot on the floor of her former home, but she lifted her head in order to see what wasn't there over the mantel, the pretty painting of a girl in a long, gray dress. Electa had taken the picture off the wall and given it to her father, who kept it out in the cabin where no one else would see his daughter's vanity. A portrait of Electa's face above a dress that had soft green highlights created by the brush. Now the picture must be gathering dust. Like John, who was also gathering dust.

The sitting had come about one day when Electa met a man in the village of Rosehill. He had his equipment in a two-wheeled cart that was pulled by a horse so dappled it looked like he'd painted it, and when he leaned forward, he lifted his hat.

Electa did not ask her parents for permission to sit for the portrait. It was an act of vanity her father would not have permitted. She made an arrangement with the traveling man and kept it to herself, going off to meet him in the front room of a Jonesville house where he had set up his easel. For this she had taken the buggy, on the pretext of selling fresh eggs. In the painter's borrowed room there was the reek of turpentine, Electa told her mother. And yet she had enjoyed her hour there because the oil painting would be eternal, existing years and years after its subject was old and withered. Clever daughter! She knew that her father would never destroy the picture if it sat in a log cabin on the mantel with a shamble of other useless objects — old saucers and forgotten keys — while in the house where she had raised her children, Lavina was scrubbing at a spot on the floor, a stain that had been there for years, as eternal as a portrait only this one was hers. It was no good turning over an imperfect house to an unseen bill collector. And no one would see her crying for all the spilled milk in the life she'd lived there. A girl knows nothing of love and its shallows. How could she have measured John's guarantee when she met him at the age of eighteen? She had looked at a pair of blue eyes. She had trusted the eyes and allowed the hands. She had accepted the embrace because a preacher can sound very full of care and concern; it's his stock in trade. A preacher does not show doubt and that is gratifying, except that intruders would now move into her house and God would no doubt look the other way and bless the fields for them. All that fertility, thought Lavina, who knew herself to be done with birthing, done with anything pertaining to her marriage bed.

29

When John called the remaining workers to the barn, it was a Saturday and the court-house was locked. Tight as a fist. Still, the sheriff would arrive come hell or high water, the sheriff or some agent of the law, and John was bedeviled by a sense of oncoming doom. He had misread the signs. His brother had betrayed all of them. How could such tenderness as he felt for Emly be blamed? Or was it something worse? His own failure to see that he and Benjamin had betrayed their father's dearest belief and in so doing had betrayed the best part of them-selves?

Habituated to sermonizing, John made a gesture that instructed the men to come up close. Rakel and Clotilde stood back, stuck to the shadows, as was their habit, while John climbed onto a feed box, thinking sight was more impressive than sound to such as surrounded him. He knew each one of them, knew each history, however uneventful, and now he must send them off in a rush without succor or preparation. Many of you have known no other home than this farm, he began rhythmically, closing his eyes and swaying so that his words carried the weight of a pendulum. Back and forth, round and round. This farm built by my father and given to my brother for the upkeep of us all . . . He opened his eyes. Jule was jumpy, as if caught in a crime. John commenced speaking again, licking his lips to encourage sound. Now that we are to be overtaken . . . He flung out his arms and raised his voice to a fever pitch, gulping back sorrow and consternation at all that had plagued them to this final point . . . Well then, now you are to have your unsought freedom! This Very Day. *Herein!* Knowing that I thank you for your abiding loyalty, you are, he continued, to be manumitted this morning by my hand, never to return here again. (He felt tears spring to his eyes at that, and shook them away.) I tell you that I am giving you each a letter to prove you are free. But you will be thrown upon your own resources from this day forward! From this day forth, you will be held responsible for your conduct, which is overseen by God, your Heavenly Father. See that you dress yourselves decently, and always be sober, be *vigilant,* because your adversary, the Devil, is a roaring lion seeking whom he may devour. Do not think that your trials are ended when I place this letter in your hands, for in truth your troubles are just beginning. He felt the sharp edge of sentiment cut at his heart and paused. He had lived with his father's disappointment in Benjamin's decision to purchase human beings and here was the awful result of that lust for wealth. He chewed on the thought of his brother's greed and the duty he owed to these servants. The woman Rakel had been there for years, cosseted and protected when she had unaccountably lost her reason. That was the system, give and take. Her manumission paper would reside in some pocket until called upon by a roadside bully. What if that person ripped it to pieces or snatched it away? Who would protect these people who had never had to fend for themselves, who had lived under the care of a man who fed and clothed them day after day? He thought of Emly's attempt to save herself and her children by whispering his Christian name. He surveyed the faces below him. Young Jim, Abe, Tom, healthy fellows. They'll be all right, he assured himself. But the others? John raised his voice: I beseech you to make haste, as there stand in your way those who will try to bring you back! He looked at them sadly, shaking his head to make the point. Those who will try to claim you! Yes. Go straight for the Northern states, even if you must follow the stars to do it. Do not tarry. Consider this letter your ticket. Avoid the cities. Stay with farming, which is all you know. The man who hires you will know your worth. Be honest in your labor and the Lord God prosper you until He shall call you home.

He wiped at the air and jumped off the feed box, almost believing he had erased the stain of his own compliant past. As he handed each man and woman a letter with the slave name at the top and his own at the bottom, he felt relief for the first time in months. Who was to gainsay such a document other than the bank, which now owned these men in all legal terms and would certainly interfere within a matter of days, might chase them down, sell or imprison them? But there were mules gathered in the pasture, specially purchased for this occasion out of his dwindling pocket cash. Three dollars each! John stood with his chin on his chest, taking deep breaths of barn air, glad in his heart to be stealing this precious property from the New York bank, resisting in this small forceful way an acknowledgment of his own sin.

At the last minute he gave a letter to Clotilde, who stood apart, the only person owned by his own household. He was sorry to send her into the wilderness but she had talent and would surely make her way. Don't look back, he wanted to say, thinking of his servant turned to salt before his eyes. But Clotilde's hands were clenched and she did not reach out for the paper. He had never impressed her is what she showed in the thrust of her chin and pressed-down lips and one piece of paper from his hands did not change that. Not forward or backward or sideways was she going to move for him. She knew her chances, and they were slim to zero of not being stopped, harassed, stolen, raped. The law required any manumitted slave to leave the Commonwealth of Virginia forthwith. It required each letter bearer to hurry to an unimagined life. There wasn't one among them who could read or write, man or woman. In fact, John thought for the first time: We might have given them that at least. And he raised his voice again and went back to the box to get some height. He said: Listen here now. No two mules are alike and every one is as smart as you are. But each of you will have a mule as my gift. *I will not let thee go . . . ,* he thought, remembering his first sight of Clotilde at the wedding feast he and Lavina had been given at Redbanks Inn, *except . . . thee bless me.* Clotilde had been an intrusion then, an embarrassment, but now she would leave with the others, forthwith. Take it! he said, thrusting the paper in her face. Lavina had not been consulted but she must sooner or later understand that nothing of their former life could be saved. All of that was finished! He watched the familiar bodies file out of the barn in the two-by-two pattern they used in the fields and he raised his hand and briefly waved. Through the door and out beyond, he could see a wagon lurching westward on the road as if his future had been fast-frozen on the lens of his eye.

30

Lavina sat in her brown linsey dress on the seat of the wagon listening to Electa complain about the oily smell of the muslin covering and the way her father was being ignored. Having dressed herself for a funeral, Lavina did not care much for her daughter's opinions. Wait until you feel this wagon shake your bones, she said coldly, believing at that moment that women were cursed by belonging to men who were cursed by ambition and hope in false things. Better to take up some practical livelihood. Take up hat making or weaving. She sat on the wagon's only seat with her shoulders high and listened to her husband haranguing their son. Yes, he had the nerve to come down to the road where they were gathering and issue forth a series of decrees. Yes, he had the nerve to express himself on a subject that no longer concerned him. And would she ever lay eyes on him again in this lifetime? Was this not the bitter end of her previously sacred married life? Leave the unholy bear, John was shouting, and everyone now looked away so as not to see his furious farewell. Drop the bear's rope or I'll hang you with it from the nearest tree! It was the one forbidden threat in the Dickinson family. It was a thing never said because in another time, in a previous, earlier, more savage time, a slave had lost his life in just such a terrible way. But John made the threat without apology. His eyes were glass as he hurried along the line of wagons, eighteen in all, front to back. Chiseled by impotence, he was raving: The bear be damned! He grabbed Martin's arm and twisted it behind Martin's boy-skinny back. But with the other arm, Martin managed to tie Cuff to a metal ring inserted in the rear of the wagon, near the words *Dickinson Partner Ship.* You are not in command here, Father, Martin said, bearing the pain in his shoulder without giving any sign of a flinch. Let me go! With his face screwed up he pulled hard and John raised a hand as if to stun his boy with a blow, but there were witnesses enough and Martin thought of the new mule so recently yoked and converted to his father's purposes. He thought of the watching neighbors who had fallen down before his father more often than salvation required. He thought of Patton taking the strap and himself taking it too, time and again through his childhood without a chance to explain action or innocence or intention, and the slaves taking it differently, more roundly, more sharply, and he wrenched away from his father, angry most of all at this indignity in front of people who were going to be his companions for the coming weeks, people he must know not as a boy but as a man, and he did not want them to see him being meek. If you will not bless us, he said to his father in a voice to be heard, you might bless the mules who will take your family away to some unknown place to live without a stick of shelter. It was, for Martin, an uncommonly insolent thing to say, during which he closed his eyes as his father's hand came straight at his face. Then Martin was on the ground, sprawled, with his nose bleeding and his jaw bruised and the pain sending shocks to his ears while grown men turned away. Most of them had listened to John call down heavenly angels one day and the wrath of God the next. They were some of them from Jonesville and most from other places. They had heard John's plan of travel and dedicated themselves to his authority.

John knew the facts, the truth, the solution to any problem. John had answers. They had forgiven his former trespasses in the matter of housing an abolitionist, since it was a Christlike error, but when word went out that John was not willing to pull up his stakes, although he had no stakes left to pull, he was regarded with a new suspicion. What did he know that he wasn't telling? Was he sending them on some ungodly mission he himself had declined for good reason? All the talk of missionary work to come, of Indians and kidnapped white children. His recent sermons had conjured up a number of demons to be overcome and then the paradise that he was now avoiding. Maybe the preacher was a fabricator, a medicine man who sold snake oil in cloudy bottles. The whole family was somewhat off-kilter. Maybe the preacher was informed of some evil awaiting and it was left to the ordinary men, the less educated men busy with harnesses and children, to face the wild west without the word of God to protect them. Their women were hugging neighbors, shedding tears, looking at familiar landmarks and at beloved relations for the last time, and all of it had been John's idea. How else could it have come about? They were sure that none of them would have considered such a rash endeavor without the mandate of a preacher who was the Lord's very mouthpiece. Now he was a defector. Someone suggested in a whisper that he should be shot in the back! More like he shot us, another said. Children were screaming, laughing, crying, holding puppies or kittens or being held by weeping grandmothers. The animals bellowed nervously, voicing a universal complaint. Where? Why? How? Martin picked himself up from the ground and wiped his bloody nose on the sleeve of his jacket. He touched it carefully and wondered if it was broken. The pain was so blinding that he truly hated the father who had flattened him in front of people he now had to join. He had friends who were watching from the sidelines. Girls too. His eyes were hard when he stared at the blood smeared over his father's hand. He thought: This is the last time. He will never hit me again.

Around them all the swirl of activity. Boots, ropes, hooves, and wheels. John grabbed little Gina as if she were his shield.

Father, hand me up the baby, said Lavina sternly, and all of them watched as John kissed his favorite child and lifted her up to the height of his hat. Gina clung to his neck and buried her face in a place at the side that belonged to her, but Lavina leaned over and pried her loose and took her up kicking and screaming and the wagon received the extra weight and creaked on its wheels. Come, baby, Judy is stamping her four little hooves. She's ready. Isn't that so, Father?

John agreed that Gina's pony was ready to be off, for though tied to the far side of the wagon away from the bear, she could be heard snorting and whinnying playfully. Martin had the four cows more or less gathered.

Quite an entourage, said a neighbor who was standing by, and John said: Indeed, in that almost inaudible voice he adopted when he had nothing to say. May God bring you to His promised land, he muttered, and the Dickinsons remembered to pray silently for one minute in the old Quaker way although the words John heard ringing in his head were his son's: *You are not in command here, Father.* He heard it. He heard it. Certainly there would be no such thing as command once they were beyond shouting distance. Letters would be of no more avail than they had been with Patton, who never responded and may not even have received his directives since he could only guess where that son might be at any given time. He saw Sister Galway running toward a wagon with a basket of steaming sweet rolls. The Lord giveth. And everything from this minute on was unstoppable. All that had happened was irreversible. All of what had been acquired was thoroughly gone. The barn, the pigsty, the smokehouse, the old lean-to, the great showpiece of brick. And his own built house. Something he should have protected since its sacrifice hadn't saved Emly or anyone else. And so wrapped was he in anger and pain and disconnection from his past that he left the road without turning to look at his family. He strode through the milk gap wondering how many cows had come through it over the past sixty years. John's mother had supported the family with the butter she sold. Butter from her own little herd. John had watched Benjamin take all her love and use it up. He had watched Benjamin inherit her herd and put Emly in charge of it. He sniffed at a blooming lilac. How much butter had been churned and how many slices of bread had that butter graced? Then Emly's fine cheeses, created to whet and to satisfy any appetite. Cows and cotton and corn and fruit trees. All to the ax, to the knife. All crumbling in his ragged mind as he walked to the cabin built by his father, its logs still holding although the chimney was showing signs of wear and the old steps sagged. John was not yet born when a slave boy named Simus had fitted those steps into place only days before he was strung up in a locust tree. And that tree had become a place where the slaves went to pray or to sing. Sacred, it was to them, and John turned to look back at the wagons now, angry for no reason he could name. The train had started to move, every separate part bumping and banging against the next. The cries of men and horses. The grumbling of cows and mules and the frightened squeals of pigs. Chickens. Dogs. John's chest was a cage. What was inside? Back on the road the talkative neighbor had taken a look at his ashen face and said wasn't it a blessing the children were headed west although, he said: That confounded Pierce! A president getting innocent people killed in the name of what's nobody's business — our way of life.

John had tried to agree. Pierce had sat down at his desk to sign into law the Kansas-Nebraska Act and now everyone wanted a piece of that good land. But Missouri was a hotbed of confederates — there were enough sparks out there to ignite a war between North and South and Patton must, by now, be there. . . . John turned up the path. He took a handkerchief out of his pocket and wiped his sweat-beaded face. Politics had nothing to do with it. Everything was survival and nothing else. With Conestogas, there are decisions about what to carry, what to leave. Should a stove be packed? If so, how much clothing and bedding must be left behind? What tools were essential? What could be better picked up in St. Louis or Independence? Some of the wives in this train had baked bread and dried it, believing that it wouldn't mold. A kettle of hot milk and a crust for those families would, on many nights, have to suffice. But that wouldn't be the case with Lavina, whose smoked bacon was double wrapped, put in the storage boxes he'd designed, and then covered with bran. Sacks of beans and rice and salt and coffee were wedged around the family medicine box, which held dried herbs and bottles of laudanum and alcohol and calomel. Hadn't John's father come from Pennsylvania in a wagon? John's offspring were born to this. (For that instant of leave-taking he felt almost proud.) He took a cigar out of his jacket and stuffed it in his mouth, although he could not allow himself to smoke. Americans will never be confined, thought John. Those wagons moving toward the Cumberland Gap must look to God like a white serpent on a dark green carpet divinely made for such a trip. Or would God liken that serpent to temptation? Was such a trip taken against nature? A breaking plow, axes, saws, spades, hoes, and carpenter tools. To wrestle, to tame, to inhabit. He was counting off on his fingers the equipment he had packed. A cookstove with its pipe running up through the muslin top. A bed frame. Two chairs. And, thought John, there are the warrants issued by the government for buying property. Patton has them, surely he does. Or had he gambled them away? Lost them in an argument? How could he have trusted his wild son to keep their last remaining treasures intact? Well, in truth they belong to the boys, he admitted to himself. One had been easy enough for Martin to obtain by trading a sow he had raised for it. And Patton had earned his one way or another. Didn't my own father create the acreage around me out of three meager warrants from the war with Britain? They will make out, he told himself. The best thing for everyone is this outcome. He saw that a button lying on the fresh grass had fallen from his cape and thought: Let it lie.

31

John, then, sitting in his father's chair with its bit of carving at the top and such a boy he was back when the chair was made, Lavina newly wed to him and both of them looking forward. Daniel had even carved Lavina's initials on the chair. It was a wedding gift, but it never got moved out of the cabin and he could not now remember whether she had rejected it or Daniel had decided against giving it to her. Was she too worldly in his eyes? Too proud? She had arrived with a slave, but it was only Clotilde, who was part of her family. And he next thought of his father's stash of letters, the hidden daughter in Canada. It was impossible to assess the motives of anyone else, most especially if they were dead and gone, but he got up and moved around, drumming his fingers against hard surfaces, thinking about the trunk at the foot of his father's bed and the wagon full of his family, each with a secret and separate heart. How could he even know his own wife, who had set off so staunchly with the whip in her hand? But it hardly mattered. He would not see that wife or those children again. He thought back on the confidence of his youth when every six weeks he had ridden to Baltimore to buy and sell for the mill their father had constructed. It had become the Mill House. The Comfort House. It had become a popular trading post and nightspot, much to their father's surprise. It was a place to buy supplies for overland travel and then it had a table or two and playing cards and brandy made from their orchard fruit and Benjamin had created himself there night by night, winning at cards, making political friends, doing business one way or another while young John was sent off to bring supplies from the Tidewater east. Tobacco, bolts of cotton, sugar, coffee. On those trips he stayed at an inn called Redbanks, where he met and courted the daughter of the house. How exhilarating to feel the wall of wind in his face as he rushed the horse over a road he could measure out by its bumps and windings on the blackest night. Each bend and bump meant a shorter time to his destination, which was his future, all shine. Each bend and bump meant a minute closer to the girl whose face and voice meant chaos and harmony in his young body, and on the way back from Baltimore, it was fury and joy until he had left the inn behind at the halfway point. Then he let the horse slow down and he would not read those ruts or care and he knew that what he was experiencing was a thing to be seized.

Serving the Lord, he had made himself a farmer. Corn, he had thought back then, along with tobacco, would be the ruination of the land, for those plants sucked the life out of the soil by requiring too much deep plowing. Cotton had been impossible until a highland version was found but now, with the gin, it could be grown in southwestern Virginia by the ton. So then, cotton. But slaves were essential to cotton and corn was essential to slaves. They used it in bread and hominy and pone and mush. They roasted the ears. Corn, then, must be planted. John was a practical farmer with a hungry affection for the women around him. For Lavina, his rhubarb grew with lush, almost tropical foliage. For her, John had grown fat muskmelons and a nutmeg melon and a citron melon from which she made an iced dessert. For Elizabeth, his brother's wife, he had grown a patch of berries for her famous pies. Later, much later, for Emly, he planted pattypan squash. It was a staple the Dickinsons enjoyed along with their slaves. Peas on a fence. Potatoes. Radishes. Cabbages. His food garden was so like his mother's that people remarked on it.

John went deliberately now to the trunk at the foot of his parents' bed and gave it a disrespectful kick. He opened it without a key, for it was never locked anymore, and he took out the letter he had been reading most recently, several times in fact. Dated *1835* it read: *Dear Papa, It seems I am mortal. I have put Eva Nell into the employ of the school she attended.*

Pray for her Papa, M

John put the letter back in the trunk. It would lie with the others that had, over the past year, fed him certain truths. *The shrike are plentiful here in September but success requires dogs, which are a luxury. Oh if only you could see with my unencumbered eyes.* John frowned. Then he lit a fire that would consume all the secrets. He added the farm account book. Go to Blazes. He thought of adding the lump of treasure stashed in the lining of his jacket, but he was too tired, too confused by the smoke filling the cabin to unstitch the seam. He was too weary even to feed himself out of that iron skillet on the edge of the old stone basin. His throat ached as if he'd been crying, and when he looked through the window glass at the barn where his father had kept his hay and his wagon and his heart, he saw that it was his father's barn and also Benjamin's and that it had never been his. He had gone out to meet Emly there where horse and cows and mules and pony and bear had until that morning resided in harmony and he had never belonged to it as the rest of them had. He had never belonged to the land that his father acquired, but he looked at the field he might have planted this year, a field smudged in uncut grass, a square of earth all his until the New York bank took it over, and he brushed the heel of his hand across his face and then looked at the hard, accusing eyes staring out of his daughter's portrait and went to it meekly and stroked the painted chin of his child and then flung her into the fireplace. He heard the wagons take up their burdens and roll very slowly and awkwardly down the road past the campground his father and the elders of Jonesville had built, a clearing for God's work, and he remembered how he had been carried to that site on his father's broad shoulders, how he had felt the scratch of Quaker homespun. He could feel the bounce of his father's walk as they set off for that place crammed with carriages and wagons and he might even then have suspected that it would all turn to gall in his mouth. His father, who hated slavery. And look what they had come to now. O Glory! he had heard a thousand people shout over the years, but the barn light never dimmed. It was the screen upon which his life was ruined. Who was Job to complain? Haven't I mounted my horse and ridden my circuit year after year after year? But I was only a man, John thought, as he tapped a thumbnail against the one plate left to him. One glass too, and the iron skillet. His life had become a series of walls without a hole to shoot through. I will go then, Lavina had said, she who had climbed up in the wagon and taken the reins.

Throwing on his jacket to cut the risen wind, John pushed at the door, the sun streaming in and casting his shadow in the doorway as if that were all that was left, and he set off across the early May grass, leaving the cabin his father had built with the help of a murdered slave. John was part of its story but a small part, and his chapter was done. First to the old well, abandoned when the water turned rank, but holding cold memories in the damp dark, memories of a fallen sparrow, a lost bucket, a thousand visits, a kitten's howl. And that patch of raspberries that had lent themselves to Elizabeth's desserts because as a very young man he had loved her for a little while, his brother's wife. Had Benjamin been amused by that? Big half-brother had waited and watched. Big half-brother had laid his traps. But Mother Ruth should be visited in her grave under the apple tree that sheltered Dickinson ghosts.

He looked at his field and remembered her wrestling there with the plow. Salvation through action. Grace through labor. He'd preached it on hilltops, in valleys. He'd preached in forests and spiritual deserts. What we do has consequence. He looked now at the subtle grasses furtive but stalwart, remembering how Benjamin had started with two grown men brought by Elizabeth to her marriage. Lend me your faith and I will bring us wealth. They had found two wives for those men, for such is the Lord's mandate. In this fashion they had built up human stock and John had found a granny to take care of the babies so the young mothers could work in the fields and soon there were acres and acres of cotton and Benjamin's growing family to be fed, and his own as well and the crops to be harvested, the soil to be worked. Each of us must live, after all. Blood brother, that land.

Behind the great house, the barn was almost as old as his father's cabin, its fine roofline a matter of family pride. Who in the future will appreciate this? he wondered. Even now, he could smell the strong perfume of hay. The barn all his now and he allowed himself to stand before its gray walls, its thick beams, its shingled roof and fine tamped earthen ramp. *We have made something to last.*

The wagon had been rolled out from the place it had stood this past month being resurrected. The mules had been yoked; the bear had been leashed and the pony tied. All were gone but for his mare, who pawed at the ground when she heard her rider approach. Sound of familiar boots, scent of familiar skin. He was coming, bearing rope in his hands. I need your back, old girl, he said, and he climbed up the gate of her stall in his boots and swung the rope over a beam.

32

Reuben was holding the button fallen from John's cape. Cape made of wool from some animal he had raised. Preacher? Them wagons movin now. Better go on down.

Go away, old man. I sent you away! Days ago.

Two weeks it was. Reuben pointed at the rope coiled around John's thin neck. What that for? He held out the button like an offering.

John sat on his mare, rope encircled. He took in air for another long minute and thought his last thoughts. You could get picked up, Reuben! The sheriff's coming any minute. He'll drag you off to the jail. Get away from me or they'll find you with my dead body.

Who want old Reuben? Can't do nothin but pick up a button. Livin off scraps. Taters and roots. Where you spec I should go off to, Preacher? Walk up North on my bare feet?

That's right. You got the freedom letter. Don't you understand that much of something? Where's your mule?

Don't like his bony back to hurt my bongs.

John blushed. He hadn't had this much conversation with one of the workers for months. Years. Actual conversation, this was, and he said: You'd do well to take care of yourself as I said that day when I explained it to all of you in the barn. Don't you remember what I said? You are responsible now for yourself. Nobody else will look after you.

Member you sayin bout that. But we b'long ta some bank up the North is the true fact you never said. That the true fact that the north bank own us. So we not yourn to make free. We not free we runaways. Reuben opened the gate and entered the stall one step at a time, watching the rope. An you never said the truth of it that we be stolen goods.

Now you listen here to me. John wanted to be finished, to leave this piece of earth besmirched by his brother where an old fool slave should know better than to bother a preacher's last earthly minutes. He wanted to pray, to think back.

Missus Lavina sittin up high on the wagon seat waitin.

No. She isn't.

Wagon made by a boy not yet bearded for a papa who told him to do it.

All right. What of it?

A wind come up and if them wagons get blowed off the groun you not there to see it. You the preacher spose ta comfort and save. Reuben looked up at John with an expression of misplaced faith, as if the sight of his master might bring him to tears.

John bent over the neck of his mare and pushed the old man hard in the ribs. He pulled the rope up over his head and then, seeing Reuben sprawled on the floor, reached down to pull on one old, withered hand and Reuben stumbled to his feet. Now you tell me this. Where is Emly? You tell me that! John commanded. Then I will get you a buggy for your mule. Tell me what happened that day when . . .

Reuben looked up at the preacher and narrowed his eyes.

Who got her, Reuben?

Tennessee man name Lucas come here that day. What I know of it.

John stared at the corner of the barn where Emly had asked him to sign his life away, remembering the hour, the light it had offered, and his heart, which even now beat defiantly. I could have . . . I might . . .

Reuben stood by the horse, his back up straight. Heard Mister Benjamin say it.

John laughed. And happiness flooded through him and old Reuben was cupped inside his arms astride the horse as they left the barn to find the old man's mule. Not another gate falls open but then this lovely sky.

33

The Wilderness Road through the Cumberland Gap, that natural mountain passage that pins the corners of Kentucky, Virginia, and Tennessee to one point on the map, was the only route west. This was the road the wagons would take, driving at a pace so slow that none of them seemed to be moving but rather wavering in the eternal present, unready to cross that steep divide into a future no one could grasp. The gap, a cleft between peaks cut by rivers and beasts a million years ago, was no fit place for a vehicle. Widened by Daniel Boone in the pay of a land-grabbing company owned by a man named Henderson, the ruts and bucks and billows would soon make the wagons unfirm.

Lavina was suffering an unparalleled guilty grief. Had she made the decision to leave in too much anger and haste? She looked ahead at the boundary of mountains and longed to turn back.

Beyond Big Stone Gap and still in Virginia lay the peaceful valley of Powell, where the Dickinsons and others in the train had bought and held on to and sold away hundreds upon hundreds of acres of land for the past many years. Sixty years for the Dickinsons, more than for anyone else in the train. Whether planted or plowed or forgotten, a field is the skin of the world, flesh of the earth, curried and fed by women and men and beasts. Seeds saved and planted, seeds dropped and blown. Shit of the horses and birds. Wheat and corn and flax transposing and now Lavina had turned from it, all of them, each of them, never to see it again. Her eyes traced the contours of the nearest field and then moved along the outline of Wallens Ridge, which she'd first visited with John when they were newly married and he brought her out to see the wonders of her new world, both of them mounted on horses; she was then nineteen. He said he had invented it all for her, that none of it had existed for a minute until he'd met her and prayed to the Lord to make a place seemly enough for her wedding trip. He said that she sat a horse better than any of the local girls, and she had brushed-back hair that was unraveling and

211

looked at him with appraising eyes because he was enough in those early days and for a long time after.

There now was Sounding Gap, which the Shawnee revered as sacred because of a cave where they hid their women during battles with the Cherokee. Or so it had been told to the bride along with the added fact that this was the land the Natives claimed as their hunting paradise. And Lavina had told her new husband that she would prefer a Heaven where there is no meal to be caught or killed or cooked. She would prefer a Heaven where the business of survival is finally put aside, and he had reached across the space between their mounts up there at the top of a windblown hill and made the sign of the cross on her lips.

The wagon train would spend the first night near the small town of Rosehill. Hoping to engage her children in their adventure, Lavina told them that the station there had been built before their grandfather left Pennsylvania and that he surely visited the place in its fatal innocence after he stopped in Jonesville to buy his first six acres. She wiped her eyes thinking of the father-in-law she had never loved because although he was soft of voice and manner, he was never good or loving to John. Daniel had blamed both of his sons for imposing slavery on the land he had won for them and yet, while he forgave Benjamin, he expected John to be a better man because he had not had the misfortune of losing his mother in early childhood. Benjamin would always need to compensate for his loss, Daniel reasoned, but John had a God-fearing mother and no excuse for moral weakness. In Jonesville, Daniel had bought land from Frederick Jones and there Daniel and Ruth had favored Benjamin so obviously that it caused people to wonder what John had done to earn their disregard. John had perhaps taken up his ministry in order to reassure the neighbors, but parental love was even then withheld, which seemed cruel to Lavina, who had vowed to treat her children equally in spite of her tenderest feeling for Patton, who was the first to survive her birthing bed and had a gleam in his eye from the very first minute of life. Now she was taking the other three children to find that brother, taking them in the company of a group of exacting Methodists bedded down around the Rosehill Station's fallen logs, women keeping to wagons and men lying underneath or beside those wagons with weapons close at hand. Muskets, rifles, hoes, and rakes. They were nervous although not far from home. The old family rifle was stowed under the wagon seat, but she had never fired a gun and thought Martin would not be up to the task. The gun had been put there by John as a remedy for his absence. Meanwhile Martin had his small knife. He kept it in a pouch at his waist.

And the world announced itself. The rhododendrons were opening beside them; the azaleas were ready to burst; the birds were finding one another after a long winter of waiting. The bluebird, the waxwing, the cowbird, the flycatcher were settling down, folding up wings in newly built nests. Sounds of the night. In the morning, the world would have the scent of beginnings and the twirl of birdsong would be overpowering, but in the dark they were dreaming of what they had left rather than what was to come.

Lavina's back ached from the tension of driving the mules and the thin mattress she had packed brought no comfort. She missed the man who always lay beside her, although how could she ever forgive him for abandoning all of them? She missed her old bed and the door she could shut between herself and her children. Gina was lying with Electa, who was breathing hard to defy her mother's hope of conversation. I am sorry, Lavina wanted to shout. All this fear of tomorrow, and none of us far enough from home to forget our losses and there is your poor brother, who sleeps on the ground with a bear.

Above them an unreadable sky.

To the stars through any difficulty was her thought.

In the morning the wagons reassembled in the same pattern as they had the day before and Lavina saw that her permanent place would be at the rear. Was it for lack of a husband that she was thus located? Was it for his betrayal in not coming or hers for leaving him behind? In any case, it seemed unseemly cruel, since skirmishes by bandits and Indians usually took place at the back of a train. But Lavina was outnumbered and as they moved slowly westward, she gazed up and up at the Cumberland barrier a thousand feet high, its sharp sides chalk white in bright sun like huge mirrors waiting to fool them into turning back. They were twenty miles from home. Men were calling to one another, horses were stamping and whinnying. Mules brayed and the cattle began to low and quiver at the sight of the hard wall of rock ahead. It was general, the foreboding, and there was no heart not quietly beating a rhythm of terror.

On the right hand the sheer face of the clean precipice and on the left a sheer drop into Tennessee. Only a few of the men had ever climbed this trail twisting over sharp boulders and slick ridges, a trail barely wide enough for one wagon, which would need sufficient brakes, and there was never a sufficiency of anything except shouting and cursing and braying and bawling as they began very slowly to climb and one wooden wheeled thing slammed back into another, wheels sliding, animals pushed aside, a child tumbling out, a rending scream.

All around the travelers meanwhile, breezes were blowing in newly leafed trees, bushes were bursting into flower while birds called out challenges. What pinned those loaded wagons to the earth as a cold wind came out of the east and the oiled tops flapped and wagons careened and one of them veered and tumbled over sideways and had to be unpacked, righted, packed again? The gap was too narrow and far too steep.

Lavina studied the line of white-topped wagons ahead. The men were making decisions without consulting her while her mind held thoughts of capsized cargo, broken yokes, and fallen mules. Dead. Children. She heard a shout and her milch cow bawled. All of them hunted by hovering fate.

Oh what have I done?

John?

She looked at Martin and gave the signal to release the brake. He was so small against the wagon, his head barely reaching the billowing top.

Last in line. Last to climb. First to be buried if all else failed.

34

At the top, the Cumberland Trail led straight down to the tangled ravine where a spring flowed through prickly laurel just come into flower. Descending, the wagon creaked and leaned and went slowly, slowly until the trail gradually leveled out in shoulder-high grass and thick canebrakes. It followed the line of Yellow Creek out of loyalty to the work of Daniel Boone, who had manfully cleared it, and it held promise and compromise every inch of the way. What if they scalp us? Gina asked, walking beside her exhausted sister and stumbling on her small, blistered feet. Carry me? Please?

The Yellow Creek basin was known as the warriors' path for good reason, since the Shawnee and Cherokee had met here to trade and hunt and make war on each other. Now the old trail led into a ravine where a sulfurous stream lost itself in deep grass and the wagons moved along its meander for one day and another and another twisting awkwardly all the way to the Cumberland River while oak, elm, pine, and poplar brightened the slopes that surrounded them warranting better things. They were moving west and north. The Cumberland ford would constitute the first test of their buoyancy and they were duly frightened and ill prepared. Who could know which wagons would float and which would sink? Who had taken such a chance before, trusting family and worldly goods to the vagaries of tar-caulked wood? The travelers spent the night before the crossing praying together, wholly exhausted, getting little sleep, hearing the river rush through undergrowth, counting belongings and frights. Some of them missed Preacher John by then, having forgotten his poor excuse for sending them off unescorted. Some of them said he would surely, certainly, definitely appear. This was the sort of thing he enjoyed, a sudden appearance after testing their faith. He would not fail them. He had ministered to them for twenty years. He had made them into a flock of believers in the word of God. He had christened them and instructed them and buried their children and parents. He had eaten at their tables and visited their sick. Preacher John, Brother John, would not abandon them for long. It was only a test. Soon he would come as a shepherd to keep them safe and escort them onward.

Brother Borden, who was new to them, insisted on telling everyone the history of every place they touched. This place had been purchased from the Cherokee by that man named Henderson, the very man who hired Daniel Boone to cut a way through Kentucky. Henderson bought a good half of it from those Cherokees, Brother Borden affirmed, in exchange for ribbons and guns and English pounds. Made himself rich, which is what men do in the West, where we are going, although the Shawnee never admitted to Mister Henderson's right to such sacred territory. I tell you the ugly facts of it. It was always Shawnee versus Cherokee. And yet, where are they now? Brother Borden was sitting on moist ground at the river's edge as he told the story. He'd lifted a rocking chair down from his wagon and set it between two granite rocks. Now the chair was sinking into land Mister Henderson had bought with a ribbon, and a small group of believers had gathered to listen to history and later to sing. Because Lavina did not know Brother Borden, when he smiled at her, she made no response. In her situation, a smile would be misinterpreted.

She watched her children stand by the rocking chair to hear that the Shawnee chief Dragging Canoe had promised revenge on all future settlers. Brother Borden said: Why, even now, scalpings are pretty regular. They grab hold of your hair . . . But Lavina hurried across the ground, tall, angular, shoulders held back, and said: There now. That will do. And she was stunned by the thrust of anger she felt, as she had been stunned by the anger she discovered while lying in bed the night she learned of her husband's defection. It was new to her, this surge of unbidden rage; she was meeting a piece of herself she didn't know. But a man who would frighten little children with stories of scalpings should be ashamed! In the dark she could feel the blood in her neck and face. There was the river at their feet and there were perhaps angry Natives ready to maim and kill and Lavina went back to her wagon and unfolded a guidebook with its biography of Daniel Boone and its description of the road he had cleared all the way to the Falls of Ohio. *A land of brooks, of water, of fountains and depths, of valleys and hills, of wheat and barley.* She studied the ragged campsite and wondered when the guidebook would prove itself. Wheat and barley! She wondered if John had any idea what this trip would entail in the way of hardship and admitted to herself that he knew perfectly well. He had traveled this area once before, in his youth when he had been converted by Bishop Asbery, his life-long hero. He certainly knew how wild and unruly and unwelcoming a place it would be for his wife and children and yet he had coldly sent them away. Like Hagar, she thought, and then she thought that Patton might well have been killed by now, eaten by savages! John had always insisted that Patton would meet them somewhere along the trail. But where? There were no boundaries or even locations in this unsettled landscape. Nevertheless, John had promised. He had said things were arranged with Patton by mail, but there was no evidence that Patton received John's letters. He had never replied. And, if they were reunited, it would be without John, who had broken the family into unequal parts and given up his role as protector and provider. Minister of the Lord no longer, but oh, if she thinks too much, she will begin to question everything.

In the morning the Cumberland ford was a battle of reason versus nature, or that was the way Brother Borden portrayed it. The water rushed along all incoherence while the men yelled for silence and demanded order, and trees broke and fell as animals pushed and pounded ground that was sticky and gnats flew into faces and mosquitoes bit flesh and the river before them flowed on unperturbed while nearby the first house made of brick in Kentucky sat on a small patch of ground as if it had been planted there and grown to full size. Someone had stopped here and refused to cross the river. Why else scratch out a living on such poor soil? The frantic travelers looked hard at the last civilized dwelling before the open frontier. It represented everything soon to be lost and they viewed it with various emotions: denial, anticipation, regret, and one by one the wagons descended the bank of the Cumberland River and miraculously, solemnly, with weighty majesty, each wagon took float while mules and horses pulled and swam and cows called plaintively and children screamed and mothers grabbed and held. There was a little ferry-boat crossing the other way. It was full of hogs going south to market and it would never hold a wagon's weight, but the women turned their heads for a minute to watch and then dug their nails into their own closed palms as the wagons bounced and splashed in the miracle of water and Lavina thought that if only they could float all the way west without the drag of soil on their wheels, without any gravity, without this terror of being swept downstream, wagons capsized and children drowned, they might relish such a voyage. Someone was shouting to a cow stuck in a ridge of sucking mud. Gee on, Susie! When at last they had made it to the other side, the dripping vehicles lumbered slowly and surely one by one up the shallow bank as if ready to be released to hard land. They were creatures alive and on that newfound side of the river there was a sky-sized bed of shallow glimmering water clear as a mirror where people had gathered salt for a thousand years. Flat Lick was a favored hunting ground, according to Brother Borden, where elk and deer came to lick the clay, where the low standing water held a strong stink of sulfur, and a tired old tavern leaned over glassy pools that reflected its slovenly shape.

They did not stop.

The wagons sloshed and slid and walking people had heavy feet. Martin was holding Beulah's halter in his fist. Beulah was fidgety. Good girl, he said off and on. He was proud of the wagon he had created, its polished planks and its oiled canvas reflecting the brand-new day. His wagon was water-tight! He said the words to himself in a whisper. Then he said: I built it, forgetting about Reuben. Forgetting every former upbraiding. He had reason to congratulate himself and to look forward. The undiscovered world ahead was going to be his.

That morning they had passed a painted sign, nailed to a wooden cross:

There the prisoners rest together;
they hear not the voice of the oppressor.
The small and great are there; and the
servant is free from his master.
Job 3:17–19.

Martin, a boy of thirteen summers, had time now to think while he steadied Beulah and kept an eye on his leash-tied bear and watched the untethered cows and the nervous tied pony. He thought about who was buried in the place they had passed. He thought that maybe nothing could be trusted on this trail where there might be a sudden cave-in or a gunshot or a wolf. Or an Indian was more likely! Martin had inherited imagination and he now compared this journey to the one his grandfather had made sixty years before. A wagon, a woman, some half-brought-up children. It was said that Daniel Boone had sometimes stopped at his grandfather's cabin to smoke and talk.

It came to his mind that Daniel Boone had once stayed alone in the wilderness for two long years, as the story went. People talked about that as some kind of feat. He'd killed a hundred and fifty-three bears was the boast, but the pelts got stolen by Indians, which served Daniel Boone right. Martin thought he was opposed to killing, although he couldn't reason on how to live without doing it. He thought of Cuff's mother falling, pawing and searching the air for her footing. He thought of the orphans Daniel Boone had left hungry in the forest. Killing just for fur, not for meat. He thought he might try living without tasting flesh but one person's diet wouldn't make much difference to the world.

His thoughts seemed to him very deep and he went on thinking.

35

On the seventh day the wagons came to a
halt on a rise and the travelers looked down
at grass all the way to a green horizon.
Never had they seen such infinite grass, and
it was anointed with millions of flowers like
invitations to something limitless with flocks
of turkeys overhead, wings open wide, and
the end of all they could see so far in the
distance that it turned into sky. The open
vastness jolted these farmers, who had never
seen such prevailing space. It stunned them
and they climbed out of their wagons and
fell to their knees so as not to appear
undeserving in the Lord's all-seeing eye.
Martin could hear water muddling through
the ground beneath him with a dark, prehistoric rhythm. He wanted to put an ear
against the earth and decipher what it was
saying. Talking water underground must be
wise to all things. Except light. He thought
about that. He thought of the school he

might have attended in the fall, but a future of learning how to reason things out had been denied to him by his father, who had sent them away to fend for themselves and there was nothing to do now but live by imagining what he could never learn of true facts. Patton had studied Latin. Patton could remember things that happened in Rome and France. Patton was right in an argument because he knew what was true and false. Martin needed a dose of his brother's cool confidence and now, walking along beside the wagon, he brought back in his mind the last trip they had made in the woods. Patton had brought the makings for several snares. His father had taught him this quiet skill when he was small. There was a time, he told Martin, when Pa could catch a grouse without hardly blinking. He was different then. Not like now.

Martin had not been invited on such a trip since the murder of Cuff's mother and yet he was uneasy about the quest for grouse, having no desire to kill anything. He had once gone with Patton on a trapping expedition and he often thought about those three days as the happiest time of his life, so he went off to the woods more or less trustingly, swinging his arms. When he whistled, Patton said: Sshh. Don't scare em away. Maybe you're still too nervous to hunt up your dinner.

Hell no. I hunt things.

Truth is Mama makes you anything you like.

I cleaned the last chicken she cooked. By myself.

Woman's work.

Well, I have things on my mind. Things you don't know about.

What things do you think about that I would even care to know?

Just things. In the barn.

Everyone knows she does it with Uncle Benjamin, Marty.

Not with him, Martin asserted. But a sudden pain over his right eye felt like a strong poke from God.

Patton was quiet for a spell. At last he said: I bet you don't know anything.

Still. Patton made strange things normal. He would have made this journey feel more like adventure and less like exile. Why did Papa send him out to Missouri all by himself? Why did he steal my warrant? He should have asked, but he didn't ask, he just took it. I could have gone with him; we could have been partners. I showed him that warrant I got, but I didn't know he would take off with it. Martin put a hand on his bear, now ninety pounds of steely weight, and remembered the joke made at school. *His papa's a preacher so it's said, goes to church but owns no land.* It was just a dumb rhyme because the boys were all afraid of God's representative. At school they stood up to sing and sat down to pray except for Clay Harmon, who did not do those things. Clay did not laugh at the store window when it was crowded with corsets. The two of them had walked back home from school a few times, three miles, and tipped their hats to babies and ignored everyone else. Clay was not afraid of Preacher John. He said his own father beat him every single night. Clay was good company. Sometimes they pretended that he was blind and Martin had to lead him by the hand down the walk-way in front of the stores. And now Clay was at school and Martin was passing a rock that grew out of nothing and Brother Borden was naming it Castle Rock as if it was his to name. Brother Borden was like a bee in your sleeve but suddenly Martin felt that bolt of guilt again, right over his eye, because of being outside Emly's house and not telling his father. He thought of how his pa would have beaten him with the strap if he'd told the truth because it was wrong to spy but now it's my fault that everything's ruined and we're poor because I didn't stop the men from running away and maybe some of them even got killed because Pa could have stopped them getting drowned and we'd still be in our house and I could still fix my rock dam with Franklin and walk home with Clay Harmon. There was all this space in Kentucky, but Martin was thinking too much to enjoy the immensity. It made him feel small and more than anything else, he missed Patton.

They'd spent two days crossing creek after creek in the boiling sun with the men ordering animals and women and one another while the children clung to their places in the wagons and sometimes dared to dangle their hot little fingers in cold creek water. Martin was supposed to be one of the grown-ups, but he wanted to run in the grass even if it was pointless and he had the wagon and the animals and his mother and sisters to worry about. The cows were good. They stayed in the herd and mowed the grass as they walked, but Judy the pony was snarly and Cuff often pulled the wrong way and the girls were annoying and he wished they'd stop talking and let him think.

The trail, log-corduroyed years before, made a bumpy bed for the big wooden wheels with their iron rims and this was the season of high water and sometimes they got stuck and people had to poke and dig and pull and sometimes a wheel cracked and held everyone up for hours. Mud is better than no place to live, Martin's father had said, although mules and cows and horses got mired in it and it was hard to sleep on swampy ground. Martin was always sleepy and wet. He lay close to Cuff and took her heat into his skin. He wanted to shout at his mother: Where is my father who wouldn't risk all this muck that never dries out or stops breeding flies and mosquitoes and bugs that are too little to swat? And my sisters are selfish and care only about gossip and Cuff is a tangle of burrs and knocked over the milk and chased a dog and chewed on the right rear wagon wheel and nobody noticed but what if the wheel falls off? The truth is oxen are better than mules, everyone says so but none of us has an ox to his name. They survive on nothing. Horses and mules can be ridden, sure, but they need better forage. A wagon pulled by mules can go thirty miles a day while an ox makes ten or twelve but the ox eats food horse or mule would never put teeth to and why should they? I wouldn't pull this wagon. So oxen are dumber than mules, dumber than horses, dumber than me, if it comes down to it. And why is it so all-fired important to go over and over the details of how Sister Riggs brought her eggs in a barrel of corn-meal, or how the swinging bucket for butter is an idea that all ladies should adopt and Sister Borden would have it that pickles are the way to avoid the scurvy. She read it in a brochure from those New England people that mean to break up the country, sending abolitionists out to K.T. to make claims. So says Brother Riggs: They want to poison us on pickles. Sister Riggs made a dried plum pie rolling out dough on her wagon seat.

Along with such items of contention as oxen and mules and pickles was every family's notion of what not to carry inside their wagon. The Dickinsons had a piece of the family apple tree put to root in a layering pot. Lavina had put the pot under the mother tree until the wagon was ready. But why on earth carry that heavy pot when it will take up space and die anyway? Sister Borden had argued.

Because I am sentimental, Lavina had replied. The big old apple tree had made a burying place for the family and now it was going traveling.

36

Lavina was in a state she did not recognize. She noticed the light around her wagon as if it came without source. One minute the wagon was ordinary and the next minute it was full of radiance. She was divided from herself, part of the light and then not. She saw that the women and children stayed out of the wagons to lessen the load but she had the driving to do; it had to be done. She was, therefore, not quite woman. She was apart. How could she trust a mere boy to handle the bulk of their lives, which was now balanced on four wheels? She had problems to solve while the other women looked for flowers and mushrooms and walked hand in hand telling life stories. She had never walked hand in hand with anyone, not even her children. If this family is broken it will mend, she thought, but she did not believe what she told herself and she felt the absence of John, although he had sent her into so much danger and uncertainty. How could he do that when they had been so close? How could he appeal to his congregation to follow him and then abandon them? Our little Gina is frail! I have to keep up her strength when I have none for myself. If anything happens to Gina . . . the thought kept her up at night, worrying. Men have their rhythms and no wife is at ease to ask, but finally, after thinking it through, Lavina decided she must have failed John in some vital way. He had therefore stopped caring for her. Perhaps, being older now, she was less ideal although her beauty had been replaced by experience. A face changes. A body too, and a voice. But the mind expands. How much did he notice? The breasts were fallen, but did he much care for breasts? The walk becomes a shuffle eventually. Soft skin becomes a hide. There was no one to ask about her appearance but she tasked herself to take up the company of the women around her in order to ease her doubts and she went to them in her loneliness when they rose before dawn, started the fires, put on the kettles, stirred the oatmeal or johnnycakes, and prepared another meal for the midday halt. With them, she put the oldest children to milking the cows while they ground coffee and

mended torn wagon tops. They erected priv-
ies using a wall of blankets and she felt less
alone with herself.

Later she sat on the seat of the wagon and
held the reins. The mules would follow the
other wagons, but they must be driven over
obstacles and kept on a narrow path. On
Sundays, they stopped to observe the Sabbath. It gave the women a chance to wash
clothes and parts of themselves and on one
occasion they stopped to take rest at a
tavern, Sister Borden insisting that they all
needed a break from their exhausting rou-
tines. She had come up from Tennessee to
join the train and her opinions were openly
stated. So, late in the afternoon, men,
women, and children filed into the shabby
tavern, which offered hot food, a fireplace,
and a few cots in an unheated back room.
The innkeeper told stories while wandering
among his guests, hoping to keep them
settled and entertained. The travelers were
captive listeners and that evening they were
regaled with a story about the famous
Harpe brothers, who had murdered a tavern
guest.

Lavina was sitting in a corner by a narrow
window but she had it in mind to speak to
Mister Ferris about his story, which should
never have reached the ears of the children,

when she suddenly remembered that this was the very place John, at age twenty-one, had met the famous Bishop Asbury and asked to be baptized. Ferris Tavern! She supposed John was running errands for Benjamin even then, as he was doing when he met her at Redbanks Inn. She rubbed a finger along the sill of the cloudy window and wondered if the bishop, a tall man with flowing white hair, had touched that same sill after making the sign of the cross on young John's smooth forehead. She bent hers down to the sill and thought of her husband's purity at that time. Virginal he had been, if a man can be so called. Those were the years when John wore the stark black clothes that Asbury wore, trying to model himself on the man who'd converted thousands. But John's fervor was never mystical. He dabbled in politics, he joined the Masons, he voiced worldly opinions. Lavina realized now that she was glad of her husband's disabilities. Who would marry a saint? She was glad of John's hands that knew the dirt of farming when he wasn't preaching. It was the John of daily toil she had loved best. She gazed around the tavern at her fellow travelers, some of them already nodding on the hard benches, and wondered if she had changed as much as John had changed. A tavern! Who was Lavina in such a place? One half of her felt the hurt of abandonment and the failure of her marriage. But there were two parts of Lavina, one hurt and one freed.

37

John's mare cantered along the road, slowing for the clumps and clefts she knew well enough while John bent his frame under branches though he could not deceive himself; he did not know any longer where he was going. Or why. The woods were his history. He'd been over the county and beyond it for years: *He That Listeneth to Me . . .* The furrows and paths were not filled with hostility; there was many a home that would take him in, offer him food and a bed, but the image he held was of his youngest child being handed up into the wagon, being given up by none other than himself. After such an act, how could he reasonably ask for shelter from a Christian family? He had taken old Reuben several miles out of the district, connecting Reuben's mule to a little cart that would serve as seat and resting place. Get along now, he'd coached the old man. Keep your letter of freedom safe.

Reuben had looked up at him without a word of thanks, climbed up in the cart, and muttered: Better you not to go lookin for more trouble.

But John had turned his mare toward Tennessee and now, miles away from that scene, he had a craving to get out of the saddle and sit in the dark and think of how Gina had clung to him. He'd started out with a clear idea of what he was doing and where he was going, *Better you not to go lookin,* and lost it on the road or in the unreadable woods. Directionless, he unclamped his hands from the mare's tangled mane and she stood nosing at a clump of green while he slid off her back and onto hard ground. Bitter and still loving all of it, he had left the brick house with the long table at its core where Emly had served a thousand meals, a thousand spicy cakes, her famous rounds of cheese. And perhaps it was his intention to find her in Tennessee, where she would be marketed as a body to be used by drooling men or perhaps he was just afraid of death. First, I will save the woman I didn't protect. That's all it was — an act of contrition. But a jab of rage hit him and he rubbed at his chest. He remembered a moment when his mother had grabbed him and then pushed him away and he had run around and around the house. Mama, he whispered now. But he could not remember the hunger he'd felt for his mother, or even the burden of her disinterest. What he remembered was Bry ten years old. They'd been born the same year, but sometimes Bry liked to play with Jemima best. They had a cave that John was not allowed to enter and maybe John ran to Rafe and told him that Bry was ten years old and it was time for him to be working the fields. Ten. Take him back. He groaned now at the memory of challenging Rafe to take Bry away. He's yours, isn't he? John had squeaked, running into Rafe on the road. How come you let him just play? And Rafe went to Mary to demand the return of a boy who had never set foot on his land, although he had been conceived there. John's jealousy had deprived Jemima of her playmate and Bry of his childhood and now he got back on his horse and proceeded southeast, catching the lay of the sun on his path and wishing his mare had wings.

Late that day, he passed an Indian farm that did not differ noticeably from other frontier farms but he hoped to find comfort among people like himself and kept to his horse until he could no longer make out leaf from leaf. Where was he, by any measure of time and direction? He made a small fire and sat by it. You must go away and grow up, he had said to Patton. Don't come back until you have done that. He'll come back to us a better man, John had said to Lavina, and she had said: It will be a shock to find nothing left!

Dear son, I am a fugitive, bone-weary, saddle-sore, and scared.

The next morning the ground was unsteady and the throbbing in his head moved down to his stomach and he stumbled to a tree, leaned against it, and was sick. Then he lay down in the road. He watched an ant carry a leaf past his hand. He saw that his hand was open. He invited the ant to partake of the salt on his skin. He tried grabbing at the mare, groping for his empty saddlebag. He could not reach the bag or the saddle and he lay faceup, still sick. In some places, there was the cholera and John considered this with sudden terror. Had he contracted the disease? The road stretched on, blocked by dead trees where clearing had been badly done. He was headed south, according to the slant of the sun when he looked into branches that shared the sky. He tried his legs again, pushing up from his knees on a road without signage. He staggered against the mare, who stood waiting without concern because the two of them had spent many a night like this. The trail stretched out with its promise of deliverance as he pulled himself into the saddle and while the mare picked her way between fallen trees, he tried to believe that the promise he'd made to Emly in the barn could still be kept.

38

On the third Sabbath, the women ranged themselves along the edge of a rushing creek, each with a pail and a bar of hard soap. One or two were using the rough rocks as washboards but most were soaping things in pails, then rinsing the soaped laundry in the running stream, wringing the water out and putting the clothes back in empty pails, wet and clean. They were laughing at the indignity of this, making jokes about their grandmothers on a washday. They were women who had conveniences at home. Some of them had a household slave left behind, but now this was the only way a baby's diapers could be washed, or underclothes or menstrual rags.

Lavina gathered her things in a pail and hauled a kettle of steaming water and soap past the men, who were working on wheels or mending boots and tools. Her pail was heavy and even the handle was hot as she headed along the path where so many women had been up and down the bank that morning and suddenly she slipped on a wet spot and the kettle spilled steaming water onto her skirt and that water seeped through the fabric and burned her thigh and there was pain so intense, so sudden, that she cried out and two men rushed to her side. Lavina felt the sting of embarrassment as well as the sting of burning skin. These were the men who had kept her at the back of the line of wagons due to her uselessness and now she was on the ground squirming in pain but doing her best to make light of it. Pulling steaming fabric from her skin, and sealing her lips, she got back to her feet, dizzy, swaying, hobbling down the gooey bank with what was left of the boiling-hot water. The river was foaming and she was in agony, wondering: Where am I? Bending over painfully at the water's edge, circling the hard soap in the hot water, rubbing it against cloth, rubbing pieces of cloth against each other, seeing spots in the space between people and trees. Reeling. Rubbing and gasping at the fury of her leg, wiping at tears or sweat on her face. Bile in her throat. One does not want to draw attention to oneself or worry the others. The pain so overwhelming that she blinked her eyes to clear them and held back the vomit she could feel in her throat, taking hold of an arm. It was Sister Borden who noticed Lavina's white face. Sit down, Sister, you look peaked. Sister Borden was a stout woman of Irish descent who had often maintained that the circles under Gina's eyes meant a poor circulation. *You must not give her the laudanum, Sister Dickinson. It will slow down her blood.* She advanced cures for any discomfort. Wahoo root tea for rheumatism. Sulfur and molasses for ague, even scrofula. Polk root, a deadly poison, covered with whiskey for any serious rheumatism. And for burns . . . oil of lavender and lard or sour milk.

Lavina said now to no one in particular: I find the syrup consoles her. The thought of Gina's syrup was a focus of sorts. She pictured the little stoppered bottle, so easily filled from a larger one she kept with the malt vinegar.

Such a mother, said the stout Sister Borden. Her young son bringing a pet bear! She smiled knowingly at the other women.

Lavina wiped her face and thought of the morning cream that was sitting cool and remedial in the shade of her wagon. She thought if only she could get into the cool creek water she'd find relief. Then she answered weakly: Martin is too tender, and added: But my eldest boy attended Emory and Henry College. And for a brief second, she forgot her leg, maternal pride consoling every injury. He is waiting for us in Missouri, she said, while the trees around her were dancing untreelike.

Missouri! Sister Borden's eyes were wide.

Lavina slapped Electa's petticoat on the edge of her pail and a spray of water moistened the air. She was keeping her face out of sight, hard panting.

It don hardly seem worth the trouble, said Sister Storey, another launderer. Stoppin there.

A third woman said: You'll pay dearly for land that could be bought for a dollar an acre on the other side of the river now that K.T. is opening up.

Lavina held a wet hand to her cheek, looking from one woman to another as if she had never seen them before. Were they seriously meaning to settle in such a heathen place, not even a proper state? She said: Martin was enrolled to attend the same school . . . but then she thought better of it and did not continue. Abandoned. Penniless. She could not admit to her shame while the burn on her skin was eating her alive.

Sister Borden repeated the exclamation about Lavina's brand of mothering and continued to wash her clothes and wring them out and slam them back in the pail. Of course, Mister Borden and I started off just the two of us, whereas you are an entire nestload, she noted, glancing at Lavina with concern.

The word reeked of vipers but Lavina, faint and nauseated, tried to imagine traveling alone with John. No picture came to her mind. A burn will continue to burn like something living, she thought. It owns what it touches until it is stopped and she held her skirt to one side and pulled herself up, taking hold of her pail of wet clothes. Then she turned, dropped the pail, and went straight to the creek. When she fell in, there were shouts from the bank and Sister Borden leapt into the water to save her, wetting boots and skirt. For Lavina, the cold brought instant relief and she pulled her bloomers away from the seared flesh and floated like a weed in Sister Borden's arms, letting the world come back into focus. She had not meant to create a scene, but that's what she'd done. She smiled a little sheepishly and apologized for her clumsiness. Took a little fall, she said. Nothing to fret about.

On shore, there were hands held out and she let Sister Borden lead her to them dripping, soaked from the neck down, swathed in heavy, wet clothes. She tugged at her skirt and picked up her pail and climbed awkwardly up the bank, making her way step by step between the scattered belongings of the other campers. She was thinking about Clotilde, who would clean the burning wound with her gentle hands and cooling creams except that John had thoughtlessly sent her away. And I am not a person who cleans my linens in a running stream, she said to the person she was passing. I do not empty my bladder on grass or sleep on a mat, she muttered, nodding at the women crouched by their fires and wondering if Clotilde was the only friend she'd ever had.

Electa had gathered wood. If it rains now, there will be nothing to eat and the laundry? Martin! Son! I need a line. She was able to get up in the wagon, but Martin was off with the bear again and that made Lavina wonder if her son was plain foolish. Maybe Sister Borden was right. Sometimes he stopped to roll in the grass with Cuff. Or he'd find a creek and Cuff would scoop up a trout. One fish, and it was Cuff's, two and a fire was started, and next thing you know the boy would be singing some invented song: *Our bodies are covered with fur and we have eyes ears nose for sense, teeth for trout . . .* Oh dear Jesus. Was she singing? Could she be heard? Worst of sins! The medicine box was equipped for emergencies. There was hartshorn for snakebites, peppermint essence, and a bottle of castor oil. There was turpentine, goldenseal, and tobacco. Gina's syrup. But Electa was writing feverishly on a piece of white paper. Another letter to her father, no doubt.

Ma! What happened?

I wanted a bath. Go wash the beans, Lavina said, wanting the syrup, wanting to scream, wanting to take off her wet clothes and inspect the burn, but waiting until Electa ducked out from under the canvas. Then Lavina reached for the laudanum and unstoppered the bottle, wondering what words her daughter would put in a letter. *I find the syrup consoles her . . .* She had recently said those words, but to whom? Some things were nobody's business, but written words were put down on paper for other eyes. Already Electa had two or three missives tucked into a pocket of the canvas waiting to be mailed. Lavina swallowed a good dose of the syrup while her mind circled the complexities of a daughter too secretive to communicate with a parent who was present and available. In another pocket sewn to the wagon cover, there were rags and she wrapped one carefully around her thigh, but that was intolerable. *Limb,* her husband would have said. Never would he say *leg.* It was the old Quaker heritage he had learned from Daniel, that cold, strict way of defining the world. Words. How would she write this pain on a scrap of paper if she had one? I am what I am, not what I say, she thought, while the pain traveled like the blade of a knife down the leg past the knee, past the ankle into the foot, and then all the way back up again to her waist. What did Lecta write? (The syrup was a bottle of the good Lord's blessing.) Was it another hopeless petition, begging John to follow after them? Or there might be remarks about Lavina, mother of the young correspondent. *Such a mother,* Sister Borden had said, and not in a kindly way. But writing it down would take all the sarcasm out of the words. No one would read the inflection. It would seem to be just what it was, which it wasn't. Peeling her wet clothes off, replacing each piece with something more or less clean, Lavina tried to climb down out of the wagon, leaking creek water from her boots, and fainted.

39

Dear Papa, We stopped in a tavern to sleep and I wanted my papa to protect me. It was frightfull. Once a guest there was joined by two men and three women who asked for breakfast because it was a cold morning and they had rid all the night, the guest took out his pocketbook which the visitors noticed had gold coins. Then he dicided to travel with those strangers who ate at his expence, and a few days later someone found him dead and the two men and three ladies were put in gaol but the men escaped while the ladies each delivered a baby and when the ladies got out, the two brothers, who were named Big and Little Harpe killed one of those babies by bashing it on a tree. Can you imagine Papa? Kentucky is a very dangerous place for us to be. I hope you will fine us in Louisville we really need you to come right away. Your loving Lecta Please, Papa!

40

The women offered tonics, although it was apparent that nothing could be done to relieve the streaks of infection on Lavina's leg until they reached Louisville, where she would find a doctor and where the train would disband and its various members would go their separate ways. Sister Borden said that her husband could help, but Lavina was not easy with that idea. In Louisville, those who could afford to travel by riverboat would find passage on the Ohio down to the bend of the Mississippi and the upward thrust of the Missouri. Others would go overland. To Missouri, to Kansas, to Nebraska, and to points farther west. The Dickinsons had planned to travel by land but Lavina was at the point of changing her mind. She could not manage the wagon in her condition. First a doctor. Then, when they found Patton, the whole process of deciding between river and land could take place.

At Bullitt's Lick, Martin halted the mules and went off to watch the salt workers where the earth was dug into a trough. We'll lose the train, Lavina moaned from inside the wagon, where she lay in the heat of her fever, but she could not stay awake to complain. She kept drifting, too hot, too exhausted to think about wagons or cows or salt workers, although Electa insisted they must hurry. Martin was in charge now that his mother was ill, which Electa thought was ridiculous. She was so much older! What advantage did he have over her? Martin would obviously be happier playing with his bear and wandering off with the other children. He was too curious and fidgety to mind the wagon properly. After the first detour with the salt workers, he stopped a second time at a place where men were making sugar by boiling up maple sap, and there he took time to bargain for a jug of syrup, then Cuff overturned the jug and drank all the contents. Does it ever go free? Lavina asked Martin. She had forgotten Cuff's history and wondered, in her fever, why a bear was tied to her wagon.

At Dowdall's Station they crossed Salt River on a ferry and that provided excitement. Later they camped in a crowd of wagons and tents at the Fishpools, where several springs were clustered along a creek. It was a scenic spot where wagon train travelers could pretend to relax and bathe and let their children romp in the sun. Martin parked the wagon in a spot of shade.

Electa said: Mama, you should be careful of that laudanum. You'd do better to get out and walk some. Gina, you come back here with me and I'll tell you the wolf story. Mama is tired.

Lavina noticed that sometimes, every so often, strange habitations grew right out of the earth along the creeks with the sod piled up two or three feet above ground. She could discern roofs and chimneys or the occasional rusted stovepipe. It was mysterious. The grass was like water. They were floating on a pale green sea.

Mama, I wish we could find you a doctor. Gina . . . come back here with me.

I want to ride Judy through the little sparkly pools.

Mama, it says in this pamphlet that it takes four yoke of oxen to break up the soil in Missouri. It says mules won't do it. Martin, will you untie Judy?

Do it yourself, you can reach.

Lavina adjusted her leg. It was central

now, the only part of her that mattered. The wash was hung on a line strung from the wagon to a poplar tree and she could hear a distant thunder roll. Who put out those clothes? Bring them in. She would not have the trail diminish her standards, having nothing left in her veins. Bring them in, Father. She twisted a piece of her sleeve between her fingers. She chewed on it, sometimes biting her hand. She said: You who spent your life within a mile of the bed on which your mother suffered your birth. Why can't you see that your brother is lost to cards.

Mama, hush! You sound silly.

How will you speak to people in valleys you never imagined or on hills you never climbed? Lavina rebuked her pain with another pull at the sweet and relieving syrup. Get the clothes in out of the rain.

41

Overtaken by a solitary rider, John felt fear and relief. Having exchanged names, the two men rode along for a while, casting quick glances at each other. The horse was Arabian, the man tall. He carried a single-bore. The woods through which they rode were lit by the sun and by the elaborate songs of unseen birds. Where might you be heading? asked the other rider as if John's destination were conditional.

Tell me first where I am.

The rider studied John. He chewed on the inside of his cheek and gave a quick kick to the Arabian's flank. Then he pulled at the reins. It seemed he was undecided about whether he would ride with John or not.

John was surveying the ground as if to find a map in the mud.

Lost your way?

John said: Slave. Then he said: A person.

The two horses moved now at the same

pace, agreeably. Ran off, did he?

John looked at the rider's fine coat, which was draped over booted legs, and at the boots, which shone. A man name of Lucas has her.

In good faith or otherwise?

John blinked. What has faith to do with it? Does not each one of us pursue his own interest?

The Arabian exhaled loudly and her rider patted her long neck, declaring: If you mean happiness when you speak of interest, perhaps it is *yours* that is the concern? He smiled at a truth shared between men.

John brushed at the long hair blowing in his face. I ask simply, do you know Mister Lucas?

He is due south ten miles, very well off, very much what . . . I assume you would expect, although I know nothing of your expectations.

They had reached a brook burbling across the path and they slowed their horses, John calling out: Over here! and easing his mare into the shallow drift of water. It rushed around hooves, clear as air. This is as good as any place, John noted, as if they had agreed to stop together. A cool breeze came through the trees. Suddenly hungry, John wondered what food the other man carried.

His companion leapt off his horse, put a blanket down, and gestured at its scratchy surface. Myself, I am heading to Knoxville to defend the state of the Union.

John knelt on the blanket while his host pulled a chunk of hard cheese out of his saddlebag along with a bundle of bread. How pleasant to lie for an hour facing the sky on his way to a meeting with Mister Lucas. He must gird his loins. Another quick prayer. And a meal.

The host unrolled a cloth bag full of meat. He cleaned his knife on the edge of his blanket after cutting two slices. Chewing, he spat up a piece of gristle and blew it downwind. After Lucas, what next?

John was watching him from a prone position through the loose weave of his hat. City bred, he thought. Those clothes were not made by a wife. Out loud he said: I have pulled up stakes. I'm going west, he added, where all parties can start out on equal footing. Fairness is the idea out there, rather than privilege. He said this manfully, not having thought of fairness as a reason for doing anything until now but picturing a log house, his children busy with lives of abiding virtue.

Equal footing? Well, if you include the Natives, I suspect those who were born on the land you will take from them in the name of fairness may not agree.

John got up stiffly and took from his saddlebag a jug that he filled with water at the brook. Well, he said. Indeed. He grabbed his hat from his head and placed it over his heart. I will take no advantage in that case. Any land I take will be fairly bought. Now he saw a vision of Lavina by the stove that his wagon was even then ferrying across Kentucky. No more slaves. Not for me. I freed one and all. His headache had returned with a vengeance.

The other man took up the blanket. So there was no ready buyer? His voice overrode a vigorous splash of urine. He laughed and noted: A vow of celibacy is not too difficult in a land of men, but tell me, do we continue on from here together?

John considered the remark about celibacy as they mounted their horses, one offering to keep watch in case the other needed sleep. He took a cigar out of his pocket and pinched off some tobacco, and with the old mare moving rhythmically, he felt the herb expand under his tongue. He kept a cigar in his breast pocket in order to deny temptation. But a tiny chew couldn't hurt. I died in the barn, he thought, feeling nothing but scorn for his body. And when he woke, the other rider was gone so completely that he thought their conversation must have been part of an unpleasant dream and he turned around in the saddle and looked at the dark hills of Virginia far behind him and at the sky that tenderly held its light.

42

In Louisville there were frame buildings along the waterfront stretching back for five or six blocks; wagons littering the outskirts; pigs and cows roaming, the air broken by shouts, boat whistles and smoke, neighing horses, the lowing of cattle and barking of dogs. Martin brought the mules in, using his new driver's voice. Hey on now, easy theeere . . . He was proud of himself and his wagon, which scattered chickens and ducks fore and aft on the narrow streets where roosters were crowing possessively. He gazed at the fancy buildings. Brother Borden said the city was owned by French Catholics, who had even established a seminary for young ladies, but the English were buying up any available property, creating social havoc. And the French were really Canadian, and the English were old enemies. But at least they spoke English . . .

I can't wait to set my feet down on solid

ground, Electa said, crawling up to the front of the wagon to sit next to her brother. We must find Mama a doctor first thing.

Oh hush up, will you? I got to drive and this road's getting skinny . . .

Watch out for that little dog! Oh look, Gina, come up here and look at this big pretty city.

Where are we? their mother asked from a folded pallet in the back of the wagon. Look out for Patton, now, when we get to town.

Mama, you just lie down and be peaceful until we get some help for your injury. Martin was holding the reins, holding his chin up, keeping his mouth straight without a smile to be seen. He thought three females were a lot to ask of a boy who was mastering roads that were full of wildlife and carts and bigger wagons, and still they went on as if there was some reckoning to come, some plan in the works, although he had no idea what was going to happen if his brother didn't show up. He wanted to shout: Patton! Where are you? Help!

A mile farther into town and there was the mighty Ohio, a big, wide wash of bilge covered by sails and skiffs and canoes and steamboats with paddle wheels and boilers mooing like enormous white cows and Martin felt a rush of joy at the sight of them and wished he could board one of those big boats that were more like the ships he had seen in pictures. They were bigger than houses. Brother Borden said the town had promised free land to anyone who would build a hotel or a factory, anyone who would stay, but down at the waterfront, even the geese were streaming downriver, going west. Everyone wanted to get away to the new lands that were opening up, lands full of fertile soil and gold. Or else they had come to welcome the boats just now docking with a set of treasures to unload. Every whistle brought an assembly to the wharf on this river that was the best passage west while Martin was following a wagon up ahead of him and worrying about his bear. How was she going to handle this mess of people? And noise? And excitement? And there was food in the streets that she wanted to grab and she was pulling, making the wagon tip, and the pony was nervous and pulling the other way and Martin wished they would find a place to stop before everything turned over in the road. As the Jonesville mules and horses plodded on, a mellow sun gilded the surfaces of the buildings in Louisville, a city of gold named for a king. Those French settlers had planted fruit trees and they were in vivid bloom, purple and red and pink all over town like overhead garlands. But now Lavina begged Martin to find a place where they would not have to pay a fee for the wagon and where she could find a latrine. Please! The bear was still tugging, pulling backward, and Martin was sure the wagon would overturn in the city confusion, its contents spilling out and all of them crushed, so he decided to stop even if they had to pay. People screamed at the bear: Dangerous! Is it trained? But those who had traveled with Cuff only laughed. Cuff had become their mascot. Martin found a place where a few of the others had parked and once they had settled, Lavina told him to see to the livestock. Quietly then, she asked for Electa's help. She needed her arm. She needed to find the latrine and then a doctor. Later, but soon, they must go to the wharf and find a ticket agent and Electa must read and decipher the contract with that paid-for education the family had afforded her. Lavina pictured an unknown doctor frowning and glaring at her, lifting her skirt, and within the hour they had brushed their best clothes and set out in a hired buggy, Lavina wearing her bonnet with silk ties and talking mostly to herself. Her dress had small tucks on the sleeves and bodice that flattered her long figure and she had added a collar that buttoned in an unusual way. What do you think?

Striking, Mama. Electa had seen the dress many times. Her mother's dressmaking was usually given over to Gina, who wore flounces that might better belong on a Romanian girl, according to Lecta.

What will your father say?

Is he coming, Mama? Do you think?

Lavina stared solemnly out of the buggy, her leg throbbing and distinct under the wrap of skirt.

Losing the farm, said Electa softly, touching her mother's hand. Probably he could not see himself starting up again, Mama. How can he ask for charity from his own sons, who own the warrants, when he has no money? So he stayed back.

Lavina was still staring at the unfamiliar city. When the buggy stopped in front of a small frame building, Electa stepped down and reached again for her mother's hand. And think of Gina and how she gets confused when you talk about Papa.

Lavina was holding her skirt, gingerly testing her weight on the ground, which seemed still to be moving. She seemed to exist in pieces. She was holding her breath. I will not pay in advance, child. Just a down payment for tickets. She wanted her syrup.

This is a clinic, Mama.

I told you, tickets first.

That isn't what you said. But there was no one to see them, no doctor on duty. Lavina would have to come back in two hours.

You are limping more and more, Mama. We'll come back right after we enlist a boat. Electa watched a woman cross the muddy street with a pram. A child peered out of it like an old dignitary. One day he will inherit all of this, Electa thought, the town, the river, this whole country we are making. Lucky baby. His mother will be dust and he will be a smiling old gentleman with a cane. He will know how our lives turned out. The young mother wore a red jacket belted at the waist. She wore short crocheted gloves and a tall, feathered hat. A hooped skirt! Electa studied the effect of its graceful swaying. She longed to ask about the hoop but it would never do to speak to someone on the street. Still, she wished she could somehow learn how this young mother's life had been arranged. Was she in love with the man she had married, or did she marry for the jacket and hat? Did she live in a house or a cabin? Was her husband a riverboat captain? Would she reduce a man to shame if he went bankrupt? Would she leave him to starve on land he did not own?

Lavina limped along the wooden sidewalk, ignoring the shoppers but staring at windows as if she had never seen commerce.

Ma, don't stare. Electa wished to press her own nose against each window but only glanced and then looked away. In one, there were French clocks and German buttons and Irish shoehorns and English porcelain dogs. In another, there were fabrics along with needles and thread and ribbon and crochet hooks and quilting frames. In another, spades and hoes, seeds and plants in damp hemp wraps. Some shops sold only one kind of thing. One sold only hats! At the livery, they could buy a horse or rent one. At the butcher's they could buy enough salted meat to last a long winter in the woods. At the grocer's there was fruit neither of them had ever seen, shipped up from the Caribbean. Lavina stopped at a stall and paid for a mug of coffee. Come here, child. Have some.

Mama, it is common to take food in the street.

It fortifies me. Lavina made an ugly sound with her wet lips to annoy the daughter whose paid-for education had given her airs.

Fortifies you, Electa said under her breath.

There be a great many saloons hereabouts,

Lavina said then, echoing old Ruth Boyd, and wishing Electa would laugh at her improvisation as she used to do. And just you look at the fancy ladies in their hoops.

Electa ignored her mother. The great white boats in the harbor reflected sunlight like outdoor mirrors. The river in surge. For these two formerly landlocked women, it was a sight to astonish, and still they walked along, trying to appear accustomed to such things. Behind them, rafts and canoes floated downstream and flatboats carried Conestoga wagons or mounds of logs across the water to Indiana.

I'd like to sit down, Lecta.

But the ticketing office was crowded and they were told to stand in a line. Some people had baggage spread around them on the floor, cloth bags with wooden handles and boxes tied up in twine as if they were prepared to embark that minute. Refugees, muttered Lavina, scanning the line for familiar faces from the wagon train and seeing only Brother and Sister Borden. Everyone knew that the river was close to flooding and there was no knowing, from one hour to the next, whether a captain would decide to leave or stay. Hadn't we better wait for calm water? a young woman asked.

Her husband was bundled in gear he

269

imagined appropriate to the West — buckskin leggings and a black bowler hat.

I would give this river all due respect, Brother Borden advised the strangers ominously.

You will be taking a later boat then? Electa was sure she had caught Brother Borden in a small hypocrisy because the worried couple was ahead of him in line. He wanted them to drop out so that his chances of finding a cabin or berth would be better.

Lavina's eyes roamed the room, unfocused.

Brother Borden said, Are you well, Sister? You seem pale.

My funds are not infinite, Lavina said coldly, pointing her eyes at his. The longer we tarry, the less we eat. She took Electa's arm with a trembling hand, pulling her head up and blinking with pain.

And the harder it becomes to pull her daughter away from city life, Electa added in order to deflect her mother's financial confession.

Lavina's pulse was slowing. She began to sway.

Sister Dickinson, are you faint?

I believe I am.

270

43

Dear Papa, Today I looked for a doctor after we got our ticket then bought a pound of beef but yankee agencys buy all the best things even boat cabins. They want their people to go out to Kansas because of the vote about slavery. I hope you come soon because Mama is so poorly. I will mail my letters today or maybe you are on the road and then you will never read them. Then you will make us happy if you arrive but we have not seen Patton. We cant find him. If anything happens to Mama we will be orphens unless you come. Mama cannot go by wagon I looked for the doctor but didn't find him. The shops are nice. I wish you could see the tools. Mama has bought two cabins which are boat rooms. Please hurry Papa. Your loving daughter, Lecta

44

That evening Brother Borden made an appearance as Electa was serving up fresh beef stew. May we offer you something good to eat? Electa asked. The question, framed in politeness, was meant to insult the visitor, to repay him for his earlier hypocrisy.

I have already eaten very well. Where is your mother, please?

Resting. Add more water to stretch it, Lavina had said before she retreated to the wagon with her head in her hands. Now, while Martin and Gina sat on the grass holding warm bowls of watered stew, Brother Borden stood as if pegged, his chin jutting out and his lips moving noiselessly. Electa tucked her wispy, unclean hair behind her ears and wiped her apron across smoke-stung eyes. When she dropped a spoon on the grass, Brother Borden leaned down to pick it up. Courtly, he was, and Electa did not care for that where her

mother was concerned, and yet Brother
Borden climbed up into the wagon very
nimbly without asking permission, hitching
his trousers at the knee and leaving the three
children behind on the grass. Then, in the
privacy of oiled muslin, he spoke softly: You
found a place on the boat, Sister? and he
stared at Lavina through round spectacles.

Lavina got herself into a sitting position
and straightened her collar nervously. She
had not changed her dress.

I noticed you seemed ill at the ticket office. Faint, I believe you said. I should have
told you that . . . I am a medic, and perhaps
I can help. Sister Borden told me that you
have an injury. It was she who sent me.

Lavina had no reply.

I am a medic. Was. Gave it up for fear of
the cholera. Not proud of that.

Well, my leg is infected but not with the
cholera disease. Limb, she should have said.
Limb, limb.

Your boat's delay may well prove to be an
advantage then.

Delay?

Just announced. Only a day or two. Is it a
burn? I am glad to examine it. Keep in mind
that I am trained.

Lavina leaned back, resting on her elbows,
panting a little.

The pain is very hard to bear?

It is constant now.

It was fire?

Water. Lavina smiled at her joke, then shut her eyes and winced as he lifted the hem of her skirt, a finger trailing up the inside of her leg as she inhaled, shivered, tugged her skirt down, her petticoat stained. But then she pulled the hem up to her waist and closed her eyes. What nonsense to feel modesty when she was at death's open door and the man was a medic. Of some kind. Almost a doctor, which she hadn't found in town. Lavina was a woman who had never exposed herself to any eyes, not even to her mother's when the first baby came, the first living one, and the old granny midwife cut the baby's cord too close, which was too much to think about now when her bloomers were loose and her stockings did not quite cover her knees and the burn was leaking nasty juices and by the look on Brother Borden's face he was noticing the putrid smell she had tried to cover with liniments. There were splashes of mud on his jacket but he was tucked in and otherwise tidy and the eyeglasses and trimmed beard gave him a look of fastidiousness and nothing had helped so far, none of the unguents or tonics, and his hands moved so gently on her skin as he advised her to take a brandy, which she refused, but the syrup was close to hand and she reached for it.

Have you linseed oil? Some carbolic?

Yes.

A cocaine solution would be good for your pain.

No.

Have another sip of the laudanum. A good swallow.

Lavina licked the rim of the bottle and felt faint with the searing pain just under his hand as he pressed.

Is your medical box nearby?

Must I be bled?

On the contrary, Sister. The circulation must be revived.

Lavina pointed and Brother Borden leaned across the width of the wagon and pulled the medical box to his side, opening bottles either corked or capped that contained liquids that he certainly recognized. Now please relax. The bladder may react, which will help in the healing, take my word for it. Just hold on to my arm and I beg you to think of nothing but your betterment, your ease, your . . .

Lavina gripped his arm. She flinched as he pressed on her lower belly. Oh dear . . .

Have no shame. Our urine is very clean.

She thought of her children romping beyond the wagon, romping with bears and cows and ponies as she wet her neighbor's hands and felt a gash of stinging pain on the burn.

Good. Good. Oh, yes, dear Sister. You must lie back. Now. Slowly. Carefully. Let me help you . . . there . . . The voice came from some place Lavina had never visited, a dark, warm comforting cave. She thought of John putting his hand on her in the place where Brother Borden was touching her and when she woke there was Electa at her side and a clean dressing on her wound. He says to stay like this for another day, Mama. Why didn't you say you were so sick? Electa was in tears.

45

All bags should be put on board before midnight. Wagons tied down. Animals aboard. Creatures to eat and sleep and relieve themselves in small stalls under the main deck and the bear to travel in a metal cage fitted out for a stallion on a previous trip. Passengers should board by eight o'clock having taken breakfast.

You must reconsider, Brother Borden said.

The syrup has such effect. Lavina dips her head. Are you hoping to purchase my ticket? That would be unkind. She smiles faintly. She looks at him sleepily as his fingers touch her swollen thigh and what a time to think of the hole she'd dug in the rain, what a thing to be doing under the apple tree, depositing a little lump of flesh with folded arms and a mushroom face, unfinished life, a failure, and she could not like John's touch afterward and he soon lost all interest. Oh! My goodness! What?

There, dear Sister. There. There. Close your eyes and listen to my words. I want to tell you that you need my further care and . . . I hope your family will stay in our wagon train so that I may help you mend. It will be so much easier for Brother Dickinson to find you on the trail rather than on a surging and dangerous river and an expense for him as well and I could mention the *Glencoe* right here in this harbor that exploded in a hundred thousand pieces. So many dead. Oh, Sister, please just lie back. Brother Borden was pouring lotion into his cupped hand and stroking tenderly, ankle to waist. Circulation, Sister. I must insist. You are in no condition, his voice was silk, to go off on your own with the burden of three growing, rambunctious children. And your awful pain . . .

Four, she said firmly, trying to focus because it was best to do something when the syrup was working its tricks. I purchased two cabins, Brother Borden, you might use one of them and look after me until I am saved. A smile. She giggled. I mean, I *am* saved, but I am not healed, am I? She drifted, reached for his very large hand that was always moving on her skin where she had no thought of connection to herself. She said slowly: Make arrangements for your animals and wife. Wife and animals.

His fingers brushed her lifted knee once more and followed the poisonous stripe.

46

Two miles away, at number 88 Third Street,
Bry was in the barbershop of Washington
Spradling, a former slave who had amassed
enough wealth in real estate to purchase
several less fortunate human beings. Since
the Fugitive Slave Act of 1850, runaways
were more often captured for gain than they
had been in the past. Even papers of manumission were meaningless to the men who
collected bounty by taking freed slaves back
down South and selling them illegally. By
purchase, Spradling had freed thirteen men
and three women without breaking any law,
but Bry now owed him two years of labor in
return for eventual manumission because,
when he was dragged off by the two men
who had bought him from the horse
breeder, he had been taken to the auction
block in Louisville, where Washington Spradling purchased him.

Penniless whites were sent to debtors' jail

but blacks without papers or with papers torn up or disallowed were hauled to the nearest market and put on display. Bry had collapsed when he was shoved into a group of bare-chested men, all of them angry, hurling insults at their captors. A contagion of terror.

But now I am legal, Bry told himself as he straightened his apron and looked in a barbershop mirror that had notes of deliverance and thanks stuck in its frame. Legal but not free. *Doc speding you mad me saif. Mister I name my child after you.* In the mirror, Bry's face was thin after his hard year of travel. He had walked up the edge of Virginia. Then he had crossed the mountainous region of eastern Kentucky on foot, hoping that he was in godly Ohio. He had gone to beg for a bite of food because he was too exhausted to be wary and believing he should be safe enough in Ohio. He had done his begging in a state of such hunger and weariness that he could not count his fingers when he held them up and now he touched the mirror and stroked his new beard, short and curly against his face. His pants were double-belted. He was thin as a sideways board. It had been only three days in that fine horse barn and then he was snapped up like a done-for horse and taken off to the auction block between Market and Main in Louisville, where Washington Spradling often came to intervene. It was the best possible outcome according to the man who had purchased him. You were a likely target, Spradling shrugged. No papers. You are one lucky old nigger to get bought by me and you'll be a trained barber, too, so I call it a fair exchange.

In Louisville, Bry came upon one woeful thing or another, such as posters about the American Party, with Washington Spradling telling him to stay clear of that bunch who were out to get Negroes and immigrants, legal or not. One day Doughty and Rilo, his fellow barbers, were given the afternoon off with him and they went to hear those American Party men in spite of the warnings, listening to church bells all over town, even a Lutheran one on Preston Street and two Catholic and one Negro, but the American Party hated the Irishman or German or Negro. They gave their speeches with a cannon firing off one bang for each of the thirty-one states and the three black barbers could see the mayor on a platform saying it was Germans who started the un-American idea of abolition, people who didn't belong in the great United States. At the word *abolition*, Bry nudged Rilo and the three of them backed away from the crowd, but there were men who grabbed at their arms and when Bry saw an opening he took off while Rilo got knocked down and Doughty went back to pick him up off the dirty street. Doughty had been in the barbershop for two years and would soon have his paper, but Bry was afraid and he ran back to the barbershop and hid, feeling something like shame as he thought about Doughty's brave act. No slave could take the risk of standing up for another on the farm, but here in the city it was what one man did for another. We, too, are human beings, Bry said to himself that day, and he resolved to start looking after those in need as he stood in front of the mirror contemplating his new beard and then he suddenly jumped seeing in the chair behind him someone he could not believe was there. There was no need for that someone to lean back for a shave since he had no hair on his face, but his locks had grown unseemly long and his parents had probably sent him in search of a cure for that and he had surely wandered into this town and come upon Spradling's barbershop, where a fiddler played in the doorway although why he was here in Kentucky was anybody's guess.

Say there, he said to Martin.

How am . . . but . . . you! Martin stopped himself because Mister Spradling was watching.

Bry said: How'd you get here?

My uncle Benjamin died, Martin said hurriedly, wondering how much to say in front of a witness. Then he added crossly: Then most everybody left us. It went all to pieces after you after you . . .

Bry had no idea that his escape had precipitated the downfall of two families, the end of an era in Jonesville, and while he stood in the inner doorway of Mister Spradling's barbershop and rubbed his curly beard, Martin looked at the boots Bry was wearing, given by a horse breeder who had turned him over to profiteers, and Mister Spradling took up a pair of scissors and put a hand on Martin's forehead. You want to do this? he said to Bry.

Bry said: Everybody left to where?

You coulda had a paper. Martin rolled his eyes at the irony of it. My pa freed the ones who stayed for us to the end.

The end. Bry thought of the squirrel he had strangled after feeding it for two days. He felt a flaming rage against the boy in the barber chair. Want to take over? the barber asked again, seeing the look on Bry's face, and Bry took the scissors in his trembling hand.

Martin plucked at the towel tucked in at his neck. Like old times, he said nervously, although he had never been this close to Bry, who began to hum something roughly similar to whatever the fiddler was playing outside. It was perhaps a jig, although which of them could know that? Bry tucked his left hand under the stringy hair of the Virginia boy and took a first snip. He had done barbering for a month at least, but he had no technique.

Don't make me look like a monkey.

Your ears sticking out's none of my doing.

Are you going to put a bowl on my head as my pa does it?

Don move. It was the first order Bry had ever given. Are you goin to tell on me?

Martin put a finger on his lips. Who'd I tell? My uncle's dead and Pa's left behind.

Bry stopped the scissors and stared in the customers' mirror. He said: This man gave me a contrack. He nodded at Mister Spradling, who was stacking newspapers on a stool by the window. Two years . . . I owe him, Martin. It was something to use just that bare Christian name.

47

The house John found at the end of a long, shaded lane was almost familiar, its four columns reminders of what he had left behind, its roof a statement against sky, its chimneys unlikely in this Tennessee valley. He put a hand to his throat, testing his ability to speak. Ah, Ah. He must offer no more money than he had sewn into his jacket but somehow convince Mister Lucas, a man he had never met, to release a woman who was no doubt serving his household with her usual stern dignity. A woman worth ten times anything that could be counted. *Your brother is . . . going to sell . . .* God in His Heaven would not see Emly spend another night on this plantation, fine as it was in aspect. Lower than low were the people who inhabited Tennessee plantations. John had three hundred dollars kept aside, squirreled away, hidden from his wife in all their adversity. He had Elizabeth's sapphire earrings because he had seen them in a bowl on the dresser when he went into Matilda's room to take her bags down to the buggy that was waiting to take her to a stagecoach. He had scooped them up and now he decided he had not really meant to hang himself; it was only a moment of desperation because he had sent his family away. A man does not line his pockets for the afterlife.

So he was admitted as one gentleman admits another. The heavy walnut door was thrown wide and he was shown in, dusty, unpleasant of smell, oily of face, and wary. Taken to a book-lined room where an unneeded fireplace offered glowing coals, he was shown to the softest chair. John could breathe now as he sat back against a cushion. Then his host left the room to order whiskey for the uninvited, unexpected, overtired visitor, never mind the morning hour. When he returned, John admired the draperies and spoke of his journey with pleasant sentences. He complimented the room, the books on the shelves. Fine-looking bindings, he exclaimed, crossing his dusty legs and then uncrossing them and scratching the back of his damp neck. He sneezed and excused himself while his host smiled and sat waiting in another soft chair.

I've been seeing to my family's departure, John said irrelevantly, brushing at his jacket.

The Tennessee host put his hand behind one ear. Whaat waas that you sayed?

How different is the length of the vowel down here, John thought. He had been in many rooms on his Methodist circuit. He had taken coffee, tea, water, lemonade, and even an occasional cider. He had offered pleasant stories on topics guaranteed to go down well with young or old, male or female, but here, in this fortress of gentility, he was about to perform the one and only act that could bring him ease. A mourning dove called from the garden beyond the bookshelves and windows and walls. John straightened his back. He cleared his throat and tried his voice. Ah ah . . . I believe you may have someone serving your wife — your household — who by rights belongs to mine. Voice loud enough to be heard by the man with a hand behind his ear.

I have no such thing.

No servant? John was trying to imagine such a thing. He looked at the painted wall above the shelves. Was it brown? Or shit yellow? There was the calling dove, the wall color varying as a slab of sun played across it. He noticed a flowering tree outside the tall window. Then the person he had come to find entered the room with a loaded tray. She held it with both hands while John traveled the whole of her with his eyes, taking in the swollen belly and the beloved face. She set the tray on a table within her master's reach as he uttered not a word of thanks. Who thanks a slave?

Emly stared at John as he came out of his chair, took hold of her arm, and pressed his fingers against its bone under the wonder of warm, human, oh-so-desired flesh. Mister Dickinson, she said, leave me be.

48

The *New Statesman.* Letters of gold. She was a back-wheeler newly tucked into the Louisville wharf with a drawing room on the upper deck and a wide promenade from which the northern shore looked almost close. Lavina had reserved two cabins, one would now go to the Bordens and one to the Dickinson females. Martin would sleep in the wagon that was parked with so many others on the cargo deck.

The family boarded the main gangplank while Martin used a lower one to bring the wagon and bear across, then the cows and the pony. After positioning the wagon, he penned the livestock and tucked the mules and pony into narrow stalls. Cuff would travel in an iron cage.

Noisy and smoky, boilers raging, engines clanging, and whistle blasting, the *New Statesman* plastered the town with loud announcements of its importance, then backed slowly out of its berth and turned upriver, passing a cotton packet and an excursion boat. The lower cargo deck, strewn with crates and wagons and farm animals, was as chaotic as a country fair. This was the place for the steerage passengers, with food already being cooked on an open grill and, without side rails, the rough water sometimes lashing at anyone who stood too close to the edge. Up above, on the promenade, the first-class passengers looked back at the southern shore, where dogs and pigs and chickens nosed through weeds and trash. A dead cat floated beside them in the water alongside a pile of rotting fruit. They heard the hiss and whistle of a train, as if all of Louisville was on the move from there to anywhere else and it was a new and thrilling sound.

Lavina was about to travel farther from home than she had ever wanted to go and she was doing it as a virtual widow, although she reminded herself of her married status whenever Brother Borden applied his gentle hands to her body producing sensations unlike any she had felt before. Relax, dear Sister, Brother Borden whispered, running a warm hand up and down the whole length of her back. Lavina curled her toes and stretched. Was this entirely medical? Her healing occurred in no certain place or time as the great paddleboat churned upriver and her heart churned and fluttered. She expected John to catch up with them while, at the same time, expecting that he wouldn't. She wanted what she could not have, but there was no way to define what that was exactly. Meanwhile, there was nothing to cook, nothing to mend, nothing to spin or plant or clean. No wagon to drive, no livestock to manage. Her children were happily romping and the leg was still horribly scabbed. I can hardly move, she moaned, lying back and lifting her dress up to her waist.

On the lower deck, Martin watched two black deckhands coil lines. Were they slaves? Or free? They looked about his age and he had an urge to speak to them about what he had done: his secret. He felt something he had never felt, a shaky triumphant sense of power, all his. Above the second deck there was a third and above that, high over the water, the pilothouse. But down at the level of water, Martin was guarding a wagon that held all the Dickinsons' goods, along with a fifty-six-year-old runaway slave.

Any food here, Martin? What'd you bring?

The plot had been Bry's at first and he had needed to convince Martin over two separate meetings, but Martin was not thinking of that now. There's bread and cheese and herring but you better be quiet, I mean it.

I get off at the first stop, Martin. Remember where I told you. (Giving him an order!)

Uh-huh. They'll still be watching for runaways there. Mister Spradling will have put out the word. Be slave catchers at the ready for sure. I thought on that and I decided on a better place.

No. I planned it all out. I studied it many a time. I talked to somebody I met down by the harbor. You been good to me, boy (calling him boy!), but New Albany's my place to get off.

Listen here, I took a chance on this plan of yours and I also heard about New Albany, that it'll be crawling with catchers. It's the first jumping-off place from Louisville. It was me who found out how wagons get loaded on — not by deckhands but by the owners. I studied up on the facts.

Bry said: I been aiming for Ohio for one whole year. What could I lose at this point?

Martin said: Your life. You get caught. Or fall in the river. Or we go to jail and they hang us. I sure can't roll the wagon off there and how else would you keep from them seeing you?

I run and jump and I'm onto the shore.

My mama would get in trouble too, you know. You better just do as I say now. Martin liked the sound of that. On this lower deck the open sides were exposed to sun and wind and rain and the boilers were so hot that no one could be close to them so everyone stood or sat in the narrow space available, where they often got wet. There were no benches, no cabins, no bunks. There were fights over any bit of shade and the water was brought up in a pail from the river and the toilet was another pail that got dumped into that same river but most men angled themselves over the side of the boat, leaving the pail for females. There was one grill to be shared. There was the ever-present danger of being swept overboard. There were hundreds of stories. When the boilers explode, people die by scaldings or drownings or burnings, someone was bound to point out. There were examples. There was nothing on offer on this deck but chance.

Even so, Bry lay back down in the bed of the wagon and complained. Maybe my last chance. I been hungry all my life, Martin, but nothing like what I was on my walk up the side of Kentucky thinkin I was in Ohio never finding myself a rabbit or a cabbage or a cake. No, sir, I don go down this river one more foot after New Albany.

Now you just listen to me! But then he could not decide how to have his way and went off to see his bear and when he neared her cage he had to stand outside it because the captain would not allow him a key. It was an iron cage and not very big, but Martin couldn't let Cuff know he felt sorry for her. Big old baby, he said, longing to pull her into his lap. He was trying to do something Good. He even felt glad when he thought about it. Brought a bear and a runaway slave aboard a boat where neither belonged. Cuff was a good ninety pounds by now at a year and a half. He had a runaway in his care and two mules and four cows and a pony and a bear. He had done something nobody knew about and he had no need for praise, not really, but he wished he could tell.

49

That first night on the steamboat, Bry knew Martin would come to the wagon to sleep, but he had never yet slept near any white person except for Mother Mary and that was a long time back when Bett made medicine and Mary Jones delivered it to customers because Bett, being Negro, was believed not to have talent or knowledge. And so, until he was ten, and Mister Rafe Fox claimed him, they had been an unusual family and now when Martin settled down beside him in the wagon, Bry would have to find the courage to explain his plan. When we get near to Albany, he whispered later that night, when we hear any passengers pushing to get off, I'm goin ta mingle. He knew it would work. He would tuck in his shirt, spit-polish his boots, smooth down his hair. There would be an amount of confusion on the lower deck as goods were unloaded and he would just mingle, as he said to Martin, making himself look busy like one of the deckhands. Already, with so many people on one side, the boat was listing and the wagon rolled against its brake and Bry moved the canvas aside to peek out. Slave-catching was a for-profit business. If a black person had papers, the papers were said to be false. Bry had learned this before he cheated Washington Spradling out of four hundred dollars' worth of labor. All I am worth at this time, he thought bitterly. In Albany, a runaway needed a contact or he would get picked up, but Bry had learned a few tricks in Louisville. That's what Mister Spradling had in mind when he purchased a slave and trained him up in the barber trade. It was better than nothing, better than cotton, which never grew in the North except on backs and arms and legs. When Bry felt the big steamboat swinging around like the hands on a compass and then bang into a dock, he put his whole head out of the canvas and saw Martin running fast at him, saying: There's a man over there on the dock with a gun.

That don't mean . . .

Get your head back in. He can see you! Martin almost believed in the man he had made up in his mind. He could almost see him. You want us to get caught? He was sorry he'd done such a stupid thing as to bring a runaway slave on a fancy steamboat. Anyone laid eyes on Bry, they'd both get caught.

Meanwhile, Bry held on to the side of the wagon. His eyes teared up. I got to get off, Martin. I can't stay here. I got to get off.

Get your hands in. I can see em, Martin hissed.

I need to stand up. My leg is cramped.

You can't.

I got to. Bry thought of the dock on the north side of the river and of his mother and maybe his child somewhere out there to be found.

50

Later, at an hour when others were looking for their bedrolls or lying in uncovered humps on the hot lower deck, Martin went to feed the pony, the mules, and the bear. The pony did not like living with the mules but the mules cared about nothing. Cows were kept in a large penned area near the bow. It was a mournful place, the animals herded together, unshaded, hot and arguing for water, but at the stern the mood was more obliging and Cuff was relaxed. Martin made the rounds and then emptied his bladder at the edge of the deck. When it was dark, he crawled into the wagon and rustled in the bag of food he had been given by Electa. Jerky, water crackers, dried herring, and sausages. He gave Bry half of his portion and Bry did not deny himself. I remember you brought a man to the field that time. Do you know what he did? Bry asked.

I know everybody started running off and

we lost the farm.

Your uncle's farm.

We lived off it if you care to know and some was ours.

Lived off us, I guess. Where do I get off? Bry felt tired from the effort he had made to resolve his difference with Martin, although Martin knew nothing of the struggle he'd felt.

St. Louis is where I'm thinking.

Where's it at?

After we get off the biggest river in the world, you'll feel us pushing against the current, and it could happen right now or almost any minute and it'll take some days of pushing.

I can't even see where I am. Could be Georgia you bringin me into.

Well, it's not. It can't be Georgia if you look at the sun.

Can't look out, can I? Take it on faith is all I can do.

The first night it had gone like this, but on the second night they began to talk in another way. The difference was that Martin was asking the questions. He said, How'd you get all the way to Louisville?

Bry was rubbing at his beard. He loved the feel of it. You know your aunt Mary? She raised me in her house. My mama was her property.

Behind them, the wheel made its grueling, rhythmic noise. Then Bry said: Missus Mary had a sister named Jemima who was my friend and we . . . he was staring at the dark because he had the nerve to tell something like this.

But Martin said: Shut up your mouth about my family.

51

Dear Papa Ladies wear gloves on this boat even to eat. I wish you could see our beds in a stack. But Gina needs her papa. In the wall is a round hole where we can see high clifs along the side and there is no sky. Mama is lying down because she is sick but Br. Borden is a medic so Gina and I go in the salone but we do not have gloves. Gina still has that cough that used to worry you. Do you still worry? I herd a lady saying the farmers are going to win the war of the west, but I don't think there is a war, is there? I hope you will fight for us if there is a war. Today we will come to St. Louis which has more French people then Louisville and maybe you will be waiting with Patton if not I will mail this because I want you to find us. I hope and cry. With love Your Lecta

52

Martin's private prayer was disturbed by sharp, blasting whistles. There were shouts from the shore. He got up off his knees and opened his eyes and made his way to the rail to see the outskirts of St. Louis. He had been praying because this was The Test. He had to get Bry off the boat on the south side of the river because that's where they were landing and that was too bad. Bry would be upset at the news but there was no way around the fact. Also the street that ran down to the river was filling up with half of St. Louis on the run to meet the boat and he did not think he would ever get Bry off in one piece.

In six days Martin and Bry had grown accustomed to each other. Man and boy stretched toe to head, listening to snores and secrets in the dark. Now the deckhands were tossing lines to men on the dock and Martin's fear pinched at him. He didn't want to move. What if his mother came down to check on the wagon, or sent Brother Borden down? When the plank was put out, men swarmed aboard, checking the female passengers as if they wore price signs. Names were called out. Maybe they had ordered brides to come out west. More and more people came pushing onto the deck. Passengers trying to get off were shoved back. More names were called. Gloria Bishop? Miss Bishop? Stewart Graves? There was a babble of French. Miss Bishop was trying to make herself heard. Tonight there would be a party on the boat with liquor, and such delicacies as came from Louisville and points east or south. New Orleans shrimp kept on ice! The locals were hoping to enjoy themselves after a winter of venison and turkey and there was no time ahead when the decks would be empty for so much as a minute. Anyway, Martin was watching for the slave hunters who would be watching for Bry. There might be notices pasted up about him. If I get the old man off, I'll be myself again, he thought. Frightened almost to death, he stood at deck edge and watched his mother begin her promenade down the upper gangplank. She turned to look down and called to him. You bring the wagon and I'll meet you over there. She pointed to a building with a broad green awning, its edges ruffling in a hot summer breeze. She went on down the gangplank on Sister Borden's arm, limping a little but not so much as before. More shouts: Men to unload! Over here! There was no end to the bundles thrown down by the deckhands. Martin went back to the wagon and lifted the cover enough to touch Bry's cold hand. Help me with the stock so it will look natural. He meant: Because you could be a servant. He reached into his shirt and pulled out a sheet of paper, which had been rubbed to give it a serious look, not too clean to be believed.

Bry angled himself down off the wagon, groaning. He had not stood in six days. He reached for the paper and examined it.

I Benjamin Dickinson owner of this man Bry herebie make him free.

Better sign it.

How can I. That's not my name.

Bry said: No matter. Put a date.

Up on the levee, men carried revolvers in plain sight. This was a city of racket and smells, its streets crowded with prairie schooners, wobbly buggies, and big, overloaded carts rolling over trash and rotting garbage. Some of the wagons were pulled by oxen. Whole teams of oxen. This was the

start of the long trip west. Martin and Bry
stood on the deck and looked at each other.
They went silently to the stall that held the
two mules and the pony, the landing now
full of more shouting and cursing and cracking whips.

That's Illinois over there. Martin pointed
across the river.

How'm I to get to it? Bry stared ahead.
How'm I to do it? You got me in a bad fix,
Martin.

On the upper deck, preparations were
already being made for the evening festivi-
ties while animals were led off the lower
plank along with wagons and carts piled
high with trunks.

Take hold of Beulah.

I never did take to them, Martin.

Just do it. She won't bite.

Bry had not eaten since the previous
night, when Martin had slipped him a few
pieces of salted herring. It was the last of
their food. He blinked now in the bright
light and swayed on his feet and took hold
of a thin piece of leather that was attached
to an animal he feared like snakes. Bad fellow, he muttered. Come along as I say to. A
fight had broken out by the boilers, two men
arguing over some piece of equipment.

This landing here's no good, Martin! You

shoulda let me off before this.

Just look normal. Just move your legs. You're helping me with the wagon, that's all. It's going to be fine. Martin was trying to think. He would have to come back for the cows. Then the pony. Or the other way around. Then Cuff. Pulling Cuff through this crowd after six days in a cage she'd be quick to take offense. Bear and slave. Both jittery.

53

The Missouri River is like no other, spilling sand and dirt from its steep sides, shape-changing by the hour, so restless and wild that it carves out wider and wider bends, making trees fall off its banks into the maddened current. The great steam paddleboats required little water but a tree snag could sink one in minutes. Martin had watched the river snapping and gnawing at the looming city of St. Louis. Then, docked, he harnessed the mules and together with Bry they got the big wagon off the swaying boat to the sound of a horse rearing madly on the street while Bry, terrified and jubilant, moved one foot and then the other as if he'd been wound up and set loose. Women passed by swathed in veils while Lavina stood across the way under the awning waiting for Patton, looking anxiously up and down the street. The Bordens had gone on ahead with their wagon. It seemed that all of them would make camp on the same ground. Who was that? Lavina asked as Martin brought the wagon up by her.

Someone just helping out. Bry had ducked into an alley.

We're taking a spot over behind that warehouse. See? Do you see where?

I see, Mother.

Take the wagon, then come back for Judy and Cuff. I'll have Lecta take the cows to graze.

But he wanted to shout. I saved a man! He wanted to scream: I did it! He climbed on the wagon, slapping the mules with the reins, beside himself and exalted, having no idea where Bry would make off to, but it's done, it's done. I made a man free. I shared my nights, my food, my whole chance with him. It was almost too much to hold in, this thing he had done, and he wanted to hurl it up in the air and give it away and make it bigger than it was. Make it as high as the sky. My Deed, he wanted to call it, even as Bry was feeling his way around the edges of a town where abolitionists and slaveholders and catchers waged daily battles over their contrasting beliefs and where he might be picked up any minute because he was still in Missouri.

54

At the St. Louis campground, Brother Borden told a story. Some time back, he said, some fellows who shall go unnamed bought a tired old schooner. Oh, it was once a fine one, having navigated the cold waters of Lake Erie back and forth. The vessel was towed down the river to within half a mile of the Niagara cataract and loaded with two bears and numerous smaller animals. Then it was set adrift. But at this point Martin walked away from the campsite. He would not listen to any story about bears.

55

The next evening the Dickinson children saw Brother Borden striding straight toward their wagon. He took off his hat, put it back on his curly hair, and stood before them, panting. He took off his glasses and wiped them on his sleeve, then put them back on his face, adjusting the wire that fit over his ears. He looked quickly at Lavina, then dropped his gaze to his feet. He put a hand over his heart and stood perplexed.

Lavina set her bowl down and came to his side. She put her hand on his and said: What is it?

I am here, Brother Borden said . . . I am here . . . He pitched his voice to be heard by the children. Because a fella down the road a mile or so says your papa is approaching. Behind the lenses, his eyes were closed, as if he did not want to see the look on Lavina's face.

Lavina could not ascertain how she felt.

There was a stirring in her that she could not assess and she could not see for the tears that filled her eyes. She looked around blindly. She said: Son! Your father! Quick!

Martin was sitting with his back against a wagon wheel (a position never allowed at home, where children stood when an adult approached), but now he got up to untie the thick rope that held his bear. That afternoon a little girl had come to pet Cuff and the bear had swiped at her and knocked her down, but Lavina had interceded with a piece of liquorice, so perhaps the child's parents were none the wiser. Lavina had managed to bargain for Cuff to travel on the *New Statesman* to St. Jo, although this captain, too, insisted on a locked iron cage. About the boat trip, the Bordens were undecided.

Martin said he thought he would take the bear for a walk. His heart was hammering and his stomach felt queasy.

Electa stood up, knocking her cup of milk over wastefully, and then sat back down. Shall I come? she called to her brother, but Martin was already striding away and did not answer. He had hold of the leather leash with its twelve feet of length, a leash easily snapped by the bear, who was led off willingly. Cuff loved her hikes with Martin,

312

although Electa once said she could imagine Cuff running home at bedtime for a cup of hot chocolate. Now she was not sure where she wanted to be. Her father was coming at last. She felt nervous and divided.

But Martin knew his responsibility to a creature he had suckled on cow's milk and honey and taught to eat from a dish. I will teach you tricks for our future, he had earlier told the bear. Civilized tricks. Not that we will find civilized anything where we are going. He had forgiven Cuff the swipe at the little girl because bears, like little girls, are ruled by nature. You shall also teach me, he added, since he had seen that if a student can be approached on his own ground, it benefits teacher and student both. He, himself, had once taught old Reuben the alphabet by walking behind the plow with him and singing the letters out. Without an alphabet, how was Cuff to be taught not to swipe at little girls, not to knock people down, not to growl or bite? Can we think without words? Words are made of letters written in our brains. Thoughts must be like that too. All this was worrying Martin as his bear, with her natural lope, went off in the direction of the trees that were clustered at the far edge of the campsite, pulling at her long leash. His father's return. Had he expected it? Along with the hammering heart and the queasy stomach, Martin felt a dull foreboding that ran up his back and around his shoulders into his chest. He wanted to stop. He thought he should maybe turn back. It'll anger him if I'm not there when he rides up, Martin thought. But I should wait for his mood to settle. And he was glad to be leaving the campsite even as he was trying to be glad that his father was back. Just for a while, he said to Cuff, we'll stay scarce. And now his mother would get better and Brother Borden would stop pestering her and the girls would do what they were told. Normal is what we'll be again, he told Cuff, whose tracks looked pigeon-toed and Martin laughed and then he remembered his father's rage at the bear on the day they left home and he decided he would stay in the woods until his father had time to greet everyone else and reclaim his wagon.

He watched Cuff mark certain trees with bite marks, advertising her size. We will have no trouble finding our way back, he thought, and from the line of trees he watched Brother Borden leaving their wagon, his back straight and his coattails flapping. In a few minutes, then, he saw his father ride up on the old, familiar mare wrapped in the black cape Martin knew so well. It covered him when he bent forward over the neck of his horse. At least that isn't changed, Martin thought, and he stood for a time keeping to the trees and shadows, well out of sight, watching his father remove his hat, slide down off the horse, and walk over to the wagon with his shoulders set. Lavina came out of the wagon and eased herself over the wheel and down to the ground so that she could cross the distance between them. They stood for some moments a few feet apart and Martin could not imagine what they could say to each other at such a time. His father had let them struggle up through the wilderness of Kentucky with Lavina's injury and illness and fever and then deliver themselves onto a boat that was defying death and now he was greeting his wife without getting down on his knees to ask her forgiveness, which seemed wrong to Martin, who walked on with his bear as the sky darkened and a handful of stars came out. Martin wondered if he would know how to read a sign if God sent him one. He looked straight up and stroked the bear's fur and felt hollow as a drum, as if there was nothing solid inside him, as if he was made of light from the unrisen moon. He was tempted by fear and then he was fully afraid. Night all around. He longed to go back to his family. The vegetation was full of heavy smells now, dew-laden, and Cuff flared her nostrils and Martin felt a sharp sorrow that was new to him. He could feel something slip away for good. He tried making a sound. He said jig without meaning it, although he'd once thought that in the West he and the bear might earn money with a dancing act. Now the bear bent her knees and took an experimental jump and Martin's heart banged in joyful response. When they had first walked together, Cuff had not yet developed her sense of smell and her eyesight was still cub-blurry and Martin remembered her loping back from the trees and missing him altogether, rushing past him and searching around in fright. A bear cub must know the shape and color of its mother, if nothing else, and he'd reminded himself to wear dark clothing on future walks so that Cuff could see his shape. Now it was a habit. Martin wore black trousers and a dark blue shirt. He wore heavy gloves and boots so that Cuff's claws couldn't slash him, and a felt hat covered his head just in case.

Cuff nuzzled and grunted and showed that she was pleased by the fur rubbing and night walking and now Martin realized that it was something rare, the way he and his bear could communicate. We are born in ignorance and must make ourselves civil, is what Preacher John always said. But Martin looked at Cuff and knew her to be true to her nature rather than ignorant. He thought: I must pray that Cuff will always be true to the way of bear. Then he thought: If our Heavenly Father cares, does He provide only if I ask?

56

Gina had slipped into her old position on her father's lap, but Electa, after pressing his stiff hands in hers, found reason to see to the cows. Greener pastures, she said, smiling, when her father wondered where she was going. Her parents would have some need for privacy. She would take Gina. Anyway, it was Saturday evening and the town was in full swing along the riverfront and this was what she'd been hoping for all day. A band played waltzes on the fairgrounds and musicians, black and white, stood on street corners with their hats turned up by their feet. Leaving their uneasy parents, Gina and Electa walked behind the cows, passing the canal, the fairgrounds, the livery stable, and, at the edge of town, a narrow street lit by gaslights. Through a window they could see a parlor with flowered paper on the walls. At the edges of the window, dark red curtains. The wainscoting was white. The floor was covered with a pat-terned carpet. Electa craned her neck and fastened her sights on a woman standing in this perfect room holding a piece of paper and an envelope. Look at the dress, she whispered, but Gina could not see over the windowsill. Electa said: The dress is blue with lace at the shoulders. The skirt is so long I can't see her feet. And her hair. Has she added a false piece to it? It is so nice and thick the way it holds to the back of her head. She sighed.

The cows began to graze on a patch of nearby grass and Gina pushed up closer to the window and stood on her tiptoes and tried to peer in. You are too short, Electa said. So listen. There are papered walls like Aunt Elizabeth's. There is a perfect little writing desk and the settee is green with red cushions. Settee — is that what it's called? I wonder if she's married. I wonder if the letter she's reading is from . . .

Gina said bluntly: It's from her uncle who died and left her rich.

No, Gina, this house belongs to her step-father. That is her only dress, inherited from her dead mother and now somewhat out of fashion! The letter is telling her she has to leave this pretty house by midnight because the stepfather is going to marry someone in the morning and he wants to be alone with his new greedy wife.

Like Uncle Benjamin, said Gina wisely.

Yes! But Electa was surprised. Had her little sister understood the family catastrophe so well? Electa had come to believe that all of their misfortunes could be laid at Matilda's feet.

Gina pulled at her arm. I'm really sure her died mother gave her this nice house and meant her to stay here forever and there's a garden at the back with a little creek and some pretty fish.

Electa said: But hardly any girls don't get to own houses, Gina. She has to leave by midnight with nowhere to go. There is a coach coming but she has only a little money for her fare and then it will be gone and she will have nothing to eat. The money is hidden in a drawer that her stepfather doesn't know about, but he's been looking for it. Electa turned away from the window. She took in the whole street. St. Louis was so much bigger, noisier, rougher, smellier, and faster than Louisville. Every one of these people had a story and she tried to imagine such variation. Her sojourn at school in Asheville was marked by a pastoral quiet that bore no comparison to this rowdy place and now, just like her mother, she wanted to see the shops and alleyways and residents and streets. Come on, let's go see everything! She was glad of the dark, which covered her rustic appearance. Then she noticed two men shoving each other. Well, I be one of em you did and I never even noticed! a young girl was shouting.

Electa grabbed Gina's hand. Hurry up!

Gina pulled back. No, I want to watch. In a minute, she had jerked away from her sister and rounded the corner, where she could watch the fighting men from a safe distance. Electa screamed: You come back here this minute! A young man standing in a doorway with his hands in his pockets said: Your cows es tekin off, miss.

Electa ran to take hold of the lead cow's halter. She touched the bell to call the others and called to Gina again.

You from herebouts? The boy caught up and was trying to help bring the other three cows, smacking a flank here and there.

Yes, she said. I live here. She caught up with Gina and slapped her hard in the face. Gina squealed and ran to the square, her braids shooting out behind her and her shoes ringing on the wooden walkway. She howled and ran until she was out of sight.

The young man was only a boy and what Electa's father called a hayseed, meaning he might not have gone to school. Electa looked at him.

You could see dancin if you like it. The boy took off his cap and offered his arm.

Electa took the arm of the boy and he led her to a corral where the cows could calmly wait. Beyond there was a place of boards and posters lacking windows and built on the slant. Inside, the beardless boy put his damp hand on Electa's waist and inched her forward between three-legged tables, some with candles, but the room was all shadows and the people around her were bulky shapes. A fiddler was at work on a tiny stage and people were moving darkly across the floor.

57

Where is your sister? John shouted when Gina got back to the wagon. He stood in the deepening twilight, glaring ahead as if any minute he might whip the drowsy mules into motion. As if they had not got this far without him.

I don't know, Papa. Gina's voice had a slight squeak of fear.

John grabbed her ear. Fiddlesticks! But this was not how he had wanted it to be and, had he looked closer, he might have seen the red mark on Gina's cheek from her sister's slap. Contracting arteries. Why are my children impertinent? Tight again with nerves so that he could not think. And where is Martin, Miss Know Nothing? His blasted bear caused trouble today is what I hear. Is that the reason I have not laid eyes on a boy who must know what's coming to him?

Having dried her eyes on the walk back to

the campsite, Gina began to cry again. It always warmed her papa's heart when she burst into tears but John, in his reunion with the wagon train, had visited several old friends and here and there taken a drink of brandy or cider or plum wine, which was not his custom and against his principles and yet it was necessary to renew allegiances. The jugs had been open on many a wagon seat, as the lack of a preacher had given the travelers license, and why seem unpleasantly righteous on such an occasion as this? The surprise reunion merited celebration and a drink was libation at such a time according to custom. Even among the teetotalers, it was a singular situation, the night air liquefied with the scent of renewed trust and fellowship. As far as John was concerned, no one must ever know where he had been and what he had tried to do. If it helped everyone to watch him quench his thirst, he would allow himself that leeway. His neighbors seemed genuinely glad to have him back, as if they had missed his leadership. As if they could not imagine that he was a man with a heart that was ripped in half, a man who had ridden night and day to catch up with the family he should never have let out of his sight. Now, where are they? Answer me!

From inside the canvas he heard the tail end of a sentence.

. . . away, I suspect.

Say that again!

I said, they ran away, I suspect.

Gina was now hysterical. John shouted at the blank canvas: My sixteen-year-old daughter is wandering the streets of a filthy city while my son harbors a dangerous creature without permission at half past ten o'clock?

Seventeen, said Lavina, poking her head out of the canvas. And we have all harbored dangerous creatures at one time or another. She closed the canvas.

In the woods, Martin had thrown himself down with Cuff, who was settled with her heavy head on his narrow shoulder. Having grown past the habit, Cuff suddenly searched with her tongue for Martin's left ear. What shall we do? Martin whispered, running his hand over her nose and loving her more than ever. Shall we go back? There was a knobby bone in the middle of Cuff's skull just under the fur, and he liked to rub it and he did that now while looking into her small eyes, which were close together and rimmed in black as if she had come from another planet. He nestled under her bristly chin and held her paw and felt each long, curved claw with his fingers and it was much like the hand-holding Electa was then performing with the boy in the shack in candlelight, for they too had found something not to be forfeited. While Martin held the bear, Electa held the boy and put her face against his neck. When Cuff rolled over on the ground, Electa threw her head back and led the boy outside. Martin lay against the bear's stomach, grabbed a foot, and found the place between two toes where Cuff was most ticklish while Electa gave her boy a tender shove and he fell clumsily onto the grass. Girl and boy. Boy and bear. An hour or more while mortals held fast to each other vowing that no one would come between them — not ever: that they would become dance partners, go into business together, learn each other's language — that neither would ever again catch a fish for anyone else. Till death us do part.

Cuff put a paw against Martin's throat, as if taking his pulse. Unaccustomed to such melancholy, the two of them got up off the forest floor and began walking back to the campsite where Dickinsons were trying to reshape their lives. Seeing his approach, Lavina wanted Martin to pull Cuff in the other direction, away from the father who had made them get up in the middle of the night because Electa was finally back and her late return had further maddened him. Wasn't he kicking at a wheel and raising his voice? Hadn't he even raised his hand to his daughter? With all the campers quiet, trying to sleep or listening, wasn't he provoking them to hear every word of his shameful, humiliating rant? Lavina, who had been fully in charge all these weeks, was now mortified.

And Martin was dragging himself back to camp.

Run, Martin! Lavina thought. Stay away. (Awful thought!) Don't come back.

But John pointed at the boy who was slowly approaching. Come here this instant! Just where is the respect due to your father, who has ridden for days to find you? My children should be here when I arrive, and yet I find Electa beyond control in a strange city and my son still smitten with the unholy creature I told him to leave behind. John was too angry now to feel any pleasure in the sight of his son. I will not stand by to see that animal ruin this venture. It should be in the woods, but now it's too late for that. You have tamed a wild creature, but it will never be tame enough! Boy, do you hear? Do you hear what I will not stand?

Do you intend to do what I say, which is that the bear is not coming on the steamboat your mother has expensively engaged? Don't you look at me that way! I'll see a smile on your face or give you something to really frown about, something to make you cry for a week. John fell back against the wagon, stunned by the intensity of his outrage.

Martin saw his father's fallen face and was shocked by its decay. His father was grasping at the lost threads of command and Martin slumped his shoulders and bowed his head as he had learned to do at such times.

John said: I require a response.

Inside the wagon, Electa was crying savagely and Gina had taken to coughing. Lavina was rummaging in the medicine box. Martin could hear these things going on out of sight and he knew in that instant that the balance they had achieved over the past weeks had come undone in a few quick hours and that he would never understand the weight his father carried against which all the rest of them were as feathers on the wrong side of the scale. He heard his mother opening bottles. He heard Cuff grinding her teeth at being bound to such a family. He moved very slowly along the side of the wagon, still holding the leash, reaching for the sturdy bear rope so that he could tether her safely. His arms were watery. We have just been out walking . . . Father . . . here he tried to firm up his words . . . is all.

We shall not proceed . . .

Please, Father.

. . . until she is disposed of.

Martin's stare an act of disbelief.

Which of us will do it?

Martin held tight to the leash, remembering the way Cuff had tumbled off the tree into his arms. The thought of it made him cry while John reached under the seat of the wagon where the old gun was kept. No! Martin leapt for his hand. Me. I. With the gun gripped hard in one hand now while the leash was wrapped around the other wrist, he began to plead. No, oh no, come on, Cuff, come on, bear. The two of them running and the father's voice ringing in each frightened head. Abraham must kill Isaac. It was this that his father had set for him. Shouting it too. Faithfulness to Father and to father, since they are one and the same. But does the Father in Heaven imbibe? Does he drink plum wine and cider? Unnerving it is and yet we are running, panting, even the stumbling bear. And let me hold your furry head and touch that

329

knobby spot between your ears and aim the gun where you have just been kissed. Let me be covered in blood and brain and then I will be someone not myself.

Martin knelt and Cuff lay willingly before him, even rolling onto her back and exposing her tenderest places so that no gun was needed, only Martin's knife, which he pulled from the sheath that hung on his belt. Easy to bring to a throat and . . . If God is directing, Cuff will be saved as Isaac was but if God . . . turns a blind eye . . .

Martin and Cuff are watching each other while Martin holds on to the knife and imagines the act, which requires a thrust. Who will he become after that? He places himself on the steam paddle wheeler in his mind, thinking ahead, moving along at full speed, bow waves fanning through dark water just as the earth itself is foaming along in its orbit. While this foaming goes on, he does his best to relive every day of Cuff's life, beginning with the first terror of fur hurtling down the black walnut tree. He makes himself remember the outing when Cuff found the tree again and smelled her mother's death. He remembers how Cuff climbed to the top and clung there yowling, as if she had heard the song of that tree above all other trees and could not forgive

that eternal thrum. Why is all learning connected to loss? Cuff had tried to climb
down, but whenever her hind feet tried to
grip, the bark chipped away and she lost
foothold, finally tumbling into Martin's
arms again as if her story could never take
another shape. Clutching the knife, Martin
saw himself on the deck of that wheel-
churned boat, boilers banging. Always and
forever, wherever he was on the river, his
thoughts would be on the bear even as the
landscape slid by. The river would change
but the fact would not. It would define him,
this murder. Guilt would be all through his
blood for the rest of his life and he would
never forgive or love his father. He remembered the tall pine where Cuff had discovered a hive and loosened a hundred bees
and Martin had been stung how many
times? The mistake of saving, the mistake of
loving, the mistake of obeying. Now Martin
dropped the knife and picked up the gun.

Behold, the Lord God comes with might . . .

And what if he were less frightened? Less
brought up to obey? For he saw now that
he was damned. If there is a God, rescue
me. But if not, the forest danced with its
meaninglessness while boy and bear began
to run and moonlight touched a spruce that
held out arms that pointed away from

331

thickly tied boats, from bellowing boys and challenging girls, from horns and fiddles and floors, away from the wagon with its butter and rules to a place where they might eat fresh berries, climb tallest trees and be free of fear for is it not ordained that the young should no sooner come into the world than milk and honey should flow for them?

58

Having charged Lavina for her goods and animals a dollar per hundredweight, the captain of the *New Statesman* refunded only half of her money on Sunday when Electa hurried into town to explain that a family member was going to be late and could he please delay departure? It was late June and the water was still high, and when the captain refused the delay, Lavina cursed her son for ruining their plans and wasting their money, forgetting that she had wished him away, wished him into the woods where he would be safe. Thoughtless child! Ridiculously and abnormally self-centered! Endangering all of them out of spite. They certainly had no way to earn back so much as a dollar of what was wasted, she announced to Electa, but later she went for a walk by herself, able to move without pain for the first time in days, and she thought of Martin's suffering and her anger vanished.

Maybe he was not staying away out of spite. Maybe he had been gone three days because he was sick at heart over the sacrifice — the murder! — of his pet. I didn't defend him one bit, she thought. I let it happen. Oh, she said very softly to herself, wasn't the bear managing the journey better than anyone expected? After all, she was really very sweet and funny. She cheered us up. But Lavina stopped herself from going on with this thought because it would not do to question John or to wonder how he could deprive Martin of something so tenderly cherished although she began to feel some complicity with her son, secretly hoping he was hiding out of spite rather than grief. She, too, had been obedient and where was her reward? Was she glad her husband had returned? Of course. But no. And that was profoundly confusing. There were moments when she wished John would go back to Virginia where he was respected more than he was here in this rugged, wavering life where he was one of too many foundering men. No one paid him any mind now, although for the first few hours they were glad to see him back. Perhaps after the gladness, they remembered his defection, still unexplained. Not so much as a word had he offered to excuse the last-minute abandonment of his flock, nor the shame he had caused his wife nor the difficulties she had faced alone; not a word of regret had he spoken to anyone.

Eight days later a steamboat hurtled down the swollen river, full of furs and tired miners. It would stay in the St. Louis Harbor long enough to take on cargo, then turn and retrace its path west and upriver. Lavina barely noticed. Martin had still not returned and she was frantic, begging the men of the wagon train who were still available to join John on his daily searches. It was an unbearable crisis of hope mixed with blame. John was either pacing the campsite, as if taking stock of something he'd forgotten, or he was riding into the woods to look for any sign of his son, who must be hiding close by. As the great white *Arabia* sat handsomely in port, the kind medic who had saved her life came to the wagon to visit his patient and see if she would be going or staying. Will you board, Sister? Any word of the boy?

Sister Dickinson requires no company, John announced, sounding possessive and contemptuous.

But Brother Borden called out softly: Sister? Do you hear?

The answer from inside the wagon was a

gasp, as if the end of a sob had been stifled.

Sister? Are you ill?

John said rudely: Your hope of free passage is doomed, Brother. We are not leaving on the *Arabia* because our son is lost in the woods as you should know, having encouraged him in his every folly, from what I hear.

Brother Borden blinked at the accusation and then at the wagon which held his patient. Then he backed slowly away, expressing his concern for both mother and child by shaking his head while retreating. When, the next morning, the Bordens were gone without warning or farewell, Lavina kept her sorrow locked in herself, unable to acknowledge the blow to her pride or her bitterness at John's stroke of mean possessiveness. Where was he when she was limping through the wasteland of Kentucky? The world had shifted. She did not know herself as Lavina Dickinson, preacher's wife. Not now when her one friend in the world had disappeared without a farewell. She would never find comfort or understanding like that again! She was alone, left in hot and humid St. Louis with bedraggled passengers who were appalling to her, traveling from west to east on the steamboat *Arabia,* a frightening preview of her future if she ever got to the place they had come from. Beggars and wastrels getting off. Miners and trappers coming home from triumphs or failures. The *Arabia* sat at its mooring, emptying and then slowly filling up again. A hundred crates being loaded onto its lower decks. Then a hundred more. The river was lower by the hour and the Dickinsons fed the fire under their iron pot and waited for Martin to recover his senses. John said he was clever enough to survive in the woods, but Gina coughed and cried in her sleep, wanting her brother, wanting to go home, refusing to believe her father's promises. Lavina knew that they each imagined Martin's unquenchable grief. They each suffered a horror of what he had done. Or what if there'd been an accident with the gun? This new fear ate at her. She saw that John went into the forest on his mare, each day riding farther and deeper into the trees.

59

Trees never seen before and rocks that Martin picked up and put down since he had no way to carry anything but the old rifle, which didn't fit well to his body. He had been a rock collector at home. He had rocks and pieces of wood and bone on the chair by his bed, but now he would sleep in a hollow and he would not keep anything in his pocket because what was the point? He had no place to store a treasure and no wish to remember where he was. He did not build a fire. It was only perversion, this running. Soon his father would come thrashing through the woods on his mare. He was tired and talking all the time to his bear. Never you mind. We did the trip without him up to now. I did it. I was the driver by the end when Mama was sick and there was no Papa then, was there? And now he just comes and says what he wants even if we were doing fine without any vote from him.

So we just wait now. Just a day or two till Papa gets over his idea of bossing everything in the world.

With nothing to eat, Martin fell into a wakeful slumber always worried about snakes, then woke up at sunrise in a pile of leaves that had turned to mush. The boy opened his eyes and looked straight up into green. He tried to remember why he was sleeping outside. He tried to imagine what drove his father to St. Louis after a month of staying back. Or the other question: What made his father hang back in the first place? He didn't care. He hated his father. Martin told Cuff: I was boss of myself for a time anyway, although he knew this was incorrect.

The bear was awake. Yes. They were pretty ravenous, but a forest is separate from human needs. Hungry and snappish, the bear climbed a tree. Martin admired her, saying: Brave bear, and Cuff slid down and they went off to find berries. The forest was a mass of thick and thin trunks, obstinate, unmoving, joined at the roots and whispering branch to branch. Vines hung down and wrapped around boy and bear so the trees had no beginning or ending. A smell of rot. Mushrooms. Should he eat one? Cuff wanted to scratch her back and leave her scent everywhere; she wanted to roll and be glad. She hid from Martin — it was a game they had played before, but now she understood the excitement of being found in an unknown place. She tried not to pant or sniff or growl and Martin called, Bear! Bear! Where are you? Martin knew she was resisting the impulse to fly into his arms. It was the first morning of the world. They were born again.

Walking was slow. Low branches tripped them or they stumbled on rocks or fell over rotting logs. The gun was a trial to be borne, heavy, useless. Crooked streams cut through the trees, some shallow, some fast. They walked downstream and upstream trying to cross, but why cross? Where were they going? Soon his father would come and now Martin told himself to leave signs, cut through root stalks or mark branches so his father would know where they had been. Or should they stop walking? There were spiderwebs hanging and clinging, sticking to Martin's face and hair. He no longer had his gloves. Bugs jumped off the trees and into his face or he stepped on them and they squished and birds were heard but not seen and they had nothing to tell. There were berries. Big plump unfamiliar berries. Cuff ate them and then Martin picked some for himself because the bear had survived her meal. They walked uphill. It was slippery with moss and Martin fell. Then he was covered with mud. He was hungrier than he had ever been in his life. He ate a handful of moss and it was filling.

Once, there were butterflies, orange and yellow, clinging to trees and flapping. Martin knew they were transformed like everything else in this forest, pulling themselves out of slug-shaped bodies and taking to the air while bees hit one flower and another, one sweet spot or another, nectaring by day, and bats were nectaring by night and the air was full of more life than any cotton field and Martin watched, unfed, purposeless. If I could fly, if I could stick my nose in a flower. A bear is happy eating ants. Why am I stuck in what I am? He got down on the ground; he crawled for a time in the damp and muck. He licked a flower and ate it and barked because that was the most likely sound he could make without words. He heard animals in holes and nests. He heard growling and thought it was male and thought male creatures made too much noise. He tried to make himself girl-like and he ran his fingers through his hair, which had grown out since the barbering Bry had given him.

He thought of Bry and wondered how he was doing. He probably found a shallow place to walk across the river or a narrow place; he's probably halfway to Ontario. Or China. It took a lot out of me, but I saved him without an ounce of help.

When they found a pond where there was a little break in the trees, Martin unlaced his boots and took off his clothes and laid the gun down on a rock. He was filthy. He had a slight rash. He felt the air touch his skin. It made him itch in one place and brought relief in another. He felt the water with his fingers and it was cold but he slipped in. Oh!

On the edge of the pond, Cuff carefully pawed at its surface, which had a size and shape unusual to her. She liked creeks, but this water's other side was not to be seen; it was a big pond and she tasted the flavor left on her paws. She paced along the shoreline and took a long, thoughtful testing drink by lapping the liquid into her mouth with her curled tongue and then she slowly, heavily lumbered in, losing her weight, lifting her feet one by one like a dancer until she and the boy could feel slimy plants rubbing against their six legs. The water was snow cold and the bear pawed her way along, muttering and complaining, and then paddled back to the shore a few feet away and climbed out slowly and shook herself very deliberately, and Martin clambered out too by grabbing at rocks and pulling himself up to dry ground and then stuffing his wet legs in his dirty black trousers, tugging them up inch by inch, and he put on his boots and hugged the bear, who was shaking herself, water flying off her fur, and he went off without the gun but then remembered and came back for it because he was lost in the woods and might have need of such a thing, although he wasn't easy about killing.

After that, they were three or four nights in the woods and he knew his mother must be worried half to death, and his father must be sorry and he thought they were making the boat wait for him and that would make them impatient. Or. Another thought . . . Had they left without him? He jumped up and down a few times to test his legs. How fast could he get back to camp? He wanted food more than anything he could even imagine. He wanted to eat something cooked. How many berries could he swallow? Never enough to feel full. How many berries would it take to keep him alive? At home his mother made him pecan biscuits and saved him the buttermilk and now it was raw mushrooms and roots.

One night he kept walking until sunup. He thought he might come upon a farm or a campfire but how would he know if a campfire meant friend or foe? A man with a gun could kill Cuff in a minute. Out here in the forest he could yell for help but there was probably no one to hear him and he kept tripping over snags and once he landed on a thorn bush and screamed until Cuff sat down by him and put her paws over her ears. It was then that Martin cried for a while. The thorn plant had sap that made him itch like a thousand bites and Martin said: Bear, we have to walk. I itch all over and we have to get somewhere before I starve. I'm telling you. I eat or die.

Try leaves.

He had never heard Cuff speak before, but now she expressed her opinion. The woods were not cold or hot but there were mosquitoes and bugs that flew in his eyes and bit his neck and behind his ears and when it got dark he tried to crawl under Cuff but she moved away and still there were bugs big as his hand, little as his tears. He could make a night fire but he might burn down the forest and stupidness is the worst of all sins. Cuff was the opposite of stupid because she used her eyes and nose and ears and never got too hungry because the forest was full of food for her and she was born knowing what to eat. Even without a mother, she found the right things. He tried getting down on his hands and knees again but it was hard to see where he was going because his head wasn't made like a bear's on the front of his neck. You have an advantage, he said to Cuff, but just remember there are Indians who eat bears and wear their skins so don't take any chances. He lay down under the confines of bear fur when Cuff would allow it and thought about the camping trip he'd made three years back with Patton. They were out setting traps. They had a small tent and one person carried it and the other one carried two rolled-up blankets and a saucepan. Martin was ten and he skipped ahead paying no attention to where he was going because he didn't have to. Really, Martin never had to pay much attention to anything because someone else was always there to look after him. Sometimes Patton would grab him and swing him up in the air. They went into a stream and splashed each other but neither of them could swim so they were always on their feet. Before Patton had killed the mother bear, Martin had loved him best of all people and even now he wished that Patton would come walking along just parting branches and laughing and making jokes the way he always did. Right now, that would be the best thing if Patton would grab him and throw him in the air.

He got up on his scratched, itchy legs and said Get up to Cuff and the two of them took off like wind blowing fast for as long as they could run straight and after a while he felt something different than he had ever felt. First Martin ran to the count of one thousand, then turned right and ran to the count of five hundred, then turned left. Straight for a thousand steps, then right again. Was it a circle? No. It was a line toward something he meant to find. Something he had always wanted. And he was close to it. He could see stars blinking through the overhanging blur of leaves. He was going to fly. He was free of weight. He was some creature no one had ever seen.

But of course there was rain and it came at them, slashing through branches, so that after a while there was a slight rift between the boy and the bear because the bear would prefer a cave and the boy preferred a shelter of branches. The boy was afraid of caves. He used the bear as his cover, was protected by the bear, and managed at least a few hours of sleep during which he dreamed of a fish that had to be carried to water.

60

The Dickinsons clung to the campsite as it filled and emptied with travelers going west. They made friends and then watched the friends board steamboats or move on in a wagon train. John rode off every morning sure that sooner or later he'd come upon his son, who should not have been given the gun. I should have shot the bear myself, John thought. The boy thinks because I was away for a time, I don't have the authority I had at home.

When news leaked out that the *New Statesman*'s boiler had exploded and the boat had caught fire, when it was heard that fifty passengers had died in the smoke or drowned, Lavina said Martin had saved their lives by running away. She said it to John, she said it to Electa, she said it to Gina. She thanked God in His Heaven but suddenly John decided they must proceed by boat even without the boy due to the descent of the water level. It was almost August. The search for Martin was finished. He'll find his way to some wagon train. My son is no fool. He's canny. He's sneaking around out there watching me hunt for him. He's almost fourteen. We'll find him settled in St. Jo with his brother. We should hurry. We should board the *Arabia* while there is still space for us.

Lavina put her hands over her ears. This was the moment when she should resist. She swallowed and looked for the strength she had grown in herself on the trail, but her courage had drained away with the arrival of John.

For a year, the *Arabia* had been serving towns on the Missouri River, sometimes going as far into Indian territory as Pierre, South Dakota, bringing dry goods and groceries, hardware, boots, shoes, and hats to the various merchants who ordered these valuable things. Bringing migrants, immigrants, and now, among other treasures, the *Arabia* was rumored to be carrying four hundred barrels of Kentucky bourbon straight from the source. There were other barrels packed with Davenport Ironstone china, including a flowered teapot with matching cups, and there were glass items packed in straw: whale-oil lamps, tumblers, and empty inkwells. There were buttons and shoehorns and gloves. There was fabric enough to furnish two retail shops. There were tools and tiles and the lower deck of the *Arabia* was loaded with wagons heavy enough for the Santa Fe Trail, all of them stuffed with bedding and family goods. This big boat weighed more than four hundred tons when loaded and there were no cabins or berths available at such a late date, but there were carpeted salons with chandeliers. There was wood paneling. The staterooms opened onto the promenade.

When Captain Terrill predicted that the trip to Independence would require a struggle upstream for seven or eight days, Lavina said she could not sleep so many nights on an open deck in public. For heaven's sake, Father, she said: Couldn't we, shouldn't we wait for another boat. (And their son?) But the river was lower and slower every day, which made a collision with underwater branches more and more likely. After Independence, going on to Westport and St. Joseph would require another three or four dangerous days. It was now or never.

Patton is waiting for us, said John, to inspire his wife, although he was operating on faith, as usual.

For passage from St. Louis to Independence the Dickinsons paid twelve dollars for wagon, animals, and human beings. They were now nearly stripped of the cash Lavina had brought with her from home, and they climbed aboard tired, shabby, and desperately sore at heart. Lavina found it difficult to muster any guidance for Electa or Gina. It was her habit to remind them to smile, to stand up straight, to speak only when spoken to, and to sit with both knees touching under their skirts but now she ignored any misbehavior and pulled herself up the gangplank, gripping the handrail when all she wanted was to run to the woods. She ignored the medley of screaming animals and shouting humans while John led the mules, the pony, and his horse into stalls on the lower deck and parked the wagon there as well. As the *Arabia* whistled and departed the harbor, Lavina and the girls sat dismally on their loose baggage, keeping an eye on the crate of goods they had stowed at the stern by the shuddering wheel. The cows had been put in a forward pen. Having spent some pleasant weeks grazing on summer grass, they, at least, were sleek and fat. There was braying and mooing and neighing from every direction. Pure misery is what Electa called all the chaos through her tears, and Lavina agreed. She was in turmoil as the boat began to churn upriver ever farther from her lost and dependent child. She wanted to scream and beg but she was enclosed in a dark, humiliating sense of her husband's power. Martin will find us, he said through gritted teeth, and she felt no will to fight back. She felt useless and depleted, too low in her mind to move from the seat she had taken on the upper deck. There was shame in her depletion, more than anything else, since she was not staying on the shore waiting for Martin but following her husband's commands. There were high cliffs on both sides of the river again, shutting the world out and closing in thoughts that were incoherent. A boy lying in grass. A corpse. How did she come to be crushed between steep earth walls under a sky bare of clouds, and where was her boy and where was this hellish tunnel going to end?

We selected her on the basis of a letter, a woman from the east was saying to someone nearby. Lavina was not listening, but she could not help overhearing. My second cousin wrote to us that the *Arabia* was next to none for comfort a year ago . . .

The words floated past while Lavina thought of Brother Borden and his abrupt departure from the campsite. He had kept his distance after John's arrival and she had missed his gentle attention to her needs. Concern such as no one had shown her for the longest time. He had made her feel happy and somehow likable and she missed the eyes behind those round glasses, wire-rimmed, eyes that studied her expressions for signs of pleasure or pain. She had looked into them, they had looked back at her, and now she had lost that regard without quite realizing what it meant to her. Lavina looked at the passengers around her and wished she could tell Brother Borden how their clothes described their destinations as accurately as their accents. He'd enjoyed her little commentaries. She'd tell him about the men wearing homespun and soft hats who would obviously buy teams of oxen to pull their big wagons and go off in search of gold, while the Yankees aboard were better dressed in order to stake a legal claim in Kansas Territory, where they could vote on the Northern side of the statehood dispute. She could see it all very clearly, but who else would care to hear her thoughts? There were Mexicans and Negroes and even a party of Indians on the upper deck. Brother Borden would be amused by that. Then Lavina heard a woman near her say that a little boy had been killed on the boat last month. He was only twelve and they sent him down on a flatboard to unload wood.

It was a slaveboy, someone chimed in.

Well a slaveboy can still have value.

Lavina looked over at her daughters, who were sitting at a table in hopes of tea, Electa swinging her leg back and forth over her knee and Gina picking at her fingernails and then her nose.

Well his owner got a settlement, said the woman whose accent was from Georgia and whose clothes were starched.

If you want to know the worst thing, there were a hundred infantrymen on this boat a year ago. And *then* the cholera struck.

How many died?

A woman, untying her bonnet, said grimly: We weren't informed.

It's all over Missouri, killing man, woman, and child.

Maybe this boat is just plain unlucky.

Lavina sat watching her daughters taking tea while their brother might well be stretched out, sick and dying alone in some frightful place. Oh, dear God, we should have sent out a search party, waited forever, offered our wagon as reward. Did the little slaveboy have a mother? She could see her husband sitting quietly on their packing crate and she wondered how he could live with himself.

61

John saw a game of cards being played and he had it in mind to interfere. The boat was loaded with nothing much better than merchants and gamblers and land agents. There were cards being slapped on a table in front of his daughters and, up by the prow, a group of Baptists was holding a prayer meeting as if their notions of worship had any business being enacted in public. In the salon, there was a game of dice run by a real professional who displayed watches, earrings, and pieces of money, inviting anyone with fifty cents to throw. John sat on the crate rubbing his hands and ever watchful, but his heart was behind him, left in the swirl of muddy water and bracken and filth and regret that consumed the St. Louis Harbor. He knew his part in the family tragedy, but he could not put a cause to it. His poverty was unimportant. Why send Patton away with the warrants, which were the only thing that stood between the family and starvation? Warrants earned by old soldiers who had no use for them and sold them or traded them cheap. Warrants Patton might well have lost. John had felt a little ashamed of his sons for collecting them, but they were often easier to come by than cash. He closed his eyes so as not to look at his wife. Then he felt dizzy, the boat plunging and swaying like his thoughts. He longed to lie down but there was no place to do that during the day and barely a safe place at night and there was the crate with everything not packed in the wagon, which Lavina had cleared of valuables because of passengers she viewed as untrustworthy. John had elected to sit on the crate. He had taken note of Baptists and Mormons, but there were wandering con men, too, looking for customers, and he kept an eye on his wife, who might be taken in by some sales pitch.

Dinner that night was delayed until just before nightfall when the captain cut the engines and the crew managed to tie the vessel to a well-rooted tree. But the boat was knocked so much by waves and current that plates flew to the floor and food fell on laps and none of the passengers could eat. It began to rain. At nine, a bell rang and everyone without a cabin scrambled for a mattress. These were to be wedged throughout the salon or under the overhanging roof of the open deck. Lavina ordered the girls to bring up quilts from their wagon but Gina refused, too afraid to descend into the dark, so mother and eldest daughter crept carefully down a ladder and felt their way between wagons on the lower deck. Regal in their white hoods, the wagons looked like monuments. To folly, Lavina was thinking. And Electa said: I'm going back to St. Louis, as she climbed in over the tongue of their movable home, unlacing the canvas.

Hand things down, said Lavina calmly. It's a boy, isn't it? Someone you met.

No. What boy?

I know my own daughter, don't I? What Lavina knew was that her daughter, even in the dark, was a looking glass where she found her own reflection. You're a romantic, she said.

Do you think we could find a latrine down here?

Just tell me anything about him. It will help pass the time.

Please don't speak about it, Mama. Please. Electa brought the quilts down from the wagon, handed them to Lavina, and quite boldly squatted. Her bloomers were conveniently split between the legs. Lavina handed the quilts back to her a minute later and did the same. What a relief. I've waited hours. They giggled and were pleased with themselves. For a little minute Lavina felt almost happy. Then everything came back.

More than forty passengers were going to sleep on the upper deck, where gentlemen and ladies were separated by a gate. For Lavina, who had never slept in the presence of anyone but her husband and daughters, it meant lying rigid with arms straight along her sides. Here is your chance to sleep under the stars, she said to Electa, hoping to keep the soft mood between them. Later she dreamed she was cradling a baby's head. It had no body but batted its eyes and smiled at her. On the deck of the *Arabia*, Lavina lay looking up at the millions of stars. What necessity did they provide? Wasn't that the new idea, that each particle of the universe was required by all other parts? Each little change created other changes — mules and trees and fish — and when a person can't sleep the mind will wander and it must not think of weather or Indians or cholera or wild animals or apple trees. She must not think of Brother Borden, whose name was James, touching places that were hers alone. James Borden touching what he called her clamorous and comparing it to the tongue of a bell. She felt the now familiar ache he had taught her to feel and put her hand between her legs while the *Arabia*'s passengers slept on their inside bunks and outside mattresses, and the river swept along, pulling down sycamores, oaks, and walnut trees that grabbed the dark water.

The next morning, passing Hermann, Missouri, John noticed nothing about the town or port. Perched on the packing crate, he was concentrating on memories that threaded through his life like sutures, and when a young man tried to draw him into conversation, he did not hear. He did not notice a man of dark skin on the dock singing a Methodist hymn. An Indian brought out a drum and danced on the upper deck while passengers threw coins. Dizzy and weak, John stared at the foam that blew off the rear paddle wheel. The overall picture was sky, shelf of land, turning wheel, and that hard spinning water. Round and round. His head ached and he rubbed it. He had lost his paltry breakfast over the rail. Along the riverbank wagons were clumped together and people gawked at him from shore, a man who had left his child to die of starvation, to freeze, to be killed. Children ran alongside the big churning boat trying to keep up.

62

Taking advantage of the melted snows of the Rocky Mountains, the *Arabia* was heading to the trading posts on the Missouri's upper waters and she was steadfast now, struggling against a current strong enough that she sometimes stood still for long moments, going nowhere. When she neared a shoreline campsite, the drone of her engines and throb of her paddle wheel brought people down to the edge of the river on foot or on horseback looking for flour instead of cornmeal, beef instead of venison, while John sat on his crate and narrowed his eyes and heard only the crumbling of the banks and the chunks of loosened earth that fell hard in the river with loud splashes.

In Jefferson City on the fourth night, the captain gave a dance and residents of the town swarmed aboard. Someone played an accordion.

What of a God who was not intervening?

At Booneville, while they waited for people to board or depart, Gina begged her father to open the precious crate and retrieve a toy rickshaw that was packed with the spice jars and flour scoop. Perhaps it was an effort to rouse her father, to remind him of her need of him, to jostle him or shame him, but John continued to sit on the unopened crate in order to remember the place in the creek at home where Cuff had liked to fish. What was it about that particular ledge that a bear would so favor it? He sat on the crate watching Lavina, who sat on a bench with her broad shoulders back and a look of disdain for the changing world. Or was it grief? Must he carry her pain as well as his own? On the lower deck there were hundreds of crates destined for the merchants in Independence or the City of Kansas or St. Jo farther upriver, but Lavina would not have her own crate mixed in with those crates and possibly lost or stolen by guile or mistake. What kind of cargo do we carry? she had asked the captain one afternoon because, she said, a few long and narrow identical crates on the lower deck gave her reason to suspect they might hold Northern contraband or guns. She had heard about this from Brother Borden. Pushy abolitionists were sending Sharps rifles out to Kansas

Territory. Afraid that they might be put off the boat due to Lavina's nosiness, John had tried to distract her, finally asking to be shown the manifest and he might then have laughed at his wife if he'd any mind to do so. Twenty crates of boots. Ten crates of horse tack: bits, stirrups, spurs, bridles, and whips. Brandied cherries from France. Hats, cigars, clay pipes, wooden buckets. There were shovels and washboards and canning jars and three cast-iron stoves along with flasks, thimbles, pepper sauce, pickles, ax heads, and spoons. There were bolts of blue wool and black silk, cases of cognac, champagne, boxes of candles, tins of nutmeg, coffee grinders, and nine kegs of pine tar and six of square nails weighing one hundred pounds each. There were thousands of glass beads to trade with the Indians. For the same purpose there were two dozen flintlock guns painted red with a brass serpent inlaid in the stock. (The white man desired furs and the Natives desired guns.) Barrels were smooth-bore not rifled, so they could shoot a lead ball or a found piece of gravel. The Hudson's Bay Company asked for twenty beaver pelts per gun. Captain Terrill was glad to share this information. He was proud of his boat and its trade mission. If there were Sharps rifles aboard, they were well hidden in the hold and unmentioned on the manifest, which also failed to list a box of lead printer's type meant for an abolitionist newspaper in Lawrence.

With every new crate brought aboard, the crew had to redistribute the cargo using hooks to pull the loads on long planks that ran from bow to stern on the lower deck while John sat on his family's treasure and heard the gasp of the steam pipe as a last breath whenever the river burst through a dam of fallen branches.

63

On the south side of the river, Bry looked for a possible crossing. The cliffs were sheer and steep and there were flatboats on the water and passing pirogues and sometimes canoes and there was not a minute when he would not be seen. Fording the river, trying to get to the north side, he would announce himself as a runaway. He thought he would cross at night or try to float on his back as he had seen it done in Louisville by the boys who dove for coins. He couldn't swim any more than Josiah could or Young Jim, who one time fell into a crick and nearly drowned. Bry couldn't see into this dark, churlish water that could have a rock waiting to meet his skull. He sat in a crouch, afraid to fall asleep for lack of a good hiding place. There were too many people here and there along the shore to find any privacy. Finally, when the sun fell behind the westward trees, he began his descent. Sliding, clinging, he was filthy and yet the river made everything clean if it didn't kill you first.

He was cold and terrified as he slipped into water so turgid he could almost walk on it. Then, in a sudden sweep of current, he was swept off his feet and pulled under. Something grabbed his legs like a living hand and in a minute he was choking, head up, struggling, head down, on his back, flapping his arms, water in his throat his nose his mouth his lungs and he went down again, grabbed at anything, at bare nothing, then pushed, rolled, head up to breathe, head down in water too fast to wrestle, and he rolled his face to one side and tried to look back at the world.

64

Trees hold out their arms. Martin made his own songs . . . *like God weaving a shirt made for me.* His voice was shaky due to hunger and a weariness such as he'd never felt. All he'd wanted was to get away from his father; all he'd wanted was to save his bear and now he was swallowed by trees and he could hear their language, could almost speak it but they were so encumbering, so tall and everywhere and wise like a community; he took in air and made it feed him. Air and sound and smell is what he ate, the being of everything and his own being the same. Beneath him, the ground, tender with forgotten life. Embedded fish bones! Embedded snails and lizards dead a thousand years. The ambling bear walked over these fragments and stirred them. She was majestic. She stalked and chewed and nudged the boy, always encouraging, fur thickening, self fattening, eating pupae and cherries and hazelnuts as she had done just this time last year when she found delicacies by some justified instinct. Then it was acorns she'd loved, secret to a good winter's sleep, and now she would find them again. Martin yawned. Hungry, he supposed these things and dreamed them into being. Sometimes he stopped and went to sleep under a tree. Sometimes he sang; sometimes he prayed. He communed with the snail that climbed the stalk of a fern and with the fern itself. All it required was breathing, simple breathing, and listening through his skin like the little salamander who crawled over his foot all glowing green. And when the hunger was too fierce in him, the bear found something good for him to eat. They could speak now as equals, although Martin was dependent on the bear for food and warmth. When it rained he was soaked to his skin and he wondered why God made a human defenseless. He remembered the birdman saying that as people cut down trees and put up houses they surrounded those houses with thornbushes and then the loggerhead shrikes had more to eat. Why's that? Martin had been so charmed by the man who had ruined their lives. The shrike has claws too small to hold its prey is what he'd been told, but it can impale a little bird on thorns and keep it for dinner.

So building a house isn't bad for nature? Bad for trees and good for shrikes.

I have no claws, said the boy to the bear. Try ants.

It went on like that. No human has ever been here before is what Martin thought. I am the very first! It was a month of Sabbaths, so tired was he of listening to God; he said: I am the first human here! Like Adam. He proclaimed it to God: This is mine for the taking. He planted a foot on the ground to prove his domain. He did not need a warrant to possess this land. But when was it made, all of this? Trees pointing like compasses. Go east, go west, and what if I never move another inch? Where is my bear? Cuff? I am so hungry. It was the longest day ever and he yelped out loud when he stumbled on a thing that laughed. Crouched over, sharpening a knife, a woman was staring up at him. A blue bead hung on a string around her neck and there was red paint in the part of her hair and some streaks of red around her eyes and she rubbed the knife on her dress, never smiling after the laugh that sounded like a sneeze.

Is that a real wigwam? He was having a dream. Cuff, I found an Indian!

The woman looked Martin up and down

and then went back to the knife, rubbing it at an angle against a stone and testing it with a finger while Martin stood in his torn clothes with his bitter breath and put a hand to his mouth. Please, he said, using a word she must understand: Hungry. He put his gun down and pointed with a finger to the pot that sat at some distance on three stones and a fire. He inched toward it and lifted it with both hands and drank down the contents, burning his mouth, having no thought for the woman's need, and when it was gone he ran his tattered sleeve across his smeared mouth and belched, wondering if Cuff had found something as nice to eat in the woods. Cuff? he yelled. Cuff? Well, thank you, he said, because now he remembered his manners. I have a bear, he said, putting the empty pot on the ground and pointing at the jagged trees. He made the shape of the animal with his hands and growled. He pawed at the air.

The woman got to her feet.

He had eaten her food and now the thought of it caught him because he was happy to have eaten but ashamed. I'm lost, he said, bowing his head, and when he lifted his eyes, it felt easier to make a bond with hers. We walked here from St. Louis, he said. I don't know how far that is. He touched his heart with a finger. I don't know how many days.

There was some movement inside the wigwam. Martin looked at it, but the woman made a sign with her arms and hands: Go. Away.

Martin lifted his feet one at a time and put a flat hand above his eyes to show that he was looking for something. I have to find my bear. And I am so tired. He put his two hands under his face and closed his eyes, to show his need for sleep. The food had exhausted him. He could hardly stand. His knees wobbled. He pointed at the wigwam.

The woman used the knife to make a drawing in the dirt. The drawing looked like a mound. It went up on one side and down on the other and there was a door in the middle that she filled with a scribble so he could see it was open. Wigwam? He used the word again and she frowned. Then she stood up and pointed. In the distance, he could see the top part of a hill.

There, she said, making a motion of wind blowing and rain coming down. She got down in her crouch again and added something to her drawing that looked like a circle next to the hump. She put ripples inside the circle. Was he taking the lesson? He nodded and she raised her hand, apparently wanting to be quit of the boy who had eaten everything she had made for whoever was rolling and groaning in the wigwam and might be about to come out. Might be a savage. Someone to kill him or scalp him. She held her hand palm out and it was a sign Martin could read, and he had her knife-drawn map in his head and he turned away and went to look for his bear: Come on now, girl. Cuff? You find food?

Acorns!

And they came an hour or two later to a body of water that might have been round like the drawing made on the ground with the knife, although he could see only one side of it, and the water was very cold and there were no ripples or stirrings and the bottom was too far down to see. There were pretty pin oaks and water oaks overhanging it, clearly reflected, never moving or breathing; waiting. He saw a muskrat dome and heard the curdling cry of a bird, but he saw no living creature and he took off his clothes and tested the water with his foot. When Cuff plunged in, she turned her head to look back as Martin slowly and carefully felt his way in, letting the water inch up his legs as he moved his feet along the lake's beginning with its slimy reeds like hairless animals and he remembered the pond where he had paddled with Cuff when their journey began. But now Cuff was buoyant. She moved her legs as if she knew how to swim, always had, and it was a joy to see his bear practicing for her future life. Honk of geese, hoot of an early owl. The big birds from the north landed in a noisy gang and began grubbing and gobbling on the water. They dipped and partly disappeared and resurfaced. They paddled and splashed and Martin stood with his bare feet clinging and enjoyed the frolic of the journeying geese until they surrounded the bear and she plowed right through them, once or twice snapping and grinning. Martin turned over on his back and tried to float, moving only his feet, but they kept sinking and he was soon standing on the mud again while Cuff tumbled and splashed among the birds and Martin wanted to join this timelessness, this floating and flapping and pawing at water covered with birds as if sky and water were a single thing. In an upright position he kicked and kept himself going and strangest of all was the fearlessness he felt and then he ducked under and knew he could breathe. He tried counting backward as he pushed through the water in reverse. When he lifted his face, he was glad of the air. I am human, he said to Cuff. He swam to the bear and took hold of her fur. The bear had such strength that she carried him without any complaint. What did she feel in her fur that was different from his skin? Why were they made so differently? Was the fish made only for the bear to eat? (Cuff was fishing.) Was bear only made for a man to eat? Dominion is what the Bible called it. Why? What point was there to dominion, domination, dominating? Only to survive longer than somebody else? Martin kicked. He paddled. He shut out every noun from his mind and opened his eyes underwater, seeing the plants and mud and sand and never naming a one of them, just seeing color and movement and shape. He made bubbles out of his nose and rose up and the air fit his need so perfectly that there was no word to describe the feeling except relief. From fire, smoke. From water, death. From air the unconsciousness of breath and he was thinking with words again. My father is wrong about everything. Dominion is not the point.

The bear and the boy got out of the water. They dried themselves and went to a bush that was loaded with autumn berries. Martin had forgotten the gun. He'd left it behind at the woman's camp. He had never shot anything, but the gun had made him feel safe. When he stretched the arm he had used to carry the gun, he noticed the pleasant lack of weight. He had found an Indian and a wigwam and his father would listen to the story if he ever saw him again. His father, who often said: Silence! Quiet, boy! He had been spanked for mumbling and beaten for speaking too fast, too loudly, too slowly. Be silent. Children should be seen and not heard, or not even seen. There should be no children, no bears, no sons. No music, no dancing, no stories. No games. Obedience. Obedience. Dominion of the fathers for keeps. I lost your gun, he heard himself say and his father said back: Never mind.

Beside the lake was a hill just as the woman had shown in her picture and the hill had an enormous tree surmounting it. Martin thought it might be a sacred place to the Indians and yet he wanted to climb the hill to see what he could see from the top, where the big tree was shimmering. He signaled to Cuff, who had a trout in her mouth and was galloping over in order to share.

Then Martin, still naked by the lake, began to cry at the sight of the offering bear. He got down on his knees. Come, bear, come to me. He used his shirt to dry his beloved, rubbing her carefully in the right direction, always toward the tail. He put on his wet shirt and then his trousers and led Cuff gently to the hill and there was a small skull at the base of it that Martin picked up to study. Eye dents and toothy jaw. He ran his finger over the cheekbones and felt the smoothness that had once supported a furry face and then noticed a small opening in the side of the hill — an opening just where the skull had been laid. Pawing at the hole and finding the ground soft, he found he could enter the hill or the mound or whatever it was by shoving his hands and knees through crusts of ground and he dropped his head to avoid the jagged roof and Cuff fit herself in behind him. Martin's hands bled from the scratches and cuts that opened on contact with the rocks, but he pushed on into the hollow hill while Cuff came after him sniffing and scooching. They sat for a few minutes in the dim quiet of the place and took their bearings. They were remote from everything else, as if they had entered a blank eternity. They were no longer hungry and there was a clean, damp breeze coming from some place in the back of this cave. Martin felt the walls, testing the surface and finding a cleft that led into darker darkness. He let the bear push past him to go in first. Important not to lead Cuff into a space too narrow for her girth, he thought, although she would be skinny come spring. He lay on his side and watched her move ahead though he was losing the thread of his plan. He could feel the hairs on his neck lift as he pushed with his feet and pulled with his hands, moving an inch, an inch, sure that his bear was hoping to find her bed in the stall of the barn. Both of them wishing such a place lay in front of them, they pushed on into the pure, cold underground.

He touched the top of Cuff's head, which was bony under the flesh, and there were the big geese leaving the lake to fly south, leaves trickling down outside, worms digging in, and the bear was sated under the tree of the world while its old roots reached under them to hold the mound and its cavern. Bellows of beasts in the upper world, and ten thousand keepers and nesters underneath. It came to Martin that here was the point. He whispered instructions to his bear and kissed her with love and crawled out of the sheltering hill.

65

Under the wigwam's strips of bark, Bry woke up for a few minutes and then fell into his nightmare again, being pulled along the ground in the skin of a beast, dragged to the wooden post and the gleaming knife hot from the fire so his parts could be thrown to the pigs. Or was he doing that squealing? He felt the sound in his chest, his throat, and his mouth after a poke of the blade bathed him in squirting blood, the pigs making riotous noises and the man with the knife wiping blood off his hands. Will I die? Is this dying? Will he sew back on what he cut away, Mama Bett? Where am I?

Here.

They caught me.

You were drowning.

So it was Emly who sat on her knees in her house where no one went in or out but her children, the master, and the hen who laid eggs and yet he was listening to her childhood, he was lying on her mat and hearing about the time she was taken from her mother's breast and sold to a woman who fancied a pet and allowed her to play at the end of a leash, given no words to know except come, fetch, rub my neck, my poor tummy, say nothing little monkey or I will send you out to dig yams.

Who does such a thing to a child?

Please, remember this for me.

They won't believe it. I'm not a man. Did the woman love you? With her leash?

She sold me when I was too big for a pet.

How big?

I was eight.

To our master.

Sleep now.

66

On the fifth day, Lavina was approached by a passenger wearing a clean, tailored jacket and vest. Tipping his hat, he said: You are among the blessed, ma'am. He clicked his heels together and introduced himself: Mister Able D. Kirk.

She was inspecting him. She, who was among the blessed.

I refer to those who are making their way to K.T. He leaned over the rail to study the current and appeared to be pleased.

We are going to St. Joseph, said Lavina, who, until a few weeks ago, rarely spoke to strange men but now exchanged information easily. Where our grown son will meet us, she added, explaining that he had been expected in Louisville and then in St. Louis but there were other ports, other stops, and St. Jo was the final and obvious place. She said: He will have found us land. She said this because an exchange of information was to everyone's advantage when traveling.

Oh, well, said Mister Kirk, and he seemed disheartened. I'm sorry to hear that you are not . . . well, I mean, I can only hope your son has already secured land, as you say. The way prices are rising. He put a finger on the shiny fabric of his jacket.

He will have it secured, Lavina said confidently, looking down at the water as if it might reveal her future.

You put faith in its rightful place above reason. Mister Kirk took a handkerchief from his jacket pocket, shook it, and then blew his nose. He said: After all, faith is exactly what brings us out here beyond the borders of a lawful society. Faith is our historical example. Isn't it? He used his handkerchief to carefully wipe the rail before he put both hands on it. Then he bent backward to examine the expressionless sky. He said: My misfortune is to fall into the category of skeptics who must always know the pluses and minuses, the dashes and dots, before assuming any risk. I admit to a lack of faith in the ways of this new world out here. He turned to look into Lavina's face, which was defenseless. He went on: I will add that I do not feel it quite fair to involve my family in an enterprise purely based on faith so I went to a deal of trouble to ascertain the situation most likely to benefit them. It has been my ardent quest. And I have indeed found the fairest piece of land between Louisville and Frisco. He studied the backs of his hands, his shiny nails, holding them out and shooting his cuffs.

Lavina put her own callused hands behind her back.

To tell you the truth, it was my intention to get ahead of the railroads. I mean, west all the way. But when I set eyes on this location . . . Why, if wheat doesn't flourish there along with anything else one could want to plant in that rich soil . . . if libraries don't flourish there and businesses and schools don't instantly spring up . . . Actually, I have a lithograph of our town plan, if you would care to see it. Only to amuse you while we chug along on this river of opportunity. He chuckled, then reached into a valise on the deck by his feet and brought out a folded brochure showing churches and houses and pretty hills with people shopping and chatting and walking comfortably on a paved street.

Kansas is only a territory, Mister Kirk.

And did I travel all this way and bring my children out of a safe home and a good school in order to set up in another finished place? I did not, I did not, madam. I wanted to get in at the groundbreaking and help make a new town according to my own values because I regard the duties of citizenship as highly as you regard your duties to the Lord, or so I suspect with regard to your faith. I am a man of this world. It is right here that I seek immortality.

Lavina had read in the *Lexington Missouri Express* a few days before that every steamer up the Missouri was taking more and more emigrants out to Kansas. By now, fifteen thousand people had passed up the dark river and as many more had gone by land, people standing in groups waiting their turn to cross the Kansas River because a hundred and sixty acres would be granted to each head of family who settled there. What about the fighting? Those abolitionists. She looked at the traveler. He might well be one of them, toting a rifle in his valise.

No little skirmish will discourage a patriot, said Mister Kirk. And it will be over before we can blink, by which time I will have an up-and-running farm with fields of wheat and I may try some cattle since this is good buffalo country and the creatures must have similarities. Let the slavers and antislavers fight amongst themselves and I will build my empire.

Lavina looked at her husband slumped on his crate.

We who go first will make of K.T. what we desire, is all I'm saying, and I wanted to offer your family a piece of good bottom land if . . . you . . .

Lavina flushed. She who no longer had any authority.

The fact is that the government has released the territory at a bargain that won't last. Civilize the place first and then we go for statehood. He touched his lips. But I'm sure your offspring will choose a fine topographical site near to markets, to neighbors, to a church and school . . .

Lavina put a hand on the gentleman's arm. She avoided his eyes. She was that much taller than Mister Kirk, in fact, that she stepped away and bent her knees and said softly: If I might prevail on you to speak to my husband?

The setting sun glazed the river and Mister Kirk's cuff links sparkled. Homes will be built. Songs will be sung. Babies will be kissed. I wish you could see how the steeples will sit tall in front of the hills . . . how the cottonwoods hug the riverbank. He waved his hands as if for an orchestra. He conducted the river's dark current. A lady friend tells me that the flour there does not

require yeast. Can you imagine? I was looking around for congenial souls, resting my
eyes on your family. Of course I will speak
to your husband.

Lavina decided that Mister Kirk would
determine her future. Because, had she ever
determined it?

67

Nistschu. She kept her face smooth, moving only her mouth. Bry tried an answer. Nitsu. He was awake. He smelled wild onions and mint and meat. It wasn't Emly's house. It was a strange bark hut where he was lying on a mattress of grass and cattail fluff, covered with a blanket that had known other bodies over time.

I crossed the river? This the north side?

You almost dead. Here is south.

Where is here?

She laughed, making a sharp sound in her nose. I am here.

I need to go north. If they catch me again . . .

Hah. I too.

Bry crawled out of the warm bed, but he could not attain his full height until he bent down and went through the doorframe. Outside, he held his arms out shoulder-high. He was healed if a man who is not a man can ever be healed. A woman had offered her bed and crouched to one side of it to feed him broth. She showed him how she had pulled him out of the river after he got dragged eastward by the current, losing all the distance he'd traveled on foot. Her laugh was unlike any he had heard, like blowing through a wide-open pipe. He had nothing to offer but the muscles he flexed, old man that he was. He saw by the cook fire the metallic gleam of a gun. He saw by the sun the late time of day, although he wasn't certain where he stood in relation to the river. He sniffed deeply, trying to smell running water. He sat down in a heap, suddenly tired again, but she brought him food after which he picked up the gun and studied it. Take, she said. We go? She made some paddling motion with her arms and watched his face.

He finished the last of her meat supply that day, a meal of squirrel and onion and pounded acorns and mint. It meant using fingers and wondering what would come next, but while he ate, she began packing things in a deerskin parcel. He watched her wrap up roasted kernels of corn, seeds of the sunflower, acorn meal and corn meal and pemmican, which she brought forth from some hole in the ground of her house.

He believed all of it was a gift for his journey but she stood in the late-afternoon sun and tied her hair in a knot and said: We go, and they then walked through fields white people had cut from the forest along the path she had dragged him over in an old buffalo skin. His boots had been lost in the killing river and there was first a cornfield, then a small creek, then a field plowed under that hurt the soles of his feet, then the river, which was only a mile from her camp, by which time his feet were blistered and cut. Goodbye home, she said, waving her arm over her head.

Under a clump of bush and bracken, she kept a canoe made from the trunk of a tree. As he brought it out into the lowering light she sang something not in words that Bry could recognize and he pushed the big canoe into the shallows and she climbed in very confidently, balancing on her knees and pointing at the prow. You.

Bry had that memory of the river that had tried to kill him, and as he climbed over the gunwale, his trembling and shaking made the canoe rock dangerously but he managed to get down on his old sore knees as she pushed her paddle against the shore. Her first strokes against the current were cautious, as if she did not have the knack of paddling, and he wanted to help but he sat looking ahead, straight of back and afraid to turn. This was the only way to cross the Missouri and if he held himself very still, hardly breathing, he might survive it. But suddenly she stopped her strange whistling song and yelped: You work! And he touched the second paddle, which lay mostly behind him in the belly of the dugout, and after some minutes of finding his balance he yanked it and lifted it and slid it into the water and the old canoe lurched and twisted until she showed him how to pull his paddle through water strewn with this and that. Showers and sun, showers and sun, and the air held more smell than color, the bottom-lands with their cottonwoods leaking, and Bry sneezed, rocking the dugout again so that it almost spilled them into the river. She kept a tuneless chant going until at last he crawled out of the dugout on the north side of the Missouri a few minutes after dark. I can make my way now. I thank you with all my heart. He put his hand over the central part of his chest.

No! she said, laughing her piping laugh. You my slave they no stop you. You be safe with me. In canoe.

He knew that even north of the river anyone could take him, report him, sell him back to the South, and slowly he began to see that her claim of ownership might help him proceed although it was a bitterness in his ears to hear the word *slave* spoken out loud. She said it again: My slave, and brought out a little of the pemmican to give him strength as the stars appeared to remind them of guidance. They slept curled apart in a small skin tent she had brought in her bundle. No dreams.

Bry had not curled around a woman since his afternoons with Jemima and even in this close company, his sleep lasted only a few minutes at a time. When he opened his eyes, he could not believe the starlight that leaked through the skin stretched above him, and in the morning the half-tree floated and swam through the land when he paddled, dabbing at the foam on the river's skin.

Sometimes in the first days, they passed campsites full of wagons such as the one that had hidden Bry on the steamboat ride. To ride a wagon on a boat. To be boatsick in a wagon. Now he was in a boat going east instead of west with this woman, Nistschu. He was bitten by insects and he scratched himself raw. The morning sun hurt his eyes and he wished the woman would sing something other than her dirge. Delaware, she told him on the second afternoon. She said it clearly. Del-a-ware. Lenape, she said next. She anointed him with bear grease and he got no more bites. On the third day they went for some miles on the Missouri and then took a narrow passage up to the Mississippi, which was not difficult if they worked together against the current. Three long days to reach the Macoupin Creek and then only five miles to the Illinois River. Was Mama Bett alive? Does a man feel mother love or does he know only the want of it?

68

The *Arabia* stopped in Independence, or Independence Landing as it was sometimes called, with its blustering frontier market. A good part of the freight was then unloaded below the quay, which sat high up on bluffs that came right to the river's edge and then dropped sheer-sided to water level. The unloading made for the usual racket of braying and squealing and cussing, while passengers stood on deck and pointed at what was left of the steamboat *Saluda* that had exploded six years before with upper parts still visible. Two hundred people dead, they said, and the Bostonian, who had first spoken to Lavina days before about the drowned boy, declared that the paddleboats should be inspected regularly.

Wouldn't account for the boilers, said Mister Kirk, the man who was heading to the promised land of K.T.

A sandy island sat in the middle of the

river, causing traffic to choose between left and right sides, but the passengers stood firm, and the river went on pouring itself eastward to the Mississippi, still in some hurry, and finally at the quay, people unloaded the wagons that would carry them west or southwest in search of glory. Independence was as far as most people would go by boat because it was the beginning of both the Santa Fe and Oregon Trails. Most groups started out on a trail in the company of seven or eight wagons. Two or three families, a few single men. They would find a longer train and join it, elect a captain. They were seekers. They were religionists. They were off to make their way in the world. A few young men had been sold to a company. Show him the ropes. Get him out where the land is clear. There were frontiersmen, French Canadians, old voyageurs who knew the West like civilized people know cupboards. There were adventurers, gamblers, fur traders, Mexicans, discharged soldiers, and criminals running away from whatever was chasing them. The women were reckless, hard, frightened, Irish and motherless, missionaries and harlots. They were Quakers and Baptists and Methodists and Presbyterians, daughters and servants, grannies and aunts, nursing mothers and virgin brides. Each of them stopped at the famous lucky spring in the center of Independence to fill their water casks and drink to success. Then, eventually, after outfitting themselves as they collectively or individually saw fit, they set off in their huge, rumbling wagons, tall ships pressing against the prairie winds, passing graves that were quick to accumulate, averting their eyes or bowing their heads.

John and Lavina and the girls stayed on board with those going upriver. John had brought Beulah to the upper deck to help someone unload a heavy packet but there had been no meeting with Patton, which meant he was waiting for them in St. Jo. Dinner was called soon after they left port and John left Beulah tied and went in to his meal.

After that unloading at Independence, the *Arabia* puffed its way upriver in the late afternoon of September 5 above a fallen walnut tree that lay just below the surface, branches twisting in all directions like hidden fingers with long claws. In the galley the cook was serving cutlets on plates stamped with the *Arabia*'s motto: *Never Too Far*. In the salon, the diners were chatting, asking their children to sit up straight and ignoring the sins of children who were not their own. Travel required social generosity. John was seated with his family at a table set for twelve. When he felt the boat lurch, he reached for Gina. Then they all knew a hard shock through their backs and legs as the submerged walnut tree pierced the lower deck and the great *Arabia* shuddered. In a matter of minutes water was rushing across the main deck.

Oh dear God help us!

The cook dropped a plate and rushed to the salon, where diners were falling off chairs or grabbing one another as the boat listed to its port side, men cursing loudly and women screaming such shrill screams that they could surely be heard on shore. A few of the men grabbed the only lifeboat, lowered it, jumped in, and started rowing in haste. They might have been disciples, fishers of men going for help, but Lavina grabbed Gina away from John, who was still clinging to the edge of the table, and carried her straddled at her waist straight to the rail where she could see the lifeboat disappear in a lowering mist. Come back here! she yelled as she had so often done when her boys went slinking off after a petty household crime. She wanted to throttle the escaping men and there was that unlikely, unfeminine surge of rage again. Come back here this minute! A few passengers joined her at the rail and added more yells, a few of them insults, and the *Arabia* continued to list, as if the river had forgotten how to balance a floating object and the packed lifeboat swung around awkwardly as the men took heed of the shouting and sheepishly rowed back to the sinking ship, climbing up to the deck where they began lowering women and children into the rocking lifeboat as if that had been their first and foremost intention. They called for a small man and Mister Kirk volunteered. He climbed into the lifeboat with the women and children. He rowed with all his vigor and the little boat pushed along toward shore, where there was a small stretch of cabins thrown up against wandering tribes and bushwhackers and bandits. Chunks of the riverbank had been caving off and it was too steep to climb, but Mister Kirk managed to ascend by docking the lifeboat and carefully clinging to outcrops of tree roots. It was a struggle since some of the roots loosened when he pulled and he slipped backward, grabbing and poking at the earth with his pointed shoes. At the top, he was able to reach down with a long branch and help the women up and they, in turn, helped the children. Lavina was still clutching Gina to her waist. Electa was crying about her belongings. Papa? Is he coming? It was a filthy scramble, not easy on shoes and skirts, but the women were soon on high ground holding the hands of children and tucking babies under their breasts, watching the boat roll over with all its remaining contents. The animals had been freed except for a frightened mule that began to bleat. Poor Beulah was tied and no one remembered to release her.

The lifeboat was then sent back for the men who clung to the rail on the high side of the boat, the only part still above water. It picked up the men and a few trunks and valises, which were carried to shore and stacked in the woods, although the crate on the upper deck that had served as John's bench joined two hundred tons of cargo on the river bottom.

It began to rain and on the shore the passengers watched the tied-up mule lift her nose and bray as the boat pulled her underwater.

The next morning, after a cramped night in several donated shelters, all anyone could see of the *Arabia* was the top of her pilot-house and Beulah's floating corpse. The trunks and valises left under the trees had been stolen while the owners were asleep.

The *Arabia* had gone down with everything the Dickinsons had saved after bankruptcy and public shame. Weighing four hundred tons, she had steamed away from St. Louis with a hundred and thirty passengers and now the river would move slowly northwest and then northeast, leaving her buried under silt and then dirt and then a stand of cottonwoods that would disappear when the covering land was planted in corn. The bowls and boots and floor joists, the glass beads and guns all lost.

69

John found his cows. He found the pony, the horse, and Beulah's frightened mate. He had an impulse to mount his old nag and ride away from the nothing that was left to him, the hand of the Lord having once more descended, but he joined what was left of his family and the other *Arabia* passengers who opted to board the steamboat *John A Lucas,* which would take them straight back to Independence to replenish their supplies. John did not speak to the other men nor to his wife. He was beyond words. Everything that counted was gone. The *Arabia* passengers stood at the rail of the sidewheeler *John A Lucas* and stared at the hills they had passed going the other way. They were on a clock running backward. Close to the finish line, they would now have to start again. How would they find the faith for another beginning? John was not standing and staring. He was circling the deck. He was thinking of the three hundred dollars he had sewn into the lining of his jacket, money stolen from his wife and children, and it should have cheered him, but how was he to explain such an unspent sum? He had enough cash to purchase a good wagon and plow, also another mule, but such buying would expose him to questions. He had stayed back. He had let them go off unprotected. He had not gone with his family when they left Jonesville and he had held on to a sum of cash. He wrung his hands, unable to explain the money even to himself. He would have to keep the dollars in the lining of his jacket now and for all time. It was lost, just as Emly was. Lost for good.

On that ship of rescue, Lavina watched her husband circle the deck. He circled for two or three hours — the length of the journey downriver — without ever sitting down. To Lavina, it seemed possible that he might circle one place or another for the rest of his days. She stood up, meaning to go to him, but then sat down again.

70

Pure drugs, chemicals, fancy and toilet articles. Patent medicines. Low Prices. In Independence signs offering comfort and temptation assailed them. They were passengers ruined by a river and they were in a hurry to purchase all manner of things. This time they disembarked. They stood speechless as huge Conestogas rumbled past, some of them pulled by six or eight yoke of oxen. The oxen were bellowing and the disembarked humans wished to cry out as well. How are we to go on? Men on the street cracked whips and the shipwrecked passengers stood watching people who knew what was next, where they were going, and why. Teamsters were putting freight on their wagons, arguing their concerns, and there was the incessant banging of hammers in blacksmiths' sheds where wagons were being repaired and mules and oxen shod. What could explain such presumption? One man burst into tears. It was suddenly clear to each of them what they had lost. John must continue on as part of the whole, never admitting his sins. He must purchase a vehicle, a plow, some bowls, an iron pot, spoons, and a scythe. Seeds. Gone the iron stove. Gone the medicines and apple tree and hope. Where was Patton? Where was Martin? Where was the protection that parents provide their daughters and sons? It would take three days or four or eight to make preparations for further travel and Lavina and the girls took cots at the primitive hotel while John stayed at the stable with the horse and pony and mule and cows. He was leading them there when a storm broke over the whole of Independence with hard rolls of thunder such as he had never heard in any place or part of his life. He was immediately drenched but he got the animals under the stable roof and stood watching the sun reappear as suddenly as it had disappeared minutes before. This was punishing weather, primitive weather, but a train of wagons set off just then on the muddy road in front of him with laughing children sticking fingers out from under the oiled coverings to feel for raindrops. A full-skirted girl rode by on a horse while holding a fringed parasol over her head. Three old men discussed the doctrine of regeneration loudly while sheltering under the stable roof. A soldier walked by holding a revolver pointed ahead. Is Santa Fe worth the trouble? John asked the stableman while he was bargaining for a cart that bore no resemblance to the wagon he had lost or even to the wagon he might have bought with some of the three hundred dollars in his jacket lining. Hadn't his been the finest wagon he could remember ever seeing? And wasn't it built by his own young son? Such a surprising child, wise well beyond his years. Thinking back, John could hardly believe the patience and skill of his boy and now that beautiful wagon was lying at the bottom of the mad Missouri and its flimsy replacement was a cart held together by wire and rope with a shaft too short for a team. He thought of old Reuben. He could not remember where he had lifted the old slave down from the mare and put him in a mule cart he had bought on that final day of the world. The day he had meant to end his life with three hundred dollars in his jacket. You're a French settlement, I hear, he said to the stableman in order to hang on to reality, any word now being better than none.

The stableman licked his mustache. Old

Robidoux père, pure Canadian French, him and the son traveled up the river dealing to the Indins and speaking their putrid tongues. Got reech enough to start thes town.

John looked at his animals, one by one.

Time of Louis Catorze, said the stableman as he accepted ten dollars for the cart. Most here head for the gold, he said. Used ta be fur for trade. Beaver's what dis part was built upon.

John studied the hooves of Gina's pony. She needs to be shod, he said.

The old Kansa village, the liveryman went on, and the Pawnee. Hides, ya know. Buflo robes. Out here's necessity for a night's sleep. He patted the pony. Wanta sell er?

Can't.

Beads, mirrors, guns, and that. Wen on for years but now de Anglish trap on dare land . . . take it without a word a tanks. He shook his head. Not like us.

John's heart was barely beating. Every piece of him ached.

An we got eight hunerd fired up Lawrence just this spring. Burn down de govnor house. Set canon to de hotel and stores so dey got ta sell out of tents, no church, no place for a guest. A shock ta them come out from Boston ta free up nigras.

John asked about shoeing the pony and added that he desired to sleep in her stall overnight.

The old stableman was apparently prepared for anything.

71

She paddled twenty-five miles or perhaps thirty north and then east to a confluence with the La Moine with the Native people along the way offering directions and food. These people lived in small clusters because the tribes had been moved southwest to Indian country but the Illinois tribe hung on in spots, sharing their calumet pipes with the Delaware woman and the runaway slave along with their melons and beans. Gifts of Nanapush, the woman explained to Bry. Word was that the Sioux in Nebraska had killed a white family and it was said around fires at night that there would be reprisals and the fires were quickly smothered at the slightest unrecognized sound after dark. Bry was surprised by these successful, communal lives, and surprised by the small white enclaves they also passed, which were haphazard and ugly. He had passed no communities of any kind until he was taken off to market to be sold to Mister Spradling for a mere four hundred dollars, but now, in the canoe, the Delaware woman spoke of Indian troubles with whites and he tried to understand her unusual English over bird-song and the whirr of bugs and sometimes the sound of trees being logged and groaning like injured giants. The wilderness was not pristine, it was busy with hunters and trappers and loggers and Indian fighters. On rare occasions, when the river was quiet, Bry talked back to the birds, red-tailed hawk his favorite, that sharp, single scream. He thought of the birdman as he paddled, one two, one two, adjusting his weight on his knees. He thought about a white man coming down from the North to talk to a room full of woebegone slaves who were hungry and sick and angry and always exhausted, a man distributing compasses and roughly drawn maps that included mistakes or neglected to mention the direction of a river's current. He thought of a man describing a black woman who had carried a baby to Canada. Then it was hard to avoid the thought of himself as an unwanted thing abandoned by that woman when she ran away. He kept all these thoughts to himself because discussion with the Delaware woman was tiring and the farther they went the more tumult he felt as the land on either side of the river was pretty here and pretty there but sometimes broken or burned or bare. It was ground he didn't touch unless they stopped to defecate or eat or sleep, although once they stopped in a place inhabited by a Sauk group arguing over a treaty the government had made with the Yankton Dakota. Here, the Delaware woman was given no welcome, although the part in her hair was red like theirs. At this place, the Sauk gave her only a handful of beans and told her to be on her way.

One night in the small tent mashed up against the woman, Bry dreamed of Jemima and he woke cold because dreaming of the dead is a sign. He pulled the shared blanket around more of himself and lay there remembering the smooth skin of Jemima's belly stretched over his own conceived child. Bry could not sleep and the Delaware woman woke to his restlessness and told him something about her mother, most of which he couldn't understand. He listened though, and came to believe that mother and daughter had stayed on a plot of land in Missouri they'd claimed when the Delaware left for a reserve in Kansas Territory. Sometime later her father and brother went to Ontario, but her mother refused to go north, where it was cold and dark a long part of the year. Later she met a trapper and left for Wyoming with him.

Bry repeated some of this story in order to understand it but she next told him about a beaver who tried to marry her. A man in a beaver hat? He thought she was mixing up English words. Time meant only more or less heat, more or less damp, more or less hunger or tiredness, and they sat in silence after the story of the beaver until he heard her laughing about what she understood as his mistake. Not me, she said, clapping a hand on her mouth. This a story we tell about a girl and a beaver, crazy Jack!

Bry turned, twisting his mouth into a smile.

You tell, she said.

He told her that he was born to a girl whose grandmother came from Africa. The girl was taught by her grandmother to heal the sick with plants. The grandmother, he added, was taught about those plants by a Cherokee woman, both of them slaves. Bry said: That is my story. He was happy that night, and the next morning they got back in the big half-tree and went on paddling until they discovered an empty cabin some distance from the river where they might eat and sleep in real shelter. The fireplace was cold and there was a smell of rot in the corner but they were glad of the roof and they spread the blanket out on the sagging floor and built a fire with logs that had been left as if to welcome them. With the rifle under his right arm, Bry stepped out into just enough light to catch the flash of a rabbit's tail or the sight of a squirrel rounding a nearby tree. He had never used a gun, but he was bound to make use of the stone fireplace and his sudden sense of tenderness for the woman whose gruel he disliked along with her unpleasant pemmican. Even so, she had fed him. She had coated his skin with bear grease. She had steered their course. Now he would provide, although he was not sure that the gun had a bullet or powder inside and he shook it lightly. Then he crept along holding it up to one eye and peering through the sight. The woods were light-featured, late sun coming down through the leaves, and when he listened, he heard a bird call and saw a whirr of brown feathers and held the gun up to the fancy display of a turkey in the bush and as he fired he heard a shattering scream and he spun around to see a white man holding the Delaware woman, both of them startled by the gunshot, both of them wild-eyed. Let her go! Bry yelled, forgetting the turkey and

411

everything else. The white man was shouting, saying she'd eaten the brains of a live cow. He pulled her against him, holding a knife to her throat, and the woman said something in her language and Bry stepped out with his rifle still raised. Let go! Bry said. Leave my woman alone.

The white man said: Well, it's a nigger, looka here. And then he put the woman between them and Bry had the sensation of enduring something that was already old.

Let go my woman, he said clearly. It was falling dark and he seemed to be standing next to himself, unbelieving.

Sioux bitch eats cow brains fore it's kilt.

Take your hands off her! She's Delaware. He felt no fear, which was the wonder of it. He felt insatiable.

A cow was tooken and she gets scalped.

The woman was shaking her head violently, although her captor had hold of her hair.

But she's Delaware, Bry said, rifle held and aimed.

Same thing and you a runaway don't need no murder to pay for, I bet.

Bry stood in the dark that had fallen on them.

We get a posse up, the white man promised, but he dropped his hands, one from the hair and one holding the knife, and then backed away into the obstruction of trees. A few minutes later a horse could be heard blowing and snorting: leather and metal and male curses.

Bry and the woman packed up and got into the dugout and paddled hard in the night over rocks and logs and unseen interruptions. My woman! she repeated and laughed and reached forward and patted his back.

My slave! he said.

For sleep, they stopped and felt their way in the dark and erected the tent and had nothing to eat. Maybe the turkey had flown away or maybe it lay wounded or dead. They went on the next day past Peoria and skirted it very carefully, the river having become so wide and open that the dugout canoe was visible to anyone on either side. Native woman and black man paddling through white people's land that had once housed the Kickapoo, now gone so thoroughly that only scattered evidence of their past lives remained, bits of bone, broken baskets, and a scalp tied to a stick showing remnants of dried blood.

They went east then through a series of channels and through small settlements that depended on those waters. The paddling was harder than before but there was little portaging and the waters were full of fish. Bry, who had never liked the taste of such creatures, learned to eat perch and pickerel blackened by fire because the woman was adept at catching them, wading into the lapping water, standing like stone, plunging at the necessary moment. The land where they rested was covered by maple and elm festooned by wild grape and bittersweet, the rocky beaches home to shore birds and gulls. But any crossing of land was a misery. The half-tree was heavy and had to be unloaded before it was carried. The two would get out, unpack the canoe completely, leave the woman's bundle hanging on the branch of a tree, and take the canoe on their shoulders. The Delaware woman's shoulders were padded with the blanket. She was supple while Bry was stiff in his legs and knees. The bundle would hang for an hour or two or three and when they returned to the site, it would have to be carried by means of a leather strap on her forehead. The woman seemed not to mind this task but there were long water detours in order not to carry the hollow tree. It was colder now and in the bright mornings the woods were full of creatures pattering and clicking over frosted leaves. Porcupines crept along bristling. Bears could be heard breaking boughs to line winter dens. Falcons. Eagles. Swans overhead. The waters were crusted with ducks and geese. Beaver and muskrats left wakes on the surface and sometimes there was ice to be broken, very thin, on cold mornings. On the fortieth day of their journey, they had their first sight of white pine wedded with maple and Bry looked down at the water where those pretty trees broke into ripples. Once, a bull moose stepped into the reflection and Bry was afraid until he remembered the running deer and thought of the duty of men and went on paddling.

After so many days, the sight of an immense, unending sea made everything small again. It was an astonishment of water and how did they dare to bring their hollow log onto such an expanse with its high, splashing waves? They dragged the canoe over sand dunes, lost their footing on rocks at the shore, and Bry remembered that the promised land was to come after the parted water, and when they plunged in, they were swamped for a minute but they paddled on, finding a different beat. They paddled all day and slept in the log boat while it floated aimlessly toward the east. Then they paddled on for another long day and when they found the mouth of the St. Joseph River they were too tired and stiff to haul the boat up to land. They were too tired to unfold the tent. They were too tired to eat. The east side of the lake had a wide, sandy shore and they lay on it and scratched at bites made by fleas that lived in the sand and they wrapped themselves in the blanket and went to sleep folded together.

Around them the next morning was a swamp and one or the other paddler had to stand in order to find leverage with a paddle as they moved through mist and heard toads sing their final songs. They passed the old landing place of Fort Miami. They passed through the town of St. Joseph as if they had business elsewhere. They passed like old voyageurs lifting their hands to signal friendship when they saw other boats. Bry had devised a hooded cape. No fear, the Delaware woman said, you are my slave.

My woman, Bry said with his grin.

They had been paddling for forty-five days and the rests at night were never adequate but the St. Joseph River was wide as it dipped south around Great Bend, which they avoided, lifting hands again in friendship and speeding on. They were not in the state of Indiana for more than four days but there was word of a sweep being made for runaway slaves. The Indiana River flows east as a tributary of the Maumee, which flows east into Lake Erie and, back in Michigan again, they paddled along a short railway line and the woman dared Bry to take his chances as a stowaway. They had jokes now that suited them.

Then, on a clear and chilly day, after three weeks of peering and straining eastward, Bry saw the land of freedom across a divide of water. There was no way to avoid the city of Detroit where, unknown to Bry, the City Bank of New York had placed a team of three slave catchers to seek out the men and women John had illegally freed as well as the ones who had earlier escaped, slaves mortgaged in return for Benjamin's loan. Those human beings were valued at seven thousand dollars, all proceeds of sale to go to the bank.

72

As they left Independence, John went into the gentlemen's cabin of the *John A Lucas.* It would not take long to get to St. Jo, where he would be earthbound again, and he was sure that Patton would be there because he had not been anywhere else. Or Patton may have joined the thieving, deadly bushwhackers and be wearing a hood and carrying out raids, but John could not believe such a thing of his son, who was only mischievous, never mean. John had slept two nights in the stable, terrified that the horse or pony or mule would be stolen by some unscrupulous Missouri thief. Now, in the men's salon of the *John A Lucas,* he was offered a cheroot. The rules of the boat forbade smoking because of the boilers, but John sat down with two men who had arranged themselves on upholstered chairs. They were beyond rules now, these survivors. They were worn down and disillusioned, impoverished by the shipwreck, failing in any known version of themselves. They had been on the *Arabia,* had lost everything to the river they were riding so precariously, had got ears for the sound of a tree branch scraping and piercing the hull of a boat and, with their throats, uttered unmanly screams. John took a light and sat back to peer through the portholes at a line of healthy trees and sound buildings on the east side of the river and a treeless, desolate bank on the west side. Kansas. Territory of. Settlers on the Kansas side got burned out regularly, the fellow smoker said, and John coughed and expressed surprise. He told then of devils like Atchison, who brought ruffians in from Missouri to rid the land of Free Staters whenever there was an election. He said that John Brown himself had arrived in Kansas, bringing Missouri slaves through Lawrence and into Iowa and up to Canada. It riled the Missourians but it riled Free Staters as well.

Why's that?

We came out here to build up towns and churches and schools. The proslavers take our quiet disposition for cowardice and Captain Brown and his hooligans feel the same way. He's determined to start a war out here whether we like it or not.

It ain't as if the Negro cun survive without us or us without them, another gentleman, sitting with his feet up on a stool, said philosophically. The last outpost of civilization has been passed, he added. I believe we will look back on it with regret.

So they were a mixed lot of men, but the topic of regret had begun to bore John, who did not think he could add to his store of it. In the Tennessee forest, he had pondered his sorrows with a whole heart. He had wondered if he'd been wrong to release his workers unprotected into a battling world. He had left Emly defenseless to predation in spite of his vow to protect her. His sincerest promise. He'd sent his eldest son into the unknown without guidance of any kind. In St. Louis he'd frightened away and lost his younger son. On the Missouri he had lost everything else, every hammer and nail, every plate and cup. His wife was now a stranger to him and he shifted in his chair and looked out at the burned riverbank, black in the twilight, a world without a speck of color in it. What do you know of St. Jo? he asked.

The smoker looked glum. Home of the ruffians plaguing us on the K.T. side is what. Proslavers one and all. Stay out of it.

John wondered if the speaker had detected

his Virginia accent. He thought not and was glad.

The other man said: John Brown and his boys hacked to death some folks down at Pottawatomie Creek. Or Osawatomie. I forget. One of them places. Killed em over nothin but sittin where they sat. The whole area's runnin blood. Folks ain't got the sense God gave em out here.

We got knocked down in Lawrence, said the smoker. Near wiped off the map. Before every election, thousands of bushwhackers cross the border stuffing ballot boxes for slavery. Then the government approves the election and they make it illegal to even speak out a word against slavery, with the threat of death if we disobey. We plow with a gun in one hand, I swear, in case of a sudden militia or gang of hooligans round the bend. We bring our cows inside at night for their safety or we find nothin but ground beef the next day.

I heard is, there wasn't a mite of resistance on that occasion in Lawrence. From your Emigrant Aid Society, said the second man.

The Lawrence resident muttered: I think we disproved that bit of bull when we took Fort Franklin and got our cannon back. Meanwhile bands of idiots ride across Kansas burning our cabins to the ground and they've blockaded this very river, sir! Were you informed of that? In Lawrence we have two thousand hungry settlers with not so much as a sack of flour and we mean to put an end to it! The Missouri boys are starving us. Look what they did to Palmyra! You'll see its burned-down ruins when we pass.

John looked through the westside porthole again, wondering about Patton, who might have got caught up in dangerous shenanigans like fighting John Brown. He listened to the story of the proslavers' raid on Palmyra, Kansas, and remembered that Patton had instructions to stay on the Missouri side, but his eldest could be hot-headed to such a degree that he might well have joined other young men of like temperament and where would that take him? John decided he had been worse than foolish to send his son out here to buy land on a battleground.

When the dinner bell rang, he stubbed out his cigar and joined his family in the galley, but he pondered what he had heard. He must get to St. Jo and stay there until he found Patton. The engines had been cut and the small side wheels slowed. A group had gathered at the captain's table and John and his family joined them. Would they spend the night aboard? Lavina asked the captain.

Weren't they close to St. Jo by now?

Better spend the night right here, said the captain soberly. I have word there is a tree down.

Tree down? Electa spun around. Papa?

Lavina looked at her husband. She took Gina's small hand, then hoisted her up around her waist.

The captain said: We'll have a better chance in daylight. Everything will be fine in the morning. We're used to this.

John's mouth opened and words fell out. I want off.

73

They were on the wrong side of the river.

May as well travel longside.

Good to have company.

Headin on up to Nebraska, so it don't matter ta me.

Give the boys some room there, hey?

These families had been together on the *John A Lucas* for less than a day, during which they had kept to formalities, but now they became comradely. The man from the salon — the one not smoking — said they must find a trail and wait for a line of wagons. His name was Bentley. Keep together is the main thing. This is no place to be shruggin off alone.

John had bought a flimsy cart instead of a wagon, saying they had not far to go. Electa was audibly crying because a reunion with Patton would now never happen. How was he to find them over here on the Kansas side? John said they would cross the river farther north. He said: We haven't stepped off the side of the earth, have we? Wondering why he blamed himself for this latest circumstance, he decided it had become a bad habit, his sense of perpetual guilt. Lecta screamed that she would never, *ever* see her brothers again and nobody seemed to care and the way things were happening to keep them from having a shred of anything they needed in order to survive just made them look ridiculous for even trying and they ought to go back to Jonesville or St. Louis or someplace that had human beings. Everyone else on the *John A Lucas* has a wagon! Look at us! She said all she'd been living for was the reunion with Patton and, in her private mind, she added colors to the picture of her brother without even trying. His scarf. His hat. The way he would lift her up and dance her around. The way he made her feel more appealing than anyone else *ever* made her feel. Something in his grin, which he made with his whole broad face, even the eyes. But the Dickinsons were on the wrong side of the river with everyone else, climbing the bank yelling Gadup and Gee and Haw and shouting and smacking their animals and no one was listening to Electa, who pointed out that the other families had replaced their gear more suc-

cessfully than her papa and, to the extent
they were weary of the river and eager to
set off on land that posed fewer hazards
than water, they were counting their blessings and the animals pulled and strained
while drivers tugged on the reins to slow
them down or cracked whips to speed them
up.

Their cart was a wobbling, loose-wheeled
mess.

They were a line of four wagons and a
rickety cart ten miles north of what had
been the town of Palmyra, which had been
burned to ashes a few days before. Some
scabby house timbers poked out of the
ground, but an hour after climbing the
riverbank, the four wagons and one cart
were strung out on a sea of waist-high grass
where the sun had set the prairie glowing.
At first there were tracks and bobolinks
sang. Later there were only wheel ruts.
Where were they going? They kept to high
ground for fear of Indians but there was
nothing, not so much as a tree on this edge
of the world. The women climbed out of
the wagons and brushed through the grasses
in spite of the burrs that clung to their
skirts. The men walked unless they drove.
They had no trouble keeping pace with the
animals and eventually they called a halt.

They had escaped the river. The sun was down and all was quiet but for distant barks and cries and calls and howls. They built a fire, one fire for all. They sat around it: men, women, children, and there was a flute played and Gina and another child danced with the wind coming at them over a thousand miles of nothing else. The two children had danced on the *Arabia,* Gina and Caroline, holding hands to whatever music was played, and now they danced to Caroline's father's flute, which made the loneliest sound, out here on the prairie, any of the listeners had ever heard.

Far far they were from anything but a cloggy river and a burned-out town.

Lavina watched Electa linger outside a small group of girls who had traveled together on the *John A Lucas* before the Dickinsons came aboard. There were enough to make up a cluster of five the next morning and now in the big emptiness they gave Electa permission to learn their histories and walk alongside them. Some of them carried younger siblings on their backs or in their arms but none would give up the luxury of distance from parents after so many cramped days on steamboats or trails. A girl named Anya could do a meadowlark. Helen could do a cartwheel, Jennifer had seen the ocean; she had been on a sailing ship. Electa observed these allies. Bonnets were taken off. Sleeves were rolled up and stays loosened. As a group they developed their voices in order to be heard in this new, hollow world. Marjorie's mother had died in Kentucky and her father would not turn back. Fathers and brothers were looking for the route west, although it was marked by fresh graves. The girls didn't speak of it. Out in the open they didn't remind one another that the ground under them was full of travelers like themselves and that the farther they moved on it, the more likely they were to join the ones in the earth. The truth of it was they were deathly afraid of death. Cholera. Brain fever. Indians. *Passed 2 graves 1 dead cow with flies on it made 10 miles.*

On the second night, camping by a stream, there were a few cottonwoods at creek edge and a racetrack was established between the two tallest trees. Gina had tucked up her skirt and double-knotted the laces on her boots although her hair was untied and so was her sash. She wanted to race. She was not coughing anymore and little Caroline, her dancing friend, was a good runner and they could go as a team. Can we do a relay? Electa and Helen petitioned Anya, the lark.

They want a race. Caroline's father wandered over with his flute and established a starting point. Teams were chosen. Three children on each of two teams. The flute was blown. Caroline and a boy named Edward flew from one cottonwood to another and back. Then Caroline touched Gina's shoulder and Gina leapt forward. Her face was flushed. She was a flying fox darting to a tree straight ahead until she heard her sister's shout, took a quick look, and ran back to the starting tree. The other runners fell in behind her, gasping and frightened without knowing why. Then they saw a blur coming out of the horizon, a storm of ponies in swirling dust. A minute later, the whooping riders circled, dismounted, and came up close, sniffing at a skewer of grilling meat. John made a motion to Electa and Gina: Come!

The visiting Pawnee were soon joined by their women, who materialized in large numbers from the surrounding dark. John squinted, trying to bring into focus these figures wrapped in blankets. His vision was blurred. They looked like mirages. One woman approached him, wanting to trade her pony for Gina's. She ran back and forth between the two animals but John shook his head, saying: No trade, and thought of the pointlessness of bargaining with people who didn't abide by rules. Most of the Pawnee men wanted gunpowder; some wanted whiskey. Everyone wanted tobacco and they rifled through the wagons looking for knives and pans and mirrors and clothes. It made for an uneasy night, the Pawnee sleeping around the fire, the emigrants hard awake in their wagons. The Pawnee had ignored the cart, so there was benefit in poverty, and the mule was valueless, but they took a cow off and butchered it while John sat on the ground grinding his teeth and rubbing his eyes and while Lavina and the girls huddled together in the cart, sitting upright.

By morning, the Pawnee were gone, vanished into the ocean of whispering grass, the mounds and gullies, the borderless sky.

But that afternoon they were surprised by the sight of a dead Pawnee on the ground. He'd been scalped. His throat was cut. John went to the body, meaning to pray. He was advised to stay back. They rise up to haunt ya, one of the men announced. Another said: Might just be playin dead.

We must bury him, John replied.

But no one agreed. They are part of nature, a middle-aged woman said. Leave him for the buzzards.

In fact, such creatures were gathering.

Leave me be. A memory of Emly's voice tore at his heart.

They were traveling across an area in dispute between the Pawnee and the Potawatomi. They knew this when a small detachment of Potawatomi stalked through their line of wagons carrying a Pawnee prisoner. The Pawnee was wearing a wolf-skin and nothing else but a rawhide knife girdle. Within minutes there were gunshots and various Natives ran through the line of wagons. Ignored in the instantaneous little battle, the white people went on somberly, facing the future in all ignorance.

That afternoon they came to a cut in the prairie at the bottom of which a stream flowed. The men unfastened their horses and rode up and down looking for a ford but there was no safe place to cross. Someone said it might be advisable to lower the wagons down the side of the creek with ropes, but the men decided to lead the animals down the bank and over the fast-flowing creek using prods and brakes. The water was so transparent that red and gold rocks could be seen in its shallows, but it was raging enough that cows would have to be tethered to the wagons or they might be swept away. Horses and mules could be ridden through the water pulling the wagons

431

but the opposite side was steep.

John and Lavina conferred. They had little confidence in their cart but John had been told it would float. Seaworthy is what the stableman called it. Good as a fish. Women and children climbed inside their wagons, holding tight. Lavina asked if Gina might ride in the flute player's wagon with Caroline. It was not the stream that concerned her, but the sand. The wagons had brakes, but on the cart, back wheels would have to be chained and sticks thrown into the front spokes to slow the descent. If the cart plunged, it would fly apart. Lavina sat firm on its narrow seat, holding the reins wrapped tightly around her hands like the bonds of captivity while John faced away from the water, faced his mule, moving backward step by step, watching the hooves, Now, whoa there. Whoa. Now there, now there, whoaaa . . . In front of the cart, the two little girls were peeking out of the back of the flute player's wagon, encircled by the white canvas cover, two heads with a ruffle around them and the flute player shouting at his wife: Hold em tight. The night before, the little girls had made flags by shredding broad leaves. Each of them now had a flag to wave as the flute player's wagon jerked to a sudden stop and little Caroline tumbled out.

John, with his back to that wagon and his over-rubbed eyes fastened to his mule, had just yanked hard to urge the mule forward when Lavina saw the child fall out and the small face get trampled by her mule first and then by the cart's iron wheel, the mother screaming along with Lavina and a cry going up, a hue and cry as the mother leapt out and tried to haul her child out of trampled sand.

John stood stunned, all hope gone on the bank of the unnamed stream where the small child crushed by the wheel of his newly bought cart was being gathered up, broken and limp. He had watched the little girl sleep in her mother's arms the night before. Bound for Oregon, was how the father had put it then, and tears ran down John's face, the flute player going along the line of wagons looking for someone to help him bury his child and the men collecting in a knot as if they could undo John's mistake. They circled and gathered, the women held to one another, all of them mothers of children who might so quickly become dead. Tears to swell the innocent creek. My fault, each mother would think if such a thing happened to her child: I did it by following my husband on his unholy trek. By now, at this stage of the journey, the encouragement they might have offered a husband back at home was forgotten and the future mythology of this journey and their brave portion was unknown to them. John moved his tongue in and out of his dry mouth, begging God to raise up the child, asking what he had done to earn this latest signal of His displeasure . . . oh God . . . and he found himself standing in front of the father, hat in hand. I am a minister of the Lord, he heard himself say.

The father pointed to the lump of muslin he held, a lump that might have held potatoes, something to eat or to plant, instead of his child, and Lavina took hold of John's elbow and pulled. What if it had been Gina? But Gina was the last of a large family and that mister and missus had nobody else and how would they go about ever fixing a meal or washing another dish? What would they do with the clean pinafores? John and Lavina's murderous cart was reconnected with solid ground and the mothers had muttering mouths and the men had shaking heads. *Then there were brought unto him little children, that he should put his hands on them* and the child's father took up his lump of muslin and everyone followed him to the hasty grave they had dug, wind blowing at skirts and hats.

74

Martin came into the town feeling saved. *All that is in the world is not of the Father but is of the world!* Chez Les Kanses, where the Kansas and Missouri rivers met and the Kansa Indians lived on steep bluffs at the landing place, where deer fed on green willows and wild apples and where, in the west bottoms, French trappers with their Indian wives had built a Catholic church and a village by the Santa Fe trace. In the woods through which Martin had come for the past several days, birds prevailed and there were Indians on small, shaggy ponies, Delaware in calico frocks or skin leggings and Pawnee wrapped in blankets. The Kansa women wore leather skirts and the men shaved their heads except for a row in the middle and they painted their faces red, which reminded Martin of the woman he had met by the wigwam who had pointed the way to the bear's winter cave. Martin therefore liked the Kansa and rode with them whenever they had a pony to spare. They were bound for the town that had their tribal name and when they arrived he asked someone to hire him to haul a load of wood in order to earn a meal because money is not much thought of in a city founded on the barter of skins although on every corner people were holding meetings. There was to be an election in two weeks.

From this point forward there would be nothing of shape or substance. Sky has no shape. He had come to the end of the trees. Such is the way of nature where it leans against prairie and Martin crept down the street in a foolish daze. He thought of his bear sleeping the sleep of winter dreams and missed her with all his might.

During a quick dinner on the open street, he experienced a genuine, everyday miracle of the frontier. It was the sight of a laughing rider wearing buckskin with rows of long fringes on his jacket. He was mounted on a big gray horse and leading another horse, pure white. A single-bore rifle lay across the pommel of his saddle and he was shouting, hallooing, lifting himself up in the saddle so as to be seen, leading the white horse by a rope, calling to a small man who was leaning over a painted cart shouting back in

French. The painted cart had been brought down from a market in Montreal, although Martin had no way of knowing that yet, any more than he could know that inside the cart were provisions for a journey across the Kansas River that Patton and the Frenchman were about to make. Patton lifted his hat like a rebel and shouted again when he laid eyes on Martin, who was eating a piece of grilled chicken on the noisy, clotted street. He swung his right leg over the saddle and ran straight to his little brother, and they danced and yelped and beat each other on arms and backs.

Where are they, boy? What have you done with the ancestors?

Left em, Martin said, bursting into tears.

Where's your bear?

Martin swallowed. Waiting to be born again, he said. Having come four hundred miles riding in a stranger's wagon or on an Indian pony, he wiped the tears off his face with the heel of his hand and shrugged and laughed and the brothers went into a tavern where Patton bought Martin his first glass of whiskey, one to grow on, he said to celebrate Martin's fourteenth birthday, and he promised that they were soon going to find the family. Patton was gleeful and Martin tried not to cry again. He swayed on his feet and Patton put him into a chair. I've been up to St. Jo twice already, he said, so I'd know if they got there yet, wouldn't I?

Martin got up on the big white horse although he was unsteady because of the whiskey, men slapping at him and nearly knocking him out of the saddle because Patton and his French friend were bound for a trading post in a day or two and this coming adventure should be acknowledged even before the fact of it. Patton had plenty to sell, even the big white horse. It was the latest venture by a brother who was bragging now as if the finding of Martin had been a laid-out plan.

As Martin nodded and tried to cling to the horse with his knees, Patton led him alongside the Frenchman and the cart on a short circle of the town in order to publicize Martin's adventure, which was more exceptional than anything either of the older men had accomplished. Then they rode off to the banks of the Kansas River at the French Bottoms, where a woman sat on the porch of a log house smoking a calumet pipe. Martin forced his eyes to stay open for a few minutes while Patton explained things and then he fell off the horse and someone carried him into the house and laid him down. Later, much later, Patton pulled him to his feet and walked him outside and Martin tried to open his eyes again. What he saw was a girl with a handful of crumbs and she threw them at some turkey birds and then came over to Martin. When Martin went back to the house, the girl and the turkeys followed him in. Patton said that the pipe-smoking woman was the mother of his French friend, and the turkey girl was his sister. The mother had desired to see her son before he made the trip to anyplace on the Kansas side of the river, where anything might happen. In this way Martin discerned that the cart man was made of two kinds of people. He was made of a Native mother and a French father, who was named Grandlouis, and who was telling Patton about the sinking of a boat named *Arabia,* which might esplain, he said, the disappeerin Dickesonne if they was on eet but none dead all save, he said, but for a mule as the sinking was just over there and we heerd it neigh. He pointed. Mos was pick up by the *Jame Lu Cass* an we gotta fine where it wen to mebe taken your famille.

You find them, Pere Grandlouis, and we will come back to get them.

Martin said: Back from where?

Patton said: Got to make a living out here like anywhere else. Don't worry. They'll be buying supplies since the boat went down and after this trip we will have cash to share.

To the old French Canadian papa the prairie was his skin. He'd come back to town after two years killing buffalo in order to see his Native bride before setting out again. He thought he might come along with his son, who was Patton's guide. They might make a foray into Lawrence and he might watch an ensuing fight as there was said to be such a thing forthcoming, but the next morning, when Martin was almost awake, they put him on the white horse and rode off, leaving the French papa behind. There was nothing to see when they crossed the Kansas River but they went on for some miles to the Kickapoo reservation so Patton could sell his trinkets. Not the horse, just yet, laughed Patton, since I can't have you weighing mine down. The horse will keep its value unless it gets shot out from under your skinny behind.

The trading post was not far into the reservation. It was on a little stream that had log houses in ruin along its banks. Stray calves, pigs, and ponies wandered close to a path that led to the trader's green-painted house. A crowd gathered at word of the Montreal cart. Wearing calico and wampum, the Kickapoo came on their ponies with faces painted red and green and black and white, and inside the green house, the trader's Creole wife was offering Patton and his brother and the Frenchman coffee and cake and the trader told them about a gathering in Lawrence, where there was sure to be a showdown, a real one this time.

Patton sold his treasures to the trader a little too fast since, if Lawrence was heating up, he did not want to miss any part of it. The cart man said it wasn't his fight and he was going home, and Martin wished they could all go back to Missouri and find his mother because he was tired of being brave and he missed her more and more, thinking she must be close. They rode off, and Martin whispered to Patton, as if there were anyone who could hear or care: It was all my fault. We lost the whole farm because I let the workers run away after I heard their plan.

Patton said: If you told, they would have been horse-whipped, Martin.

The brothers set off at a bumpy trot — Martin clinging to tight reins. He had never been a good rider; he had never had the chance. They rode for some hours and he was sore all over and more and more angry because he thought they should be finding their parents and sisters and not looking for trouble.

75

Astride her swaybacked vehicle, Lavina took her sorry place in the line of wagons. All those white tops, the insides of which were lined with pockets full of necessities, and she without so much as a medicine box or a sewing basket and that headache that assailed her when she needed a draught for her leg and now, after weeks of traveling on water surrounded by trees, everything was bone-bare and hard of surface. Grass and more grass, flattened by constant wind. They had left the great eastern forest and the sun bore down on this world of horizon meeting sky.

A nice town of well-built houses, Lavina was thinking. A church. A school. They might come upon lights in the distance, steeples set solid before mild hills. She pictured herself at a glazed window looking out at a field plowed up and ready. And beyond that a pretty, new town. She glanced back at her horse-riding husband, whose shape was as familiar from a distance as ever it was close by. She saw his isolation; he'd been abandoned by the other men.

Mam! I got a rabbit!

Good girl, Lecta! How in the world did you do it?

A boy helped me. That boy over there.

Climb up here, child, and keep me company.

It makes too much weight, Mama. Will you stop so we can skin this fellow and eat? But she climbed up, holding the soft long body by its ears, and the cart took her weight.

Again, Lavina looked back at her husband. She looked at his horse, his last possession, and glanced at the shabby, woebegone cart she was driving. Hold tight, my girls, she yelled, cracking the whip and pulling her cart out of the string of wagons that continued along without pausing, each wagon keeping another in view for lack of anything else in the world to see.

John came up to Lavina at a gallop. You lost our place!

We have no place.

Mother! John was within reach of the reins and he grabbed for them.

She lifted her whip.

They were on a ridge with a broad valley on each side. There was a scattering of creeks running into the valleys, their various courses marked by timber growing sparsely along their banks like weeds. The tall grass reflected twilight like a silvered mirror and John put his fingers under his saddle for something that felt familiar. Alien beauty without a reference point. No animal. No bird. He brought his right leg over the saddle of his mare and slipped down to the brushing rustle of grass. It's St. Jo we want, Mother. We won't find it on our own. We go north to a decent crossing with these wagons.

Let me go!

John took off his hat as the wagon train passed. Later he sat on the endless ground and thought about the father on his way to Oregon without a child. He thought about the Native people who belonged to this place and how they must despise the sharing of any piece of it. The horse, grazing as if there could be a reason, was lumpen in the dark and he watched the cart driven by his wife for a long time as it receded and then was lost to sight.

76

They had come to the Detroit River, the last road to Canada, and they needed food before crossing. There was no knowing what they might find on the other side and they had nothing left but a little wild rice they had been given two days before that required arduous boiling. There were said to be catchers around Detroit so Bry would stay under the shelter of a pier and she would walk far enough to find help at a Black church near the river's edge. Rumors and suppositions were part of the territory.

Indeed, she came upon the Methodist Episcopal church, which was known as a last stop of the Underground Railroad, where there was a group of black citizens who haled her in a friendly way, calling her sister. They invited her in to pray and when she demurred and explained her purpose, they told her about catchers in the area seeking a bunch of Virginia runaways. Keep him where he is until after midnight.

She had hoped for food and she next walked along a street of darkened buildings, wood and brick. The Delaware woman had never been to school, but there were papers nailed or tacked to a board on the wall of a building that had an empty flagpole by its doorway. One piece of paper had a line of words going down and she stared at it, but what was the point? Why had she bothered to walk all this way? She backed up and moved across the cobbled street, then turned toward the river, where she once again entered the church, opening heavy doors that slammed behind her. Someone was preaching in there but the sermonizing stopped abruptly. Sister? The preacher came down off his perch while those who were listening turned to watch.

My friend he want food . . .

Ralph, you go with her to the tavern.

A slim man stepped out of the small congregation and touched the woman's shoulder. It had carried the canoe for so many portages over so many rocky miles that she barely felt the weight of the stranger's hand, but he led her out of the church and they walked quickly to a small ill-lit room in a back alley where people of color could buy warm food. At the river they went down underneath the pier where she had left Bry. Gone! And they turned and ran back to the church, where the small congregation was still gathered and when they heard that Bry was missing they rushed for the door. Wait, wait! the preacher coached. He could be anywhere.

The cellar under the abattoir?

How would he know it?

The lot behind the post office?

Ralph, go have a look.

The Delaware woman told Bry's story using every important English word she knew. She said: He run from Kentucky. He save me from white man. He come for the mother in Canada.

The church people assigned specific areas to particular men and told the women to keep the church open. This was something they knew how to do and now the men fanned out like experts to find Bry before he was shipped south. All over again.

77

In Franklin, nearly a thousand men in red shirts and red-ribboned hats had assembled with various guns to outshoot the Sharps rifles and pitchforks of two hundred or so abolitionists hiding behind two big lumps of earth on the main street of Lawrence. It was going to be a lark, Patton said, and Martin was given an old red scarf full of spit and dirt and he put it around his neck. He had never thought about Kansas and he wondered what his father would think of this plan and told himself: So what? It was fine to be on a horse even if it hurt his backside but he thought about his mother with a hand on her brow looking eastward for him and wished she would turn around and face west. Crossing over the river to Kansas had felt like going the wrong way and now they'd met men who were shooting their guns off and yelling cuss words at the dusty air. There were those who wanted Kansas to be a club for Yankees, but it was no farther north than Missouri, which was part of the South. Martin thought about Bry, who got as far as St. Louis. I'm the reason he's free, Martin thought, so what side am I on?

As they galloped off toward Lawrence, the swarm was whooping, packing bullets and powder into guns, shouting and standing up in their stirrups and threatening to find John Brown and hang him or shoot him or skin him alive. That's him, that's him, some of the horsemen cried, as they got close to the center of town, pointing at a shape so distant it could not possibly be identified. Suddenly there were gunshots coming from every side and Martin was grabbed by his brother, who took hold of his horse. Out of here! he shouted. Now! This is too much! Martin wanted to look back but Patton screamed that this was no place for a boy, no place, no place, and when he slapped the white horse, they both galloped back the way they had come.

78

Bry was laid in a coffin on the back of a funeral cart. It was long and narrow and he folded his hands over his chest in the horrible dark. Draped in a blanket the coffin and cart rumbled to the graveyard and then it paused before it went down to the river, where Bry climbed out and got into the dugout with the help of the Delaware woman and his rescuers. The church people used the coffin for escapes. It got pulled down the street with a long line of silent mourners, its wheels clacking against paving stones and a frightened runaway slave lying still inside. They had found him under a porch after he'd walked a little way into town, where he saw the list tacked onto a wall.

REWARD FOR *MISSING VIRGINIA* PROPERTY

Tom — reddish complexion, age 30+, bad

eyes; Jule, stout yellow, 40, bald; Edward — birthmark on right side of his face; Sutter: crossed eyes, having some white marks on his lips; Rakel: Past bearing but strong; Young Jim: 20+, round face; Bry, castrate, fifty-five, or six well spoken; Reuben: skilled carpenter, old; Nick: yellow; Josiah — large hands, scarred back; Billy — well muscled, five feet 3 inches; Abe — very black, thumb missing, middle age

Reward to be paid by
City Bank of New York

Back in the dugout, what the two paddlers could see through the dark that hung over the river was the distant line of promised ground some miles away. Bland it was, that far shore, having awaited these two immigrants for centuries, but the river was still swarming with barges and boats and ships transporting goods between Canada and the United States and there was a small rowboat following them closely, veering as they veered. A river belongs to everyone; and in the heavy dugout, they moved awkwardly through flagrant traffic and Bry pulled the makeshift hood around his face. After an hour of paddling, he heard the Delaware woman speak as they headed toward a landing downstream of the spot they wanted because she had not the strength and he had not the skill to beach the canoe in the better place. The woman was making that chant of hers while they rode into the sharp smell of pine and made a soft landing under a wall that rose up like a barricade black on black. Perhaps it had been erected during the war with the States, but it stood against the invasion of two renegades who scrambled out of a dugout and fell on dry ground, gratitude in each of them in spite of histories too separate to connect. Can you walk? They were stiff in back and arms and legs but they stood up and hobbled, groaning to prove what they had accomplished. Bry said: Free! It was all he could think. Free, safe, touching the arm of the Delaware woman because with that arm she had delivered him. Her dress was stained by grass and blood. Her hair had unfolded around her face. He knew she had lived on land that was whittled away by treaty or thieving and still she sowed every spring and reaped in the summers and autumns and there was much she could not describe but now in the dark, he and a Native woman walked out of their former travails. They walked the distance of the wall, sinking at times in soft ground, until they came to a spot where the stones had tumbled into a formation of steps and they mounted them bent over and poorly balanced and put the wall behind them as one more overcome impediment. The woman was carrying those grains of rice and they ate them dry and uncooked, never slowing, finding a road that provided no welcome other than its surface. Bry talked to himself but also to the woman. It was coming back a little at a time, his belief in himself after the dark fright of the coffin. He was free except for a portion, left over, of antique fear.

The whole journey from Missouri had taken nine or ten weeks and now there was mold underfoot, the leaves on the ground so moist there was no sound of walking, and they set up the tent they had slept in together all those nights of the past and on that final night she lay next to him and told him how the grandfathers were pushed out of the east by the Ojibwas, who had guns, of which she said: We never knew them. She told him that her people had never farmed until the years in Missouri, that they were hunters and warriors but never with guns. She could not now remember the hunting song but some of the words came out of her throat and Bry was polite because he did not recognize her mistakes. Long time before when grandfathers go west, some stop to Ontario, she said.

The next morning, she put her strong hands on Bry's shoulders and said: You to you I to I. And then she walked away from Bry, who was not one of the Lenape people and would not be welcome where she was going and at that moment, with the sun coming over the tops of the pines, he called after her, but she was running along the shore and would not look back.

Bry paddled through the old Carolinian forest, with its broad-leaf trees and squirrels he knew by sight. The dugout was difficult to manage alone but the river was placid at this time of year. He met whitetail deer, otters, and small creatures he could not name. Snakes. Turtles. Unfrightened birds. The river flowed through all these occasions, through trees on one side — a swell of trees, a thousand thousand trees with height enough to see every place he had been if he climbed to the top of one and, on the other side, the bowl of water that connected this new world to the world he remembered without longing.

Chatham, his first stop, was a town of former slaves, runaways, black soldiers from the War of 1812 and another Methodist church. These people were nicely dressed and there were fields that belonged to none but themselves, private property for black settlers who had come up with Loyalist owners or who had run from owners loyal to the South. Now they each had one hundred acres. This he learned from the first person he met. He had pulled the canoe up to a stand of trees and walked a short way on a street, holding his head up and his shoulders down and trying to look each person he passed in the eye. It was harder than paddling the canoe to manage this face-to-face inspection. He felt in his bones that he might find Josiah or Nick walking the street. Rakel. Bry could dream of meeting them on a Chatham street.

He chose a door and soon he was taking a cup of coffee in the house of a woman called Mamma Chad. She wanted to feed him and show him her house. In a frame hanging on one of her walls, this motto was cross-stitched in yellow and red: *With pleasure let us own our errors past . . . And make each day a critic on the last.* Bry read the motto with more contentment than he had expected to find in words. He counted back his errors past but also the things he had done to get this far. He admired the old woman and took her hand and stroked it and she looked down as if it belonged to someone else. Afterward, when he was getting on his feet to leave, Bry said he meant to find his mother in a city of Indian name, and Mamma Chad covered her toothless mouth and explained that it was called Toronto: It's a ways to go, son, and God keep you on your feet. Bry wanted to joke that he walked on water, but he thought she would take offense. When she closed her door, he went down her path, which had flowers right and left, and he wandered through Chatham town for a while, seeing the children of his race playing, noticing a poster nailed to a tree about a circus that had come the year before with *Clowns equestrians the intrepid maitress de cheval,* and clutching the foreign dollar Mamma Chad had given him.

A town of people like himself. He imagined the various reactions he would receive if he ever went back to the start of things and told what he had seen.

79

There were stands of box elders on the river flats, with their leaves turning yellow and the white pine lifting branches and cones under the autumn sky. There were places to get food when he came to a village and in one he spent some part of his dollar on bread and cheese. He did not like the cheese but it served his need.

In London, he got out of the dugout canoe and left it behind. The river was impassable and he would have to walk the rest of the way so he was directed to Governor's Road, which had taverns at intervals where he might eat a meal and shelter overnight except that he had no money left so he found a stable where he was allowed to sleep, although the smell of hay and horseflesh brought back memories he had put aside.

In this way he came to the city of Toronto and it was nothing like Louisville or St.

Louis to the runaway slave. Here, he would not be apprehended; all that was finished; here, he belonged to himself although he asked about a Negro woman who might be working to heal the sick with the herbs she blended. There were buildings of stone and the noise of creaking drays and of constant hammering and digging and horses whinnying and human languages he did not recognize. He stayed for a night in a shelter where people asked if he was Protestant or Catholic. It seemed to be a question of some importance but he shrugged and accepted a bowl of oatmeal and stirred it with a finger as he sat on the cot he'd been given for the next six hours. This shelter was in the thick of a midtown place known as The Ward, a place of vagrants and immigrants and those too misfortuned to make a good life, and the next day he found work carrying stacks of wood and bags of coal and earned the first money he had freely made and he kept it under his shirt in a pouch and there had never been a more pleasant weight to carry.

80

Lavina proceeded north, traveling by inches in the cart. Late in the late afternoon she saw the sun in a hollow like oil in a pan and knew there was water down there where red grass was rippling. She stopped the mule, wrapped the lines around the cartwheel, took her skirt in her hands, and stepped down. She was so close to her destination that, had she kept going, she might have reached it in an hour but, far off, they could hear the longing of coyotes and she decided to stop for the night in the smells and light of an unlikely place. Kansas! Grass and more grass into eternity is all it was.

They had left behind the trees and stepped off into this! Had they gone blind? Where was the beauty in a world of horizon always meeting up with sky? Nothing, nothing in between! A hawk wheeled overhead. Electa was sent to look for buffalo droppings. Gina pulled grass for kindling. Lavina cleaned the rabbit, keeping the skin as an heirloom since all of her personal things had been drowned. She thought of the crate her husband had tried to protect with his body. She cut the rabbit into pieces and washed it in the water they had collected at the morning ford. She built a cooking rod with two forked sticks and a third laid across.

Electa took the pony and mule to be watered. The three remaining cows had followed them and they were resting and chewing after a meal of bluestem grass. Electa came back with water and buffalo dung and threw herself down on the ground. The water will not be fit to drink, John would have said, but he was not there and for a while they watched the sun like a letter slide into the ground.

Lavina put the rabbit in the new iron pot John had purchased in Independence. I have an iron pot, she said for no reason in a singsong voice, speaking foolishly to the two children left to her and thinking of the little one named Caroline who was killed by her cart. When the meat browned, she added cream skimmed off the milk that morning, and mother and daughters lay around the fire as if everything they might have to say had been said in the months that had gone before. All this long time they had been surrounded by other families — children, animals, parents, babies being born and babies dying. The entire movable world was all one family to which the Dickinson women belonged, but now they were plunged down on the softened ground in the darkness of Kansas Territory, with its stars that held up the sky. *Appoint the cities of refuge* . . . A city with churches and tolling bells.

Gina was asleep on Electa's lap and Electa was spitting small bones at the fire that burned on grass growing out of rock laid down by prehistoric seas and below the rock more rock and fossilized fish. Lavina lay on her back, arms spread, and took inhalations of sky. In the morning I shall have a bath in that pond even if it is lively with snakes. She patted her scarred leg where the skin resembled the striated ground. She had a bowl of rabbit stew kept aside for John when he was ready to be seen. What had he taken in the way of victuals that morning? She studied the stars, knowing she would spend the night where she lay. *Ad astra per aspera.* It was warm enough and the planets bristled. Then a low sound reached her ears, something more human than feral, and she saw a rider, then another splashing through her future bath. The apparitions hovered for

a time in the evening mist of the disrupted
pond as if they carried the news of something forthcoming.

81

The next day, Patton cut down a cotton-wood tree — there were ten of them by the creek they claimed. Why the tree? Because the house was to be built of sod and must have a frame. It was close to the Nebraska border where they stopped after traveling a few paltry miles from the meeting place, the bathing pond, the scene of frantic and joy-ous reunion, and John sat on the ground smiling while Patton and Martin chose a site for the house. John could see the horizon, the overwhelming sky, the general color and shape of everything past and pres-ent. He watched Patton take his brother into the prairie, where they made two furrows of even width and depth with the spade he had bought during the second visit to Indepen-dence. He got himself down to the place where his boys were cutting through earth that had never been cut by hand or tool, grass that had never been cut except by teeth. He could see that Patton was up to his old tricks, covering protectiveness with horseplay. Patton used the spade to cut sod pieces three feet long between the furrows while Martin piled the soft bricks in the bed of the topless cart. John waited with his sons until dark, then helped them draw a line for the wall plumb to the North Star. Against the hard sky, they worked as shadows in firelight, placing bricks side by side. Where the door was to be, they left a gap. Cracks were filled with dirt and two more layers of bricks were laid, breaking the joints. Eventually, they wiped their faces on their sleeves and lay down on the waist-high grass.

It was from the cottonwood tree that they fashioned posts for the doorframe and window the following day. These were placed in the wall as the sod piled up around them. Martin went back and forth between the wagon and the walls, carrying the soft bricks that his brother and father laid.

When the walls were six feet high, Martin climbed up on the cart to lay enough bricks for gables at either end while Patton worked on a ridgepole and rafters. John felt the wind against his brow. He felt the essence of time, which was merely a rotation of duties. They had set down in a place that had no name and now John watched Gina build a miniature house out of Kansas clay. The sun was indiscriminate overhead, but the boys added a sheeting of brush to the rafters and over that they put a layer of sod and prairie grass. They cut the earth with a scythe and laid it on in batches as if they were creating a lawn on the roof or a grave.

In due course, Lavina was picked up by her jubilant sons and carried into the tiny sod house. They had built her a bed. They would make her a stove out of clay. They would cover the door with a blanket, which could be raised to let in air or lowered to keep out rain. Lavina sent her daughters out with pots for water from the creek they had named Wolf. Wolf! cried Gina. It was her favorite story, or the one they most often told her. Never cry wolf. Never declare an untruth or it will come back to bite you. After months of travel, the family had shelter. Thick-walled and dark, the sod house gave respite from sun and wind and later from cold. Everyone clustered inside it. They stood and breathed in the dark, moist air. John prayed. Martin stood off to the side. Patton said: How bout I make us a table? The roof crackled and a sifting of earth fell over them.

It was nine by twelve feet, their new home,

and they would learn to sleep inside on summer nights when rain soaked through the roof and ran down faces and necks. When it came from the north, they moved to the south side of the dwelling. When it came from the south, another move. When the roof was soaked through, it dripped for three days and nights. Lavina managed to cook with one of the girls holding a pan over her head. At the first sound of thunder, she put all the dishes on the floor, on the stove, on the bed, in order to catch the water.

Meantime, there was only to walk from one place to another since the cart had no road to hold to. They walked to fetch water, to hunt, to plow, and to plant although sometimes they went on horseback. They walked or rode through the tall grass, through brush, and over creeks. Together, Patton and Martin acquired four hundred and fifty acres with their warrants. This was the whole of the world. There were no trails, no bridges, no stores, no churches, no neighbors, no place to mail a letter or buy coffee or sugar, not within fifty miles. No barber, no mechanic. There was no legal framework, no law, no doctor to call when they were sick. The prairie sod was so heavy that their plow cracked on its first attempt at breaking ground but sod was used to build a corral, a henhouse, a corncrib.

Sunflowers appeared on the roof.

And Patton went down to the creek with the cart to gather up rocks. The barn he planned would be three feet thick and made of native limestone with holes through which to shoot Indians or abolitionists or bushwhackers.

John sat in the shade while the barn went up stone over stone and his thoughts went back all the way to Bry and the fort they had built as children. They had played all one summer in the woods, trapping and snaring and fishing, having battles. Redcoats and Yanks. Happy. They seemed to be friends until John went off to school and Bry was taken away to Rafe's fields. Friendship was impossible then. He passed a hand over his eyes because his sons were losing their edges. Too much light. The fort was designed by Bry, the point being not to defend but to create. And they had used stones gathered from the creek. It is right firm, Bry would say. He had the speech of two educated mothers, one white and one black, although he had no doubt lost that speech over the years and John thought then about the magic of language and the fort built piece by piece, a little at a time.

Of course stone was more work than sod

and harder on the hands. But it is not so different building a stone fort or a stone barn, John decided. Square off the corners, lay the pieces down true. Break the joints and turn every third row crosswise. How did Bry know about plumb lines and clay mixed with sand? Those walls had held for so long that Bry had gone off to belong to Rafe Fox and John had been left to rule over their kingdom. He took the long piece of grass he'd been chewing out of his mouth. It had gone from sweet to bitter, from dry to moist, from tough to soft. He watched the boys toting stones. Patton had engineered a sleigh that he loaded with small-sized pieces and towed across the future barnyard. He stood in the cart and threw the stones down and then rolled them along in a kind of scrimmage, sometimes using his two feet, sometimes bending down and pushing with his arms. In this way, he managed the biggest stones and felt justified in demanding the biggest supper. They judged the hours by the position of the sun. And later they sat with the stars and ate close to the fire, as if nostalgic for the limbo they had come through. Lavina was stirring the food. Metal plate. Tin spoon. Biscuits and beans. Round and round. This sky. The shelter of stars.

82

The city was large and confusing and it began to seem unlikely that Bry would find Bett without a surname attached to her. He had been asking about her for three frustrating weeks. Has she no surname? He was asked that time and again. Nor could he claim such a thing for himself. Son of Bett, he might have said in the old-world way. Bry Bettson.

One day, he was directed to the door of a woman known to everyone as helpful in such matters. And she healed the sick.

It brought a stir to his heart but The Ward was full of runaway slaves and free blacks and immigrants who were homeless from Ireland or some part of Europe and he would not assume anything. There was a horse-drawn taxi driven by a black man, and there was food growing on the edges of city streets, and wandering pigs, and with its upright stone and mortar banks and office buildings, it was apparently British in its intent although here, too, there was a river cutting through ravines with somewhere to go, an inland sea to be endlessly fed. It was that unsalted sea he had kept on his right side as he paddled through forest and farmland. He had slept by its lapping and fished in it with a string. He had squinted and looked for the other side and never found it, which meant he was safe. Now he knocked on the door of a woman whose patients came to her daily with complaints and illness and killing fatigue. They came to her during epidemics of cholera. They came with measles and scrofula and ague, with lice, with rat bites. She had a place with two cots and a room for herself, and her days were full of the old and the sick and the destitute. She was, in fact, on her way out the door when she heard a light tap and found Bry on her doorstep gentle of bearing, not very tall, somewhat old and rather bent. How did she know him? Why did she throw herself into arms so strong from the paddling of a dugout canoe that he could lift her off her feet and hold on to her? Would know you anyplace, she cried. Dear Lord, I would know you as my son anyplace. Tears and tight holding body to body until they were too weak to stand and found chairs by the table that served as her desk and her place to eat.

How did you never let me know where you were?

I thought you were lost. We thought you never made it to . . . the . . .

Bry waved her next words away and both of them cried for uncounted minutes. It was crying that encompassed all the people they'd known who would never arrive, and those who had been wounded in the process of unknotting the bonds of heart and flesh. This mother and son had not seen each other for too many years. Forty-one! She went over his face and neck and shoulders and arms with her eyes and then with her warm mother hands that he recognized from the press she'd exerted that had so often sent him into comforting sleep, and now she fastened him with such a piercing examination of muscle and bone that he was glued to the chair and she said, not knowing the lasting damage done, Well, you look all right.

He said: Mama. You know where my child is?

And so it was that my mother stood in the doorway of a small sod house, earned and yet never hers in the way of an ancient relationship to the land, while Bry's mother stood in a doorway far from her starting place, picking up the broken pieces of the oldest relationship in the world. Don't do that to her, Bett said, taking his big, hardened hand in hers. Leave her be, my son. Let her live this life she can understand. She knows me as her mother's servant.

A month later, when he came to her house, he stood outside for some time wanting to touch the skin of Eva Nell's pinewood door, the door of a home where she'd lived first with Mary Jones and now alone because it was a proper place to weave or write or teach, all the likely occupations a white woman might pursue at that time. He watched through a window as she sat at her loom and he imagined the conversation they might have. Come in and sit down, for heaven's sake, she might say. Let me give you a glass of beer. Or water. What do you like? In truth, she would have no idea. Mother Mary had come home with the frame of that loom years ago, balancing the wooden object in her arms. Bett had helped Eva Nell warp the web and then taught her to weave. It was what she did now. She could weave a shroud or a Christening gown. Sunshine for white, logwood for black, or a pattern of both, interwoven.

ACKNOWLEDGMENTS

I thank my beloved Michael for his encouragement and advice during the years I worked on this story, for reading it gently and believing in it fiercely, and for his affection, which sustains me. I am grateful to my daughter Esta Spalding for her careful study of the manuscript followed by her brilliant recommendations about structure, content, and expectation. And thank you, Esta, for the title! I thank daughter Kristin Sanders for interacting with my characters so entirely that they found more courageous paths through the narrative than I had expected, especially Martin. Chris Dewdney helped track the Thames River in Ontario, and I thank him. Stan Etter charted the complex route of a dugout canoe from St. Louis to Chatham, Ontario, however unlikely that may seem, and I am eternally in his debt. Rachel Hall found the truth of the current in a section of the Ohio River. Oh rivers! I thank you for refusing to give in to our demands. Lead us and bewilder us. Move and meander and be covered sometimes with corn and bury your secrets. I thank the Arabia Museum, which displays some of those secrets as testament to the willfulness and pride of the pioneers. To Michael Redhill and to Barbara Gowdy, who read the manuscript, I am grateful for your meticulous care and concern. Each of you is irreplaceable as advisor and friend. Martha Kanya-Forstner of McClelland & Stewart read, reread, edited, and consulted throughout. What a gift to this book she has been. Ann Close at Pantheon has kept close watch and her sensitive and considered point of view has been invaluable. Ellen Levine has represented it and championed it. My gratitude to Martha, Ann, and Ellen should be shouted. And I want to mention, here, the learning I received from Ellen Seligman when we worked together on *The Purchase* and on ideas that led to *A Reckoning.* I still hear her dear voice questioning, suggesting. I thank Janet Yorston for medical notes regarding third-degree burns. My very sincere and heartfelt thanks to St. Andrews University in Scotland for hosting me as resident writer in 2016 and to Don Patterson and John Burnside for making that possible. Special thanks to Tara Quinn for the red deer; to Leah Springate for the beautiful map; and to the poet Forrest Gander for the translation of the epigraph by Pablo Neruda, from poem "19" ["Roa Lynn and Patrick Morgan"] in *Then Come Back: The Lost Neruda.* Blessings on Karen Solie for keeping the house warm and on Jasper and Jack for consistency of affection and mettle. And on Shelby Morgan for the last word.

ABOUT THE AUTHOR

Linda Spalding was born in Kansas and lived in Mexico and Hawaii before immigrating to Canada in 1982. She is the author of four critically acclaimed novels, *The Purchase* (awarded Canada's Governor General's Literary Award), *Daughters of Captain Cook, The Paper Wife,* and (with her daughter Esta) *Mere.* Her nonfiction includes *The Follow* (published in the United States as *A Dark Place in the Jungle*), *Riska: Memories of a Dayak Girlhood,* and *Who Named the Knife.* Spalding has received the Harbourfront Festival Prize for her contribution to the Canadian literary community. She lives in Toronto, where she is an editor of *Brick* magazine.

The employees of Thorndike Press hope you have enjoyed this Large Print book. All our Thorndike, Wheeler, and Kennebec Large Print titles are designed for easy reading, and all our books are made to last. Other Thorndike Press Large Print books are available at your library, through selected bookstores, or directly from us.

For information about titles, please call:
  (800) 223-1244

or visit our website at:
  gale.com/thorndike

To share your comments, please write:
  Publisher
  Thorndike Press
  10 Water St., Suite 310
  Waterville, ME 04901

LP Spa
Spalding, Linda,
A reckoning /

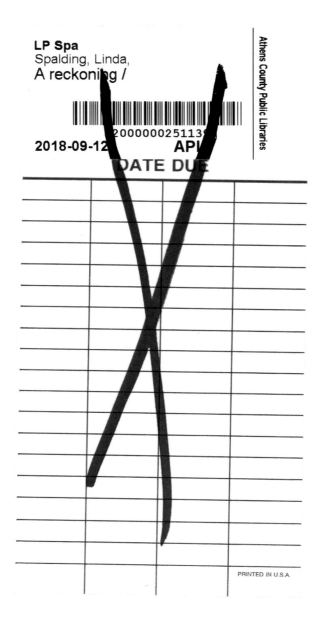

200000025113

2018-09-12   API

DATE DUE

PRINTED IN U.S.A.